T0106522

Into the Frying Pan

Also by Sarah Osborne

Too Many Crooks Spoil the Plot

Into the Frying Pan

Published by Kensington Publishing Corp.

Into the Frying Pan

Sarah Osborne

LYRICAL UNDERGROUND
Kensington Publishing Corp.
www.kensingtonbooks.com

To the extent that the image or images on the cover of this book depict a person or persons, such person or persons are merely models, and are not intended to portray any character or characters featured in the book.

LYRICAL UNDERGROUND BOOKS are published by

Kensington Publishing Corp.
119 West 40th Street
New York, NY 10018

Copyright © 2019 by Sarah Osborne

All rights reserved. No part of this book may be reproduced in any form or by any means without the prior written consent of the Publisher, excepting brief quotes used in reviews.

All Kensington titles, imprints, and distributed lines are available at special quantity discounts for bulk purchases for sales promotion, premiums, fund-raising, educational, or institutional use.

This book is a work of fiction. Names, characters, places, and incidents either are products of the author's imagination or are used fictitiously. Any resemblance to actual events or locales or persons living or dead is entirely coincidental.

Special book excerpts or customized printings can also be created to fit specific needs. For details, write or phone the office of the Kensington Sales Manager: Kensington Publishing Corp., 119 West 40th Street, New York, NY 10018. Attn. Sales Department. Phone: 1-800-221-2647.

Lyrical Underground and Lyrical Underground logo Reg. US Pat. & TM Off.

First Electronic Edition: May 2019
ISBN-13: 978-1-5161-0808-4 (ebook)
ISBN-10: 1-5161-0808-6 (ebook)

First Print Edition: May 2019
ISBN-13: 978-1-5161-0811-4
ISBN-10: 1-5161-0811-6

Printed in the United States of America

To Dan and Alix

Acknowledgments

I want to thank my beta readers who reviewed this book in different iterations and helped improve it each time: Marjorie Bufkin, Jayne Farley, Abigail Gilman, Mary Louise Klimm, Ann Komer, Linda Newton, Laurie Pocius, Lynne Roza, Margo Schmidt, and Kate Shands.

A special thanks to my technical experts. They patiently explained and re-explained what could and could not happen on the battlefield, during an investigation, and in a refugee clinic. Chris Burns, Georgia Division Infantry Commander, was my expert on reenactments. I took liberties with the reenactment dates for the sake of the plot but otherwise tried to stay true to the facts. John Smith, my dear brother-in law, now deceased, was a Deputy Sheriff and then Investigator for the Monroe County Sheriff's Department in Forsyth, Georgia. He described how an investigation involving county sheriffs and investigators would proceed. A pediatrician friend, who wishes to remain anonymous, helped make scenes with sick children true to life. All inaccuracies are my own.

Once again, I am indebted to the usual suspects: my writing group, which includes Larry Allen and Mike Fournier, and my 241 Fitness buddies led by Wendy Bryant.

And a new thank you to my recipe finders: Jeanne Lee and Judy Alden. I found some old recipes, but they found the rest on family recipe cards or tucked away in journals. I tested them each more than once. Mandy and Paula Haddon (Molly's Tea Room in Falmouth) tweaked the soup recipe to make it more flavorful. Marjorie Bufkin, a remarkable cook, and I did our best to make Mrs. Cornelius's Molasses Apple Pie work, but our attempts failed, i.e., the non-molasses variety of apple pie remains superior. I was sorry to give up such a simple recipe with such a wonderful name.

Thanks also to John Scognamiglio and the staff at Lyrical Underground Kensington Publishing Corporation who helped me with every stage in the publication and publicity of the Ditie Brown Mystery series. They include Michelle Addo, Lauren Jernigan, Karen Auerbach, Rebecca Cremonese, Amy Boggs, Marketing Intern James Akinaka, and Maryanne Lasher.

Chapter One

Car horns bleated, tempers flared, and people were as prickly as the sweat that beaded on their bodies. It was the usual muggy July in Atlanta, Georgia.

Every summer I wished for a condo by the sea, but the kids seemed content with the public Glenlake Pool in Decatur, ten minutes from our house. I made sure they got in the water every day it wasn't raining.

We'd just returned, and the shade of my giant magnolia gave us a moment's relief from the oppressive heat. Jason, age five, was becoming a swimmer, and Lucie, almost nine, already was one.

Four months since the death of my childhood friend Ellie—their mother—Lucie was beginning to act like a kid again and not a second mom to Jason.

"Stop hitting me with your water wings, Jason. It's not funny. Make him stop, Aunt Di."

"Jason, come here. Let me have those wings. You hardly need them anymore."

Jason looked at me as if he were debating the possibility of running into the house, but I was too fast for him. As a pediatrician, I knew how to capture children, if not with my charm, then with the speed of a firm hand.

I took the water wings and scooted him inside to take a bath.

"You can use my shower upstairs, Lucie."

I entered the house two steps behind them. The swim had been refreshing but already I was perspiring from the sultry air.

The air conditioning took my breath away. I started when I saw Mason settled on my sofa with my dog Hermione lounging beside him. I didn't work Fridays, but Mason did.

"Why aren't you tracking down murderers?" I asked.

"I got time off for good behavior." He must have seen me shivering. "I hope it's not too cold in here." He held out his hand and tugged me, wet suit and towel, onto his lap. Hermione jumped down—she wasn't fond of anything or anyone that might get her wet. Mason wrapped a throw around me.

"That will get soaked," I said.

"You have a dryer—I'll take care of it."

"Really, why aren't you at work?"

"I pulled two all-nighters. They'll call me if they need me. Right now, I just wanted to see you." He pushed my short dark curls away from my face. "You look good enough to eat."

I probably did look like a nice plump muffin, but no matter how I looked, Mason made me feel gorgeous. I slipped off his lap, so I could see him clearly.

"What are you up to?" I asked.

"A man has to be up to something because he wants to see his girlfriend in the middle of the day?"

"Yes, if that man is a detective with the Atlanta Police Department."

For a moment, Mason looked hurt. "You really don't know what day this is?"

I searched my memory and shook my head. "It's not my birthday or yours. Jason had his, and Lucie's is in September. I give up." I looked into his warm gray eyes, rubbed his bald head and gave him a kiss. "I really don't care why you're here, I'm glad you are."

"It's exactly four months since we met," he said. "You forgot."

"I'll never forget that," I said.

It was the worst night of my life and my children's lives. It was the night their mother was murdered. Mason Garrett, the detective on the case, gave me the news. He was kind and gentle, and my view of him had never changed.

I cuddled up to him, wet bathing suit and all.

"I can't believe it's only been four months," he said. "I feel as if I've known you all my life."

"I feel the same way."

"You mean that?"

"Of course."

As soon as I said that out loud, I realized where Mason was headed. When would be the right time to ask me to marry him or at least to move in together? The children, I'd say, as I said every time he brought up the issue. The children needed stability right now, no new upheaval.

We were spared this conversation by Jason who ran into the room with his mitt in one hand and a bat in the other.

"You didn't wait for me to run your bath," I said.

"Uncle Mason is here," he said, as if that justified never taking a bath again. "Wanna play ball?"

"You got a ball?" Mason asked looking around.

Jason searched the room. "Hermione," he shouted.

My wonderful patient shepherd-collie mix trotted into the room, head held high with a softball in her mouth.

"Jason," I said. "I told you to put that up where Hermione couldn't get it. She thinks it's her toy now and she'll chew it up.

Jason pulled it from her mouth. "It's fine, see?"

It was fine except for a few toothmarks.

"If it gets chewed up," I said, "the next one comes out of your allowance."

Mason stood up. "I think we men better leave, before your Aunt Di starts yelling at us." He ushered Jason out in front of him.

Hermione trotted after them into the front yard. From the porch I watched Mason lob the ball to Jason who threw it back with the fierce attention of a five-year-old. After Lucie appeared, ready to play shortstop, I went inside and took a shower. I was barely dressed when I heard Hermione barking.

Mason shushed her and said, "Can I help you?"

"Is Ditie available?"

I recognized a familiar voice.

I ran downstairs and out to the porch, a towel in one hand, trying to do something with my curly hair.

Before me stood Phil Brockton IV...in a Civil War uniform. Despite my best efforts not to notice, he looked incredibly handsome. Six feet tall, one hundred eighty pounds, straight brown hair that fell casually over one eye—elegant in his gray uniform.

"Phil? I thought you were going to call when you were coming to town for a reenactment."

"I did call and emailed as well, but you never responded, so here I am."

It was all true. Phil had emailed me a few weeks earlier and given me the date he was coming. I hadn't responded because I didn't know what to say. He'd called, and I'd deleted the message almost as soon as I received it. Somehow I'd managed to 'forget' those communications.

"I'm on my way to a pre-battle planning party and thought I'd stop by," he said. "I hope you can come to the Battle of Resaca tomorrow. It's the biggest of the Atlanta Campaign reenactments."

Before I answered, I introduced him to the three people clustered around me.

"Philip Brockton, this is Mason Garrett and these are my children Lucie and Jason."

"Your children?" Phil looked shocked.

"Long story. They're my children now and forevermore."

Mason and Phil reluctantly shook hands.

"You're the boyfriend police detective, right?" Phil asked.

Mason raised one eyebrow and nodded. "You're the doctor obsessed with the Civil War who took off for New York abruptly after residency."

This wasn't going well.

Phil looked at me. "What have you told this guy about me?"

"Never mind," I said. "Why are you here, Phil?"

"When I didn't hear back from you, I assumed you hadn't gotten my messages. I'm hoping you can come tomorrow. For old time's sake."

"Like Civil War old time's sake?" Mason asked. "Or something else."

I gave Mason a look meant to say I could fight my own battles. Phil was the only man I ever thought I might marry before Mason. He'd stood me up seven years earlier—not at the altar—but by leaving town and moving in with an oncology nurse.

"Why didn't you just call me again today?" I asked.

"I thought you might be avoiding me, and I wanted to see you. Can you come tomorrow? All the action starts in the afternoon, around two." He looked at the family group. "Everyone's invited."

I wasn't sure he meant that. It sounded more like his polite Southern upbringing speaking. "I don't know, Phil."

"A lot of the old gang from med school will be there—Harper and Ryan Hudson, Sally Cutter, Andy Morrison. I don't know if you remember Frank Peterson—he was in the class ahead of us, but he and I stayed friends."

"To be honest, Phil, the only person I'd really like to see is Andy. I haven't kept up with your other friends, and didn't Sally drop out of school second year? I'm surprised you're still in touch with her."

"We're friends, and she loves this reenactment stuff. Please come."

I looked at Mason. He didn't look happy.

"I'm not sure I can."

Why couldn't I just say no? What was wrong with me? He'd hurt me more than any man ever had before or since. Did I need him to take responsibility for what he'd done? I'd fallen hard for Phil. Do you ever get over your first love or do you always imagine how it might have ended differently?

I felt an old longing mixed with hurt.

"I'll see if Lurleen can stay late with the kids, and I'll have to see if I can leave a little early from the refugee clinic. I work there Saturday mornings, so I don't know if I can make it."

"You'll have a great time. Maybe we could visit before things get started."

"I'll see."

Phil left and Mason turned to me. "Are you seriously thinking about going tomorrow? I thought you were over this guy. Do you still have feelings for him?"

I looked at the children, who were staring at us.

"Let's go inside," I said. "I think we all need to cool off."

I headed for the kitchen. "How about some lemonade? We'll make it fresh. Jason, get me six lemons from the bowl by the sink. I'll cut and you can squeeze, Lucie."

Standing in my cool white kitchen with its tin ceiling and gray quartz countertops helped me calm down. It was always my go-to place when I needed comfort. I ran my hand over the marble island and waited for Jason to bring me the lemons.

Mason remained in the welcoming archway between my kitchen and breakfast room, but there was nothing warm in his look.

I turned to him. "Maybe you can find a family movie for us to watch unless you need to check in at the office."

Mason didn't say a word, just headed for the family room.

Lucie leaned toward me and whispered. "Something's wrong, isn't it Aunt Di? You have that look."

"That look?"

"You know, the look you get when you're worried and don't want us to know. You get those wrinkles in your forehead and your mouth goes all serious."

"Lucie, it's nothing to worry about." I hugged her. "It's just that a man I knew years ago turned up on my doorstep, and it shocked me a little."

Jason was walking toward the island trying hard to balance lemons in his small hands, intent on not dropping any. I placed them on the chopping board, and he counted them out.

"Look Aunt Di, six."

I smiled at him. "Perfect."

"That man who came to see you," Jason said, "was he wearing a costume for Halloween?"

"That's months away," Lucie said, "in October."

I could see Jason's lip start to quiver. He never liked being criticized by his sister.

"He was dressed in a Confederate Civil War uniform," I said. "He came to Atlanta to play a part in a pretend battle."

Jason looked completely bewildered.

"Jason, you remember how much Danny likes to talk about the Civil War, the war that took place over a hundred and fifty years ago."

Danny was the live-in boyfriend of my best friend Lurleen, and he'd become an important part of the children's lives.

"Uncle Danny calls it the War of Northern Aggression," Lucie said proudly, "where the Northern states got mad at the Southern states and everybody fought everybody. We read about it in school, and they called it the Civil War."

"I love Danny like a brother, but we don't see eye to eye about everything. The Southern states wanted to leave the United States and form a separate country. You've heard about Abraham Lincoln?"

Lucie nodded.

"Lincoln was president and he didn't want the United States to fall apart," I said. "He fought a war to save it and eventually to free the slaves."

I'd lost Jason halfway through the conversation. He'd wandered off to the living room and was trying to teach Hermione a new trick—walking on her hind legs to get a treat. She was a big dog, and this was unlikely to work no matter how sweet the treat.

I cut the lemons in half, and Lucie squeezed them into the pitcher. We added sugar and ice water and stirred like crazy. Lucie tasted it and agreed it was sweet enough. We put together a tray with glasses of lemonade and some homemade ginger cookies.

I poked my head into the family room where Mason was watching TV.

"Twilight double header," he said when he saw me. "Just started. The Braves hit a home run." He glanced at the kids. "I can find a movie if you'd rather."

"No need," I said.

Jason scrambled up on the couch. He was never one to miss a baseball game or time with Mason. I left them with the cookies and lemonade.

Lucie and I sat on the porch swing outside. Hermione flopped at our feet. Majestic, my orange cat who lived up to her name, settled on Lucie's lap.

Lucie stroked his head, and neither of us spoke. I was grateful for the time to think.

Phil Brockton shows up expecting me to drop everything to watch him play soldier. Just like old times. When I could be of use to him he wanted me around. He even let me think he loved me. But, no matter what *he'd* felt, I *had* loved him. I thought he was like my father—smart, funny, and compassionate.

I sighed, and Lucie looked at me.

"It's nothing," I said. "I guess I'm bothered that Dr. Brockton showed up."

"Did you love him, Aunt Di?"

"Whatever made you ask that, honey?"

"You have that look you give Uncle Mason sometimes."

"Good grief, Lucie. Do you spend every minute studying my face?"

Lucie blushed. "It's not hard, Aunt Di. Even Uncle Mason says he can tell what you're thinking before you say a word." Lucie sat quietly for a moment. She started picking at the wooden planks in the porch swing.

"What is it, Lucie?"

"It's just…if you loved him once, maybe you still love him. Uncle Mason wouldn't like that, and I wouldn't either."

"Not to worry, Lucie. I'm no longer in love with Dr. Brockton."

I hoped that was true.

"And you are in love with Uncle Mason?" she asked with the tiniest grin.

"Say, I think you have a wobbly tooth in that mouth of yours. Let me check."

I poked around in her mouth and tickled her until she was giggling so hard she nearly fell off the swing onto Hermione. Majestic had jumped ship at the first sign of a disturbance, and Hermione had the good sense to move away.

Mason must have seen us through the bay window in the family room because he and Jason came outside a moment later.

"I can't leave you guys alone for a minute," Mason said as he closed the screen door. "I expected more of you, Hermione."

She trotted up to Mason in hopes of a good rub, which she got.

Lurleen and Danny arrived moments later, and we made plans for an ad hoc dinner. Danny and Mason would grill steaks. I would handle the salads, and Lurleen would watch the kids. She was always my backup. When her aunt died and left her a fortune, she'd quit her job at Sandler's Sodas and spent almost as much time with the kids as I did.

Over dinner I told Lurleen and Danny the story of Phil's abrupt arrival and his request that I watch a Civil War reenactment on Saturday.

"Boy," Danny said, "would I love to see that!"

Danny looked like a kid at that moment, all six feet four inches of him.

"You could come along if you don't have work to do," I said.

Danny was a former cop and now private investigator who set his own hours. "I'm free tomorrow."

I turned to Lurleen. "It'll be a longer day for you. I probably won't get home until after five."

"I don't mind," Lurleen said. "No offense, Danny, but the idea of watching grown men play war doesn't really interest me."

"It's not playing war, Lurleen, it's creating living history," Danny said.

"*Ah, mon Dieu,*" Lurleen said. She returned to her unique version of French when she got frustrated.

"I'll try to leave the clinic around noon and get to Resaca about one," I said, "but you can probably go earlier if you want, Danny."

Mason had been silent throughout the meal. I looked over at him. "Would you like to come?"

"Can't. I have to work tomorrow."

His response was curt, and I didn't have any inclination to draw him out. Danny and I made plans to meet on the battlefield.

Mason barely said two words to me when he left at the end of the evening. Worse than that he didn't kiss me good night. Could he really be jealous of a relationship that had ended seven years ago? Or did he know me well enough to recognize my ambivalence.

* * * *

My supervisor Vic had no problem with my leaving the clinic early. I arrived at Resaca shortly after one. It was hard to imagine a bloody fight in such a pastoral setting with rolling hills dotted with pine trees. I'd never seen a reenactment, and the idea intrigued me now. In med school it was the last thing I had time for.

Perhaps having a boy of my own made me realize something new about the excitement of guns and battles. I suppose, to be honest, the idea of seeing Phil once more in uniform also intrigued me. Phil was a handsome man, and I didn't mind seeing a handsome man in uniform. I tried hard to convince myself that was the extent of my interest in him.

When I arrived, tents lined the hillsides, and men sat outside them dressed in blue or gray. I walked over to a row of larger tents where women and men were selling goods. I asked inside one of them where the battle would take place and they directed me to the top of a hill.

"You can see everything from there," the man told me. I walked past an EMS Gordon County ambulance—I guess they were prepared for anything that might happen—to a tent at the top of the hill selling bottled water. It was a humid day with no breeze, so I bought some and stared over the field.

To my left were a set of at least four cannons. Across the field I could see members of the cavalry running their horses along a line as they poked with their bayonets at balloons on posts. The horses were beautiful. Clusters of men stood near the edges of the field. I'd never be able to spot Phil.

One tent with two women inside was nestled near the bottom of the hill. I asked where I might find the Confederate organizers of the event.

One woman dressed in a period costume greeted me warmly. "We're with the Army of Tennessee, dear. We know the men. Who is it you might be looking for?"

"Phil Brockton," I said.

"Colonel Brockton? He's a fine man. My William is under his command. They're over yonder near those trees."

She never broke out of her role and pointed to a clump of pine trees fifty yards away.

I spotted Phil about the same time he noticed me. He motioned me to stay back and I watched as he sketched something in the dirt to a dozen men dressed in gray uniforms. Then he strode over to meet me.

"I'm glad you came, Ditie. Pretty impressive, isn't it. Wait 'til the action starts."

He was in charge of maintaining the cannons on the Confederate side. He gave me a history of the battle as we walked to the cluster of cannons not far from us.

"General Sherman's men and our Rebs under General Johnston fought on this field in May 1864. Sherman wanted to hold the railroad and telegraph lines south of Dalton, and he did. We didn't win this one," he said, "but they lost more men than we did."

As if on command, a train rattled past at the edge of the battlefield.

Up a small hill, three cannons were positioned behind bunkers. A fourth stood separate from the others. Phil inspected each one, shining a flashlight into the bore. "We use 12-pounder smooth bore Napoleons if we can get our hands on them. Most are reproductions." He stood beside the one that was separated from the rest. It was a shiny bronze, not the dull green color of the other three. "This one's special. It's the one I'll be using today."

Danny ran up before Phil finished speaking. "Gosh, I've never seen one of these up close." He ran his hand along the glistening five foot cannon. "This is a beaut."

Phil nodded.

"They used solid shot in these?" Danny asked.

"Or canister in close quarters," Phil said.

Danny turned to me. "The canister casings were filled with steel balls, sawdust, anything they wanted to put in there, Ditie. They could do a lot of damage over a wide area."

I nodded and tried to look interested, but I was ready for the battle to start. "I think I'll join the spectators. You two carry on without me."

Ryan and Harper Hudson caught up with me before I reached the people settling onto blankets and portable chairs they'd brought for the event.

"We heard you were back in town," Harper said, "but we never knew if you'd taken off again. I didn't expect to see you at a reenactment—I thought you hated them in med school!"

"They demanded more time than I had available. I came to see what Phil has always been so passionate about."

"Can we take that to mean you and Phil are getting back together now that he's divorcing his wife?" she asked.

"I didn't know he was in the middle of a divorce, but our relationship is ancient history. I'm here because Phil invited me."

"We're here," Harper said, "because we just love this kind of thing, don't we, hon?"

Ryan shrugged and gave me a kiss on the cheek. "Nice to see you, Ditie."

"I have to be a Federal today," Harper said.

"A Yankee?" I asked.

Harper nodded. "Too many Confederate reenactors showed up. I don't mind. At least I'll be on the winning side of this one."

Phil saw us and ran over. "Hi Harper. I don't think they need you today. Sorry, It looks like a flood of Federals showed up at the last minute. You could help us out on artillery—we're a man or two short."

"No thanks. I'll just see *my* man in action." She motioned to Ryan but winked at Phil.

I watched them as they walked away across the broad expanse of green. Ryan and Harper made a handsome couple, both tall and fit. Harper was blond. Ryan's hair was brown. They looked like Ken and Barbie in uniform. They had a dermatology practice in Buckhead, but I'd never bothered to look them up when I came back to Atlanta. They'd always been more Phil's friends than mine.

Danny waited for me near the edge of the battlefield. We joined the dozens of spectators, families mostly, getting settled for the battle. A few of the women were dressed in period costumes including a two-year-old daughter. I got a picture of that.

"This is great," Danny said. "Phil told me I could participate the next time he's in town. Man, I'd love that."

We sat on a hillside under a large oak tree that provided shade and waited for the action to begin. We could see Phil gathering his men. Someone stepped out of line and offered a prayer. Then Phil got everyone situated. Several men wandered off with guns at the ready.

Clusters of Confederate soldiers and Federal forces were hidden among the trees at various points on the field.

Six people including Phil stood near the one cannon we could see clearly. Large carts stood fifteen feet behind each cannon with more men standing around them.

"Those are the limbers," Danny said following my gaze. "They carry the ammunition. Normally there are nine men to a gun, including the man in charge—the gunner. That's probably your ex, right?"

"Probably. Phil said they were short a man or two. Can I borrow your binoculars, Danny? I forgot mine."

Danny lifted them from around his neck and handed them to me. I made a survey of the people near the cannon. I thought I saw Sally Cutter, but I couldn't be sure. Andy was recognizable with his hat off and his red hair flying in the breeze. He was laughing with someone standing next to the cannon, Frank Peterson perhaps.

Wait a second! I saw someone else I recognized talking to Phil.

"That is Carl Thompson! I swear it is!"

"Should that mean something to me?" Danny asked. "Is he famous?"

"Phil and Carl hated each other in med school. Carl hated everything about the South. They traded barbs throughout first year and stopped talking after second year. I wonder what brought about this great reunion."

Some signal seemed to start the battle. Drummers could be heard as clusters of men marched onto the field. Bugles blared and shots were fired. I watched as Phil's crew stepped up in a ritualized dance. One man stuck a long stick into the bore of the canon.

"A sponge," Danny explained, "to make sure there are no leftover sparks from a previous shot."

Next someone put something in the tip of the bore. Another tamped it down.

"Black powder," said Danny. "And now, see that rope Phil is holding—that's the lanyard. It's attached to a wire that's fed into the powder through what's called a vent. When it's pulled out friction makes the powder ignite and the canon fire."

"Thanks for the artillery lesson, Danny."

He looked at me as if I were making fun of him.

"No, I mean it. I can understand what's happening now. Everyone has his role."

Danny nodded.

Then we heard the boom, boom, boom of three cannons firing in succession. The sound was louder than I expected. It vibrated beneath our feet. I saw one little girl covering her ears and thought I should join her. Smoke filled the area around the cannons. When it cleared it was obvious Phil's crew had not yet fired.

It looked as if Carl and Phil were having a discussion while everyone else stood around waiting for something to happen. After a minute Phil handed the lanyard to Carl, who was standing alone on the left side of the cannon. Phil stood to the rear of the gun and signaled to Carl. Then he turned his back.

I watched as Carl pulled the lanyard and the gun banged.

Boom! Was it louder than the other cannons?

Then I heard the shouts and screams!

"What the hell?" Danny yelled. He grabbed the binoculars out of my hands. "That wasn't supposed to happen!"

When the smoke cleared, I could see something was terribly wrong.

Several of the people around the canon had been knocked off their feet and the canon itself was split.

Phil stood, looking dazed.

Carl had been on the other side and I couldn't tell what happened to him. I *could* see that everyone was staring in that direction.

I asked Danny to let me look, and he handed me the binoculars as he ran onto the field.

I watched as Harper came running up the hill. She helped Ryan to his feet. I saw Sally and Andy look to the other side of the canon. Even from where we stood I could hear Sally's scream. Frank stood silently several feet from the shattered cannon. Phil had gone to where Carl lay and returned shaking his head.

I ran toward the disaster. Two members of the Gordon County EMS raced past me. Danny motioned me back and pulled out his cell phone. I assumed he was calling 911. I didn't see Carl. I didn't have to. The two med techs knelt beside his body and then stood up and backed away.

"We need the police out here, now," I heard Danny shout into the phone. "We have one man dead. I'll cordon off the area."

Chapter Two

Danny tamped down the grass with his foot and marked off an area thirty feet square surrounding the shattered cannon and the body. The Gordon County EMS techs spoke briefly to Danny and then remained standing on the other side of the gun near where Carl lay.

Danny motioned my six classmates to stand in one corner and ordered them not to speak to one another. Me, he called over to where he was standing.

"Make sure none of them is injured," he said.

I started to walk away and Danny waved me back. "No interrogating them, Ditie. Leave that to the police."

Phil started talking to me as soon as I approached him.

"I don't know what happened. One minute I'm talking to Carl and the next minute we're all knocked off our feet."

"Are you hurt?" I asked.

Phil did a quick inventory of his body and shook his head no. "Most of the blast was to the front of me."

One by one, I spoke with people I hadn't seen in years.

Ryan and Harper assured me they were okay.

"Of course I wasn't anywhere near the explosion," Harper said, "but Ryan was."

"I'm all right," Ryan said. "More shaken by what happened to Carl than anything else."

"You weren't knocked unconscious?" I asked.

"No, just lost my footing," he said.

"You've checked him all over, Harper?"

"Of course."

Frank Peterson and Andy Morrison were standing together. They looked battered. Frank's uniform was covered in grass stains and dirt. Andy always looked as if he'd been through a war, but I could see a cut above his eye.

They were silent as I approached. Frank stood tall in his makeshift uniform, his black hair trim and his bearing suitable to a military man. Andy slouched as he'd done in med school, always looking as if he'd just rolled out of bed to make it to class. His hair was in disarray, and I couldn't tell if it was from the blast or the way he always wore it.

"I'm supposed to make sure you're okay, not that you guys need that from me. Did you look at Andy's cut?" I asked Frank.

"Yeah. It's superficial."

"I'm fine, Ditie," Andy said. "No internal or external injuries, except the cut, and it's not bleeding anymore. I can't believe you're here. I heard you'd come back to Atlanta and I kept intending to look you up, but this is a terrible way for us to meet again." He ran his hand through his red hair repeatedly. It was like a nervous tic, and I remembered it from med school whenever we were about to take a test.

"I guess you two would know if you'd been hurt," I said.

"Yes, we're fine," Frank said. "I don't know if you remember me. I was a year ahead, a friend of Phil's."

"Sure, I remember you," I said. "Where are you now?"

"Upstate New York. I have a busy internal medicine practice near Ithaca."

I glanced at Danny to see if he was looking in my direction. He wasn't, so I did what he told me not to do and asked a question. "What do you think happened?"

"The whole god-damned gun exploded," Frank said. "It's a miracle we weren't *all* killed."

I nodded and moved on to Sally Cutter. She was standing alone, staring at the other side of the cannon.

I followed her gaze. Carl lay on his back. I couldn't see more than an outline of his body, and the EMTs made sure no one came any closer.

She looked at me and pushed her short dark hair out of her eyes. It took her a moment to focus. "Phil said you might come today."

She spoke as if we were meeting at a casual gathering. People react to sudden death in all kinds of ways. I imagined she was still in shock.

"Are you all right" I asked. "Do you want to sit down?"

She didn't seem to hear me. "Carl was the only one on that side of the cannon. The rest of us knew to turn our backs before the cannon was fired, but Carl didn't know that. Phil didn't explain that to him."

"Please," I said, "let me make sure you're okay." I led her unresisting away from the view of Carl's body. I checked her out. She was a tiny thing, as she'd always been, sprite-like literally and figuratively. She still looked more like a child than an adult. She shook her head, no, when I asked if she'd been knocked unconscious, and her short black hair fell back into its pixie cut.

"You do know everyone here hated Carl—Phil most of all," she said. "They stopped speaking second year." Sally paused. "After the cheating scandal."

"I didn't know much about that, but that was ages ago. Surely, they'd put that behind them."

"I don't think so. Phil let Carl come to the reenactment because Phil's dad insisted on it. Carl's working for him now."

That information stunned me. "Why? Carl hated the South. Why would he possibly be working for Phil's dad?"

"I'll tell you the whole story over a drink sometime. Phil wasn't happy about it, not one bit. He wanted Carl out of the picture, and now he is. Permanently."

"Are you suggesting something about the accident, Sally?"

"How do we know it was an accident? Phil inspected the cannons. Why didn't he see something was wrong with this one?"

"You can't possibly be saying Phil orchestrated this."

"Think about it," Sally said. "Phil hates Carl and lets him pull the lanyard. That's a big deal. Carl is the only one on the side of the cannon that explodes."

Before I could respond, a deputy sheriff from Gordon County arrived and spoke with the EMTs near the body. Then he began closing off the area with stakes and the infamous yellow tape. A few minutes later another officer arrived who apparently knew Danny. He introduced himself to us as a Gordon County investigator, Officer Barden. He was a small man with a no-nonsense expression and the most intense blue eyes I'd ever seen. "You both here at the time of the explosion?" he asked Sally and me.

I shook my head.

"Then I'll ask you to leave, miss. Stay near the tents, and someone will question you later."

I did as I was told. As I walked up the hill toward the tents, my cell rang. "Are you okay?" Mason asked. "Danny called me."

"I'm fine, but a classmate is dead—Carl Thompson."

"Yes, I heard. Sounds like a terrible accident," Mason said.

"At least one person here isn't so sure it was an accident," I said. I told him briefly what Sally had said.

"Sally Cutter thinks Phil might have killed the guy over a feud from a decade ago?" Mason asked.

"The feud might be more current," I said. "Carl was working for Phil's father. When I last spoke to Phil four months ago, he was considering taking over his father's concierge business and didn't say one word about Carl working there."

"Concierge business?" Mason asked.

"You know—the VIP service where your doctor is always available. You pay an annual fee for that. It's popular these days."

"Are you saying what I think you are—that Phil would have hated the idea of Carl working for his father and may have doctored the cannon, no pun intended?"

"I'm not sure what I'm saying. I can't imagine Phil committing murder, and frankly I can't imagine he'd do anything to mess with his precious reenactments."

"Leave it, Ditie. The right people are there to figure out what happened."

We hung up and I called my supervisor Vic at the refugee clinic. She took the information in stride.

"I just heard about it on the news," she said. "I can't believe you saw it happen."

"I can't either. I was calling to see if you might need me this afternoon. I'll be better off at the clinic than trying to act like nothing happened with eagle-eyed Lucie hovering around me."

I waited half an hour until a police officer took my statement and said I was free to go. It was a relief to leave, and I didn't realize *I* was still in shock until I drove away from the scene. I only saw Carl's body from a distance, but it was enough to take me back to the image of Ellie lying in the morgue.

Everything about the night of her death washed over me. The anger I felt that Ellie hadn't called the children to say good night. The shock of hearing a detective's voice saying he needed to speak to me, and then the overpowering wish that the woman shot to death would not be Ellie but some stranger. For weeks afterwards I woke up at night with a start, seeing her face torn apart by a gunshot wound. It took me most of the hour on the road to clear my head of the picture of Ellie's lifeless face.

A bustling afternoon in the clinic did the rest. I worked nonstop from four to six thirty. Many of the refugees could only come on Saturday, so we had extended hours. We didn't have interpreters on site on the weekend.

We could get one on the phone, but fortunately we didn't have to do that. We did wellness checks and shots for school, which would be starting in early August.

I got home before seven to find Mason sitting on the porch swing watching the kids play in the yard with Hermione. He jumped up and gave me a warm hug. "I fed the kids, I hope that's okay."

"More than okay."

"I'm glad you're all right," he whispered in my ear.

I gave each of the kids a hug and looked around for Lurleen.

"I sent her home," Mason said. "She was eager to be there when Danny got back. They'll be coming over later."

Lucie and Jason roughhoused with Hermione in the grass while she licked their faces. Lucie tried to shove her away and pushed Jason instead. He squawked and shoved her back.

"Hey," I shouted. "Knock it off. It was an accident."

Jason wrapped his arms around himself. "You always take her side, just cause she's a girl!"

"Really? What do you say, Mason? You saw the whole thing."

"I say it's Hermione's fault, and she didn't do it on purpose."

"Agreed. So are you two safe out here with the dog?" I asked.

It was meant to be a joke, but Lucie gave me a serious look and nodded her head. I walked over and pulled her blond ponytail gently. "I was teasing you," I said, "but maybe you could give Mason and me ten minutes of private time. I'll bring out a pitcher of water, and if you get too warm come inside."

Lucie ran into the house and returned ten seconds later with a notebook.

She took Jason's hand. "Come on, Jason. I'm sorry I shoved you. We'll sit inside the magnolia tree and I'll read you one of my stories—you can be the star in it."

I'd already put two small chairs near the root of the tree inside the circle of its glorious branches. It was the perfect place for storytelling.

Mason followed me to the kitchen as far away from curious ears as we could get. He waited while I carried the ice water and glasses outside. When I returned, he looked at me expectantly. I settled on a stool across from him, my hands on the cool marble island.

"Has Danny filled you in about any of it?" I asked.

"You both said a man died when a cannon exploded—someone you knew in med school."

"Yes. Carl Thompson. I can't believe it even now."

"Neither can anyone else apparently," Mason said. "If Brockton is telling the truth, Carl wasn't supposed to pull the lanyard—Phil was. His story is that Thompson begged him to let him do it, so he did."

"Phil thinks *he* was the target?" I asked.

"Yes, if it wasn't an accident and if your old boyfriend is telling the truth." My heart thudded to a stop. "You think he's lying?"

"Danny wonders if he might be. Did he say any more to you?"

Before I could answer, Phil called me on my cell. He didn't give me time to say a word.

"Ditie, I'm in real trouble. You have to help me out. You have to."

"Did they arrest you? Do you need bail? Surely your father is helping you?"

"No to all of that. I'm back in my hotel for now—the Whitley in Buckhead. Can you come over?"

"What's this all about?"

"That guy, that investigator Barden, kept interviewing me like I'd done something on purpose to the cannon, like it wasn't an accident. I have to stay in town for now and see them at their office tomorrow morning. I have to get my head straight. You've always helped me do that."

"I can't help you right now, Phil. We'll talk later. What you need is a bath, a drink and sleep. I'll try to stop by tomorrow."

I hung up while Mason looked at me, one eyebrow raised. "You'll stop by tomorrow?"

I put my elbows on the island, my head between my hands, and stared at Mason.

"What's wrong with you?" I asked.

"Why would you get involved with him again? He dumped you."

"I know, Mason, I was there." I paused. "I'll go because he said he needed my help."

"Maybe Phil Brockton isn't as innocent as you'd like to believe. Apparently Brockton told the police about his long-standing feud with Thompson."

"I'm glad he did. He'd never have admitted that if he'd been involved with Carl's death."

"Unless your boyfriend was sure the police would find out about it eventually."

"Ex-boyfriend." Mason was starting to annoy me. "I loved Phil once. I don't love him now."

"*You* may not love *him*, but what are his feelings about you? You're the person he runs to when he's in trouble."

"Phil doesn't love me. He's asking for my help because I've always been the one to bail him out of trouble."

"And does he get in trouble a lot?"

"No." I got up from the island and walked over to the sink to pour myself a glass of water and clear my head. Mason was acting in a way I'd never seen before.

"Look, Mason. I don't love Phil. I love you. End of story. Phil never got into any serious trouble, but when he needed my help I gave it. If he went out with the boys and got drunk, I picked him up and tucked him in bed."

Mason took a deep breath and his tone became more cop-like. "You know why Brockton and Carl Thompson disliked each other so much?"

"Phil is a 'good old boy' from way back. He's a fourth-generation Southern doc. His great, great, great grandfather fought in the Civil War. Phil lives and breathes the life of a Southern gentleman. That was one reason I was so shocked when he went to New York."

"He and Carl couldn't have been more different. Carl was from New Jersey, turned up his nose at our medical school, and always made cracks about Southerners, their lazy habits, their crazy accents."

"You think that's why they became bitter enemies?"

I shook my head.

"No. It was something more than that. Something that happened in med school second year. Suddenly they weren't speaking, even to slam each other with insults. Phil wouldn't tell me about it, but there were a lot of things he didn't tell me about." I sighed. "None of that makes me believe he could kill a man in cold blood. This whole thing has to be a terrible accident."

"It may be."

Mason took my hand and squeezed it. He rubbed his other hand over his face.

"I'm sorry if I've been hard on you about Phil. I worry you may want someone younger than me, a wealthy doctor perhaps."

"Mason, sometimes I wonder what you see when you look in the mirror. I see the man of my dreams. I couldn't imagine loving anyone else."

Mason wrapped his arms around me and kissed me. The next thing we heard was a loud giggle. I thought it was from Lucie but it wasn't.

Lurleen and Danny stood inside my kitchen, their heads tilted to one side as if they were studying a work of art.

"*Très jolie.* Don't stop on our account," Lurleen said. "We just came in to get something to drink."

It was impossible not to smile when those two walked in a room.

Danny was five years younger than Lurleen, but he could barely keep up with her. They made a striking couple. Danny, sandy blond hair with the body of a linebacker, and gorgeous Lurleen, tall, thin, auburn-haired.

Lurleen glanced around the kitchen. "I know it's been a terrible day for you, but we still have to eat, and cooking always calms you down. What's for dinner, *chérie?*" She sniffed. "I don't smell anything delicious."

I glanced at my watch. "I haven't had time to think about dinner."

"You want us to go home?" Lurleen asked.

"No, not at all. Could you bring the kids inside? Mason fed them, but I need to get them ready for bed."

"They were inside when we came, watching TV in the family room."

I wondered how much they might have heard of the conversation Mason and I were having.

The four of us settled in the living room and closed the door to the family room while Lucie and Jason watched the end of *Diary of a Wimpy Kid 4*.

Danny told us what he knew about the day.

Lurleen listened with rapt attention as Danny described Phil's situation. She'd known Phil from med school and never liked him much. She thought I deserved better.

"Poor guy," Danny said. "They've closed down the reenactment for the rest of the day and probably for tomorrow as well. These guys spend their entire year getting ready for their battles and to have one shut down, that's rough."

"Not as rough as it was for Carl," I said.

"Yeah, I know," Danny said. "Don't get me wrong. It's just a big deal for the guys that are really into it."

"That would be Phil," I said. "Even in med school he took his vacations so he could participate in reenactments, and everything had to be authentic. Everything! He's sewn his grandfather's buttons on his jacket."

"I've always wanted to participate," Danny said. "Either side."

"With your Southern accent, they'd assume you were a spy if you fought for the North," I said.

"Danny knows everything about the Civil War," Lurleen said. "Maybe he could help with the investigation."

"I know the investigator—Doug Barden," Danny said. "He's a competent guy. He won't need my help, but I do have a thought. If the reenactment is on for Sunday, I could infiltrate the group."

I could see his eyes sparkling.

"If you go, I'm going with you," Lurleen said. "You've already told me some women went to battle dressed as men."

"You looking like a man, Lurleen? That would take some work," Danny said with a grin.

"I think you're all getting ahead of yourselves," Mason said. "If it's deemed an accident, then you won't need to go undercover, Dan."

I breathed a sigh of relief. Of course, it was an accident. It had to be an accident!

Lucie stuck her head into the living room. "The movie's over. Are you done with your grown-up talk?"

"Done," I said. "But it's late and you two need a bath."

Lurleen jumped up. "I'll help Jason."

While the children bathed, I fixed a quick meal of summer pasta and tossed salad for the grown-ups.

The kids joined us in their pajamas and nibbled on what was their favorite dinner in the world.

I looked around at my family and best friends. Despite what a horrible day it had been, I was in fact a lucky woman. No one, not even my mother, perhaps especially my mother, could have believed my good fortune. I was sorry she wasn't alive to see it and wondered if she would have become a better grandmother to my children than she'd been a mother to me.

A sadness caught me off guard as I thought about Dad dying of cancer before he even knew I went to medical school, much less had children of my own. The sadness passed as quickly as it came. I hoped he was somewhere smiling at my perfect life.

Phil called while I was putting the children to bed. I let it go to voice mail. When I picked up the message later I must have looked upset because Mason asked if anything was wrong.

The message was terse. "It's me, again. They think someone deliberately damaged the cannon, so it would explode. I'm at the top of their list of suspects, and they've cancelled the rest of the reenactment. It's a crime scene now."

I couldn't tell what was upsetting Phil more, that he was a suspect or that they'd called off the second day of his precious Battle of Resaca.

"I think I need to call Phil back," I said, "in private."

I headed upstairs to my bedroom, leaving Danny and Lurleen happily sharing a piece of chocolate cake with Grand Marnier icing. Mason looked far less content.

Phil barely gave me time to say hello.

"I was just about to call you again. You got my message, didn't you?"

"Phil, I have a family now. I can't drop everything for you the way I used to."

"I've never been in trouble like this before. The truth is someone wanted to murder *me*. I swear it, Ditie."

"I don't know what to say, Phil, or what you want me to do?"

"I need protection. There's another reenactment at Tunnel Hill next weekend. I'm going to participate."

"Phil, be sensible. If you honestly believe someone is out to kill you, why would you make yourself a target at another reenactment?"

"I have to go. If I don't go, people will think I'm guilty of something, or worse, they'll think I'm a coward. What I need is a bodyguard. You must know someone who could do that for me."

Sadly, I did.

Chapter Three

I promised Phil I'd do what I could to help him. Then I got off the phone and walked into the living room.

"Well?" Mason asked. "Did he confess?"

I gave Mason a look.

"Okay, I apologize. What did Dr. Brockton have to say for himself?" Mason asked.

"They shut down the Battle of Resaca, but apparently reenactors are free to join the Battle of Tunnel Hill next weekend. Phil said that's where he's headed if they don't arrest him first."

"I'm sure he's got the best lawyer in town, aside from your brother," Mason said. "They won't arrest him until they figure out if this was murder or an accident."

"Phil also said he wanted a bodyguard. He's certain someone meant to kill *him*, but he still won't give up the reenactment next weekend."

Danny jumped up. "I'm his man."

"And I'm his woman," said Lurleen.

"Hang on," Mason said. "I know the Sheriff in Gordon County. Let me give him a call and see what I can find out."

Mason headed for the kitchen. While he was gone, Lurleen and Danny talked Civil War battles. That gave me time to think.

Phil claimed he should have been the one pulling the lanyard. He was the gunner, meaning he was in charge of the whole operation, but because they were two men short, he took the position of the man who pulled the lanyard. When Carl begged to do it, Phil let him. Could anyone else verify that? These 'progressives,' as Phil called himself were all about detailed plans. Other people called them stitch counters, meaning every detail had to be authentic. That was certainly true about Phil. So what could have motivated Phil to hand the lanyard to a man he hated?

Mason returned and sat down beside me. "The Sheriff's an old friend. He told me what he knew—that Brockton was in charge of maintaining the cannons, and Brockton claims they were in good shape before the first round of the battle. The cannon's now in the crime lab in Atlanta and they'll get experts to see if the misfiring could have happened by accident— maybe a bird or squirrel getting into the bore. It could take a couple of weeks before they know for sure. Brockton's right. He's been cleared to participate in the next event. After that, he'll probably be free to leave the city if they don't find more direct evidence against him."

"That's settled then. I'm between jobs," Danny said. "I'll be happy to be Phil's bodyguard. This guy will pay me?"

"He'll probably pay you anything you want to charge," I said.

"It'll be my usual fee. Heck, I should be paying him to participate. This is going to be a blast."

"I hope not," I said.

"Sorry. It's just that Tunnel Hill is a great place for a battle. There's the original tunnel from the 1850s that you can walk through—talk about living history. It was part of Sherman's efforts to take over the railroads and block the South from getting supplies."

"I want to come to the battle," Lurleen said.

"You could probably be a sutler," Danny said.

"A settler?" Lurleen asked.

"A sutler is a person who supplies goods to the soldiers, like a makeshift shopkeeper."

"So I wouldn't have to dress like a boy. I could look more like a Southern belle."

"I don't know about looking like a *wealthy* Southerner," Danny said.

"I'll make it work, and that way I can keep an eye on everyone who comes and goes."

I could see Lurleen was getting into this a lot more than any of us might have liked, but there was no point in arguing with her.

I yawned.

"Okay, everyone out," I said. "I have to get some sleep. We'll meet at the Silver Skillet tomorrow around ten—whoever wants to that is."

The Silver Skillet, a retro diner, was our favorite breakfast place in Atlanta, with waitresses who knew us and the kids. We went there at least once a month. Everyone agreed except for Mason.

"I may have to work," he said.

"On a Sunday?"

"Some of us don't have the luxury of a nine-to-five job."

He was being difficult, which wasn't like him.

I turned to Danny. "I'll get in touch with Phil tonight and give him your number. You and he can work out the details of your assignment."

Mason was the last to leave, and I wasn't anxious for a long discussion. We'd likely get into another argument over Phil.

He pulled me close. "I can't help it that I don't like this guy."

"I've never seen this side of you before, and I have to say I don't like this jealousy thing—if that's what it is."

"It's not just jealousy," Mason said. "Phil Brockton is a prime suspect in what may be a murder investigation."

"I know."

I closed and locked the doors after I made sure Majestic was hiding somewhere in the house. Hermione followed me upstairs. I sat on the bed and called Phil. I told him about Danny.

"I knew I could count on you, Ditie. You're the only person I've ever really been able to count on. I've missed you."

"Don't start, Phil. I'm happily involved with a man who treats me great. The last I heard you were still married."

"It's easy to get married and a lot harder to get divorced. But we're in the process. All Tiffany wants is a good settlement. She claims I never had time for her, but my practice is huge with multiple research grants to oversee."

"Not to mention your reenactments," I added.

"Don't knock it. Today was awful, but that isn't how they're meant to be. Maybe you should bring the kids next weekend and let them see history in action."

"Phil, you think you're the target of a murderer and you need a bodyguard—how could I possibly put the children in a mix like that?"

"I'm calmed down now. This whole thing must have been an accident."

"Why the change of heart?"

"It's the only thing that makes sense. There's no way someone could know who'd be killed in a blast like that."

I was silent.

"You know, Ditie, you'd get a chance to see more of our old friends. Andy will be there."

"If the police say it was an accident, I'll consider coming. Jason would be thrilled to see a battle, and I know Lurleen would like some company."

"I think Ryan Hudson will come. You liked him in med school."

"I did, although he had a hair trigger when things didn't go his way. I remember how upset he'd get when he didn't do well on an exam. I'm a little surprised he and Harper have lasted. I didn't think he'd put up with her flirtatious ways."

"Flirtatious ways—what an old-fashioned term, Ditie, and I always took you for a modern woman," Phil chuckled.

"I always wondered if Harper did more than flirt," I said.

Phil was briefly silent. "Ryan keeps a pretty close eye on her, now that they're married."

"What do you mean? I thought they'd been married forever."

"Hardly. You do know Harper was engaged to Frank Peterson during their residencies?"

"You're kidding. Where was Ryan?"

"He was hanging by her side, doing the same dermatology residency she was doing. Biding his time I'd say."

"I guess it paid off," I said. "Why didn't Frank and Harper marry?"

"I can't say."

"Can't say or won't say? Did they split over Ryan?" I asked.

Phil laughed again. "I don't think Harper was ever that into Ryan. He was her fallback guy—a solid Southern doc her father would approve of. You heard of her dad?"

"Not much. I heard he had a big Texas ranch."

"One of the biggest, and according to Harper, the best beef cattle in the state. I met him once. He was a tough rancher and ran a tight ship. He had a lot of expectations for Harper."

"Like what?"

"Like she was supposed to bring home a smart Southern husband and breed children as pure as his line of cattle."

"Phew," I said. "Makes me have more sympathy for her. Maybe that explains why she went wild in med school. It was probably the first chance she'd had to get out from under his thumb."

"Yeah. There was a younger brother, but he didn't amount to much. It was Harper who was supposed to carry on the family dynasty."

"How do you know so much about her?" I asked.

"We're friends. I visited the ranch once or twice."

"I bet *you* would have qualified as a good catch—with your prestigious Southern lineage."

Phil changed the subject. "I'm surprised you never reconnected with Ryan and Harper when you moved back to Atlanta."

"I don't have a lot of doctor friends," I said, "and I wasn't that connected with them in the first place."

"You still think doctors are elitist and that offends your sense of fair play."

I sighed loudly into the phone. "You have an amazing capacity to try to make me feel bad about myself. I used to think you were right, but I've grown up in seven years. I like a wide range of people—just not those who see themselves as better than others."

"All right, let's drop that old discussion. What I meant to say is, I have a week before the next reenactment. Maybe we could get together with some of our old med school friends, and if you want to be egalitarian you could invite some of the reenactors who are staying for the Battle of Tunnel Hill?"

"*I* could invite people? Where are you thinking of having this reunion?"

"You have a nice house. I'd do it, but I'm in a hotel room."

"Why aren't you staying with your parents? They still live on Tuxedo in that beautiful Tudor house, don't they?"

"They do, and it's a long story. I'm happy at the Whitley for now, but there's no place for an informal party here."

"Carl's dead, and you want to have a party?"

"Bad wording. A gathering. I'm sorry this whole thing happened, but maybe if we all got together we could say farewell to a classmate."

"You hated Carl," I said.

"I won't lie to you. I did. He wormed his way into my father's good graces and then into his office. My dad made me invite him to the reenactment."

"You let him pull the lanyard—why?"

"It was no big deal. He asked to do it, and I let him."

I was silent.

"Look, Ditie, call this whatever you want. Why don't we do something to take our minds off what happened? We could make it a Civil War gathering—people could dress up if they wanted. You could find some old authentic recipes."

"It's a terrible idea," I said. "A classmate was killed, and you want to invite people to my house for some kind of celebration?"

"Not a celebration. I need to make peace with Carl's death," Phil said. "Why don't we try to create something decent out of a monstrous accident? Reconnect as a group, catch up on our lives. I'm going crazy here, wondering what the police are doing and thinking. I really need your help!"

Phil was begging for support. My brother would have pointed out that's all it took to make me jump in—someone in trouble asking for my help.

"Who else is still in town?" I asked.

"Frank and Sally may be forced to stay for a while. I don't know if they'll be going to the Battle of Tunnel Hill, but I can find out. What do you say? Just an old-time medical school reunion with a few extras."

"Let me sleep on it." I gave Danny's number to Phil, and we left it that we'd talk the next day. I knew Danny, Lurleen, and the kids would love the idea. I knew Mason would hate it.

I turned on the news and heard in detail about the disaster at the Battle of Resaca. The newscaster announced the death of Dr. Carl Thompson in a cannon explosion during a Civil War reenactment. The investigator Barden said it was too early to determine if the explosion was a freak accident or something more suspicious, and several people of interest were being detained for questioning. No names were mentioned.

I switched off the TV and tried to sleep. Was Phil telling me the truth? Like Mason, I wondered. Phil made it sound as if he were simply doing what his father ordered him to do—teach Carl something about reenactments. Phil also claimed *he* was the intended victim, assuming the whole thing wasn't a terrible accident.

But if Phil was lying about his encounter with Carl, perhaps he was lying about much more. I remembered how viciously the two of them attacked each other verbally our first year in med school, and how they never spoke after second year. The silence felt more deadly than the cruel banter.

Phil was a careful man, conscious of his image, his status, his work. I couldn't see him killing another human being and risk losing everything he valued.

But what if Carl had something on Phil that would destroy Phil's professional career or keep him forever out of his father's good graces?

Four months ago, Phil had talked about taking over his father's business. Now, for some reason, he wasn't even staying in the family home. And why does Carl show up in a part of the world he used to hate? I thought he'd taken a residency somewhere in the Northeast in internal medicine. What could have brought him down South?

So many questions.

A reunion was starting to sound like a good idea.

Chapter Four

The kids and I met Lurleen and Danny at the Silver Skillet and waited twenty minutes until the corner booth opened up. It was the only booth that could accommodate six people if Mason decided to show. I slid across the pea green and mahogany-colored vinyl seats, 1950s style, and got the kids settled beside me. Danny sat next to Jason, ready to keep him occupied if he got restless.

The smell of bacon and sausage and the sight of fresh biscuits, grits and gravy delivered to the table across from us made it hard to focus on anything but breakfast.

We ordered and then put our heads together to be heard over the noise of the diner, which as usual was filled with university students and locals.

I presented Phil's idea.

"You want to have a party when a guy just died?" Danny asked.

"Not a party exactly," I said.

"More of a wake then?" Danny said.

"No. More of a gathering, a reunion of my old medical school friends, although truth be told, most of them were Phil's friends, not mine."

"I thought you were over this guy," Lurleen said, "but it seems he asks for a favor and you say yes."

"I didn't say yes, just that I'd sleep on it."

"Maybe, but I can see you've already made up your mind. How does he do that to you?" Lurleen asked.

I shrugged. "I am over him."

If that were true, why couldn't I put him out of my mind? Why did I keep replaying our last dinner together? Maybe I wanted him to see what a mistake he'd made by leaving me.

Lurleen was continuing to talk and I picked up the second half of the conversation, "...don't know what you saw in him. Sure he's handsome and maybe he's good in—" Lurleen glanced at the children. Jason was playing with a miniature Caterpillar dump truck, scooting it along the edge of the table, but Lucie was hanging onto every word. Lurleen caught herself—"good in other ways, but he wasn't considerate of you."

"He was never mean to me," I said, "until the end. He encouraged me to do well in school. We had great conversations about history and the state of the world."

"You sound like you're working hard to justify your relationship with him," Lurleen said.

Our food arrived, and I found some welcome relief in concentrating on the soft scrambled eggs, crisp bacon and biscuits that were the best in town. The others seemed equally content with their choices.

Why *did* I still jump whenever Phil asked me to? I had loved him once. I thought he was like my dad. I guess I still found it hard to believe he didn't have a kind heart. Maybe contact with Phil was a way to make me believe I still had my father nearby.

"No matter the reason, I think a party or a 'reunion' is a fantastic idea," Lurleen said, putting her fork down for a moment.

"Why the sudden endorsement?" I asked her.

"There is a mystery here, Ditie. You know there is!" Her eyes brightened, and her usual French accent settled into a more comfortable Southern one. "I can be a Southern Belle and charm all the men who come without partners."

"Wait a minute, Lurleen. I do plan to be there," Danny said.

"Silly boy," she said, waving an imaginary fan. "I will be a femme fatale spy, nothing more. I can find out what's going on with that odd group of friends of yours, Ditie, and no one will know what I'm up to."

Lucie giggled.

"What, you don't see me as a spy?" Lurleen asked. "Did I never tell you about Richard and his work with the French CIA?"

"Richard?" Danny asked.

"No one of consequence," Lurleen replied.

"Just another one of Lurleen's many conquests," I said. I doubted there ever was a Richard, but it made a good story.

"CIA?" Lucie asked.

"Those are spies that work for the government, Lucie," Lurleen said. "Anyway, Richard needed some help from a woman, so he asked me to accompany him to a den of iniquity—"

"Okay, Lurleen, this story has gone far enough," I said. "Back to the question of a reunion, you think I should do it?"

At that moment Mason arrived.

We went silent and returned to devouring our pancakes, eggs, grits and gravy.

"Did I come at a bad moment?" he asked.

Rita, our favorite waitress, appeared, ready to take his order. "It's never a bad moment when you arrive, Detective Garrett. You want your usual—scrambled eggs, biscuits and gravy?"

Mason smiled. "Yes. With a little corned beef hash on the side, I'm pretty hungry."

"Coffee coming right up, hon." She returned seconds later with a full pot and made sure we all had what we needed.

Mason took two sips and turned to me. "What's going on? This group never stops talking. Let me hear it."

"You're not going to like it," I said.

"That's what I thought. Tell me anyway."

As Mason drank his coffee, I started at the beginning and tried to make it sound innocent. His food arrived as I finished.

"Let me get this straight," he said. "Phil Brockton asked you to entertain him and a few close friends because he was afraid he might get bored waiting for the next reenactment."

Danny stepped in. "You know, Mason, it's not a bad idea. Phil called me late last night, and I've agreed to be his bodyguard. A gathering might be a great way to get to know some of the players, see who looks or acts suspicious, that kind of thing."

I nodded along as Danny spoke.

"With the kids involved?" Mason asked, looking at me.

I hadn't stopped to think there could be any danger. "If you don't think they should be there, I'll get a babysitter."

"I'm your babysitter," Lurleen said, at the exact same moment Jason said, "I'm not a baby."

"Now see what you've started, Mason," I said.

"What *I've* started?"

"I'll be there, glued to Phil," Danny said. "Nothing's going to happen at the party. No one would be dumb enough to try something at a small gathering."

"According to the Sheriff, it could still be an accident," Mason said. "They won't have the final word from the crime lab for a few more days or even weeks. Am I invited to this reunion?"

"Absolutely," I said, "but you have to dress in costume."

"Maybe I'll come as a cop," he said.

"A Civil War uniform," I said.

"That's not going to happen. Are you cooking?"

"Of course. I'm going to find old recipes from the 1800s if I can."

Mason looked at the kids and paused before he spoke. "It seems an odd time for a celebration."

I put my hand on Mason's arm. "I understand what you're saying. It's not great timing. On the other hand, maybe it's a way to say good bye to someone we all knew. It will be a quiet gathering, and I'll make sure it ends early. I'd like to know what my old classmates have been up to since I saw them last."

"I'll watch the kids," Mason said, "but I won't be in costume. I'll bet Mom would like to come. She loves to get a taste of the Old South."

Mason's mother Eddie was a great cook, along with being an ex-cop.

"She might even like to help me hunt for authentic recipes," I said.

"I'll check with her," Mason said.

We planned the party for Wednesday evening on the early side. Wednesday was my half day at work, so I'd have plenty of time to cook. I could do most of the baking ahead of time. The kids were excited but not nearly as much as Lurleen—or Danny.

"Man," Danny said. "I've got an old belt buckle from the Atlanta Arsenal, and Phil says he can get me a uniform, maybe a saber."

"No sabers allowed," I said.

"Sure, sure. I was thinking of the reenactment on Saturday and Sunday," he said.

"And now it's Phil, is it?" Mason asked.

"That's what he asked me to call him. I can't very well go around calling him Dr. Brockton, IV, can I?"

Mason didn't comment.

Lurleen insisted on handling all the decorations, naturally. That was her forte. We'd have the party in my backyard if it didn't rain or get too hot, and we'd move inside if it did. Lucie would be my sous chef and Jason would be whatever Jason would be. I'd put him in charge of managing Hermione and Majestic. Majestic would simply disappear and Hermione would be her old sweet self once she'd greeted all the guests.

Lucie and I skipped plans for a swim that afternoon, so we could get down to work. Lurleen and Danny took Jason to Piedmont Park.

I called Phil and told him to invite people for a casual dinner on Wednesday, in period costume if they liked, no weapons allowed—starting around five and ending by eight thirty.

"Eight thirty?" Phil said. "Who ends a party at eight thirty?"

"I do. I'll need to get the kids to bed. If you want to go off with your buddies after that, fine. Let's keep it to a dozen people. And I'll want a list of guests, so I know who's expected."

"I'm surprised you're willing to do this for me." Phil was quiet. "I wasn't sure you'd ever talk to me again after I moved away—that's one reason I showed up in person at your house."

"Is that an apology, Phil?"

"I guess maybe it is. I didn't want to hurt you."

"Don't you mean you didn't want a scene when you told me you were leaving?"

"That too. I admit it. I hate scenes."

"You did hurt me, Phil, but now I have a terrific man in my life."

"I'm happy for you, Ditie, I really am. I didn't know what I had with you."

"Don't go there."

Phil paused, and then he spoke in a more animated way. "I know why you're really doing this! My dad couldn't stop talking about how you solved the Sandler's Soda case after your friend died. You're just itching to figure this one out, aren't you?"

He didn't give me a chance to speak.

"I'm glad you are. It means you believe I'm innocent. You want me to bring all the likely suspects on Wednesday, don't you?"

"Phil," I said, "do you want this reunion or don't you?"

"You know I do."

"All right then. You handle your part, and I'll handle mine. If you're free Tuesday night, why don't you come by around nine and we'll go over the details."

Even as I said it, I knew Mason would be unhappy, but Phil was eager to come.

"Sure. Great. Thanks. I'll pay for the food and decorations."

"Wow, Phil, have you become a more thoughtful human being than the man I used to know?"

"People do grow up, Ditie. You should give me a chance. You might like what you see."

I hung up not sure what I was feeling. I'd put Phil in a category of lousy human being and now he was trying to ease his way out of that box.

Lucie and I spent the rest of the day searching the web for authentic recipes from the mid-1800s and trying out some of the simpler ones that I had the ingredients for—like old fashioned tea cakes. Mason's mother Eddie called to say she'd be delighted to help and already had found some interesting recipes. She'd test them out and let me know.

Danny and Lurleen arrived with Jason in time for dinner and sampled the tea cakes for dessert.

"Fantastic," Danny said. "These are just like the ones my grandmother used to make. Not too sweet. Can I have one more?"

"You can take some home. We'll make a bigger batch for the party."

Lurleen got the kids to bed while I finished baking and cleaned the kitchen. She and Danny left before Mason arrived around nine. I poured us both a glass of wine, and we sat on the porch swing to talk.

"I've told the Gordon County Sheriff what we're up to, so he won't feel blindsided," Mason said. "He's okay with it as long as I give him any information we uncover."

"So you do think we might find out something Wednesday night?"

"We might."

"How shall I introduce you? If they know you're with the Atlanta Police that'll shut down the party."

"I know. I'll think about it."

It was a beautiful night and we sat in the swing pushing it gently with our feet. We didn't speak for a while. We listened to the crickets, heard a door slam down the street, and the backfire of a car on Highland. Mason put his arm around me, and I snuggled against him.

"I'm sorry I've been acting like a jerk," Mason said. "I just can't bear the thought of ever losing you. I've never been this content before."

"Me neither. A year ago I thought I'd always be single and always on the move. Now I can't imagine being anywhere but here in Atlanta with you and the kids. Funny, isn't it?"

Mason smiled. "Phil doesn't stir up a different kind of longing?"

"No, he doesn't." Was it the tiniest lie? I gave Mason a lingering kiss meant to erase any fears, and it seemed to do the trick. We made sure the kids were asleep and then we went upstairs. Mason left reluctantly around midnight.

I got up early for work on Monday. Lurleen would come at eight. I stood at the sink cleaning up the breakfast dishes and watched Jason in the backyard playing tag with Hermione. Lucie was settled on a stool in the kitchen reading *Harriet the Spy*. She had a notebook beside her.

"That's a wonderful book, Lucie, but don't get any ideas from it."

Lucie smiled, showing her latest missing tooth. "I won't."

"What's the notebook for? I saw you reading from it to Jason."

"Oh," said Lucie blushing, "that was my story notebook. This one is more like a diary."

"You're not keeping track of people, like Harriet did?"

Lucie didn't answer me directly, except to say, "It's Lurleen who wants to be a spy."

"I know."

"Aunt Di, is Lurleen really French? She doesn't sound French like our French teacher in school."

My perceptive Lucie. "That's a hard question to answer. I think you should ask *her*."

I hadn't pried into my dearest friend's childhood, and she'd never told me much about it. I suspected it wasn't a happy one, and I suspected Lurleen had invented a history that *was* happy. She told stories, usually about French boyfriends and occasionally about a French aunt. I never knew what to believe. Someone had left her a lot of money a few years ago—that much was true. I thought she might one day tell me the rest of her story, but if she didn't, that was okay too. I knew Lurleen the way you want to know a person. I knew her good heart, her humor and her intelligence.

Lucie watched me as I put breakfast dishes in the dishwasher and finished cleaning up the kitchen. "You know, Aunt Di, when I ask Lurleen about when she was little, she looks sad sometimes. Do you think something bad happened to her, and she doesn't want to talk about it? I know when people talk about their mothers, it makes me sad, and I don't want to talk about it."

"I think you may be right, Lucie. I don't know because she's never told me."

"Then I don't think I'll ask her about being French. Is that all right with you?"

"Absolutely."

Chapter Five

I got ready to leave for work as soon as I heard Lurleen pull up in her yellow Citroën. She came in like a small tornado. That was how she always entered my house. Her auburn hair was pulled back in a low ponytail, her Gucci knock-off dark glasses sat on top of her head. I was pretty sure Lurleen could have bought the real Gucci, but she was always more excited when she got a bargain.

"*Ooh la la*, the plans I have for you and Jason today," she said, kissing Lucie on both cheeks. "Where's my boy?"

Jason must have heard her car. He came running in through the kitchen with Hermione at his heels. "Hi Lurleen." He pretended to pull away when she tried to hug him, but it was all a game. "What will we do today?" he asked, "Will we look for spies?"

Lurleen smiled at me as if to say she had no idea what Jason might be talking about.

"We'll go to some stores for costumes and decorations for the party and then, if we have time, and you are both very, very good, we'll go swimming. I'll have them back here around five thirty. That suit you, Ditie?"

"Perfectly. Get whatever you want for costumes and decorations. I trust your judgment and I'll settle up with you tonight."

"My treat," she said and smiled. "Do you have any tea cakes left? I'm starving."

I brought out a plastic container. "Have all you want."

I left and managed to shift mental gears before I reached the refugee clinic. Mondays were full days. We had help from CDC volunteer physicians and the local medical school, so the place was packed when I arrived. Several clusters of families were waiting to be seen, seated on red vinyl chairs in the large waiting room where a television provided early morning cartoons for the kids. A few interpreters were already talking with some of the adults.

Vic waved me over as soon as I entered. "Someone's here to see you."

"What?" I asked and entered her office. There sat Phil. "What are you doing here?"

"I thought I'd see where you work. Ryan and Harper are super anxious to visit with you. They can't believe you've been back in Atlanta for two years and never looked them up. I'm an emissary to see if you can come to lunch today."

"I eat at my desk. Sorry. Make sure they come to the party, and I'll see them then."

Vic listened to the conversation. "You can take a lunch hour and see old friends. We've got It covered."

Normally, I loved Vic's generosity and her ability to stay calm in the face of any emergency. She was a powerhouse of energy packed in a compact body a little taller than me at 5'4" and without my rounded edges. She and I both complained about our curly hair, but hers always looked as if it obeyed her orders. Today I wished she'd made things harder on me. I wanted to focus on work, and the last thing I wanted to do was spend extra time with Phil.

"We've got more help coming in the afternoon," she said, "so we're fine. You probably don't need to come back."

I tried to smile. "I'll be back."

"I'll pick you up at twelve thirty," Phil said and left.

"He seems nice," Vic said.

"You think everyone is nice," I said.

"Oops, did I do the wrong thing?"

"No. Mason won't be pleased, but I can deal with that."

Vic nodded. "An old boyfriend?"

"Yep and a long story."

We left it at that. We looked over the roster and divvied up patients who were already waiting. Some had appointments, but most were walk-ins.

I greeted a family from Syria, a father, a mother and three small children. "Do you speak English?" I asked. The father nodded.

"It's our four year old, Bana. We've been here two months now and Bana has never been well. She sniffles and coughs and acts tired all the time."

I nodded and led them back to the examining room. The rest of the family sat in chairs near the wall as I helped their sick child up onto the examination table. I looked in Bana's ears and down her throat. I peered in her eyes and had her lie down and poked on her belly. The whole time she just stared at me and said nothing.

"Do you speak English?" I asked.

She nodded. "A little."

"Does anything hurt?"

She shook her head.

I turned to her parents. "We'll get some blood work, but I think your daughter may be suffering from allergies. Atlanta is known for that. If the blood work comes back normal we'll give her some medicine for allergies. Are you fine with that?"

The man nodded. "These allergies—that is not a bad disease?"

I smiled and called in an interpreter. "Could you explain to Mr. Abadi and his wife that I think their daughter has allergies from the pollen in Atlanta. Let him know it is not serious and once the pollen clears his daughter will feel better at least until the fall when it starts over again. We'll give her some medicine if the family is willing to have her take it."

The interpreter spent several minutes explaining what I had said, and I watched the relieved expressions on the part of both parents. They nodded when asked about medicine and shook my hand before they left. A nurse took Bana down the hall to draw blood. Her mother went with her.

"Thank you, thank you," Mr. Abadi said. "In Syria we lost our baby. She couldn't breathe and we couldn't get help, so you see my wife was very worried."

I nodded and showed him to the waiting room. He held tightly to a small child with each hand.

"Your other children are doing well, not bothered by allergies?" I asked.

"They are strong as bears. No problem."

The morning picked up its own rhythm as it always did. Sometimes we had to move quickly and at other times our pace was more relaxed. We had no emergencies that day and people as always were grateful for their care. It was twelve thirty before I looked at my watch and one of the nurses called to let me know a man was waiting for me in the lobby. I finished up what I was doing and signed out to Vic and my nurse.

Phil took my arm and walked me to his rented Mercedes.

I must have made a face because he responded defensively. "What's wrong with that? It's what I drive at home."

I got in the car and settled back into the plush leather seats. Nothing but the best for Phil. That hadn't changed. "Where are we going?"

"Ryan and Harper insisted we try a bistro they love in Buckhead, cleverly called the Buckhead Bistro." He gave me his boyish grin, and for a minute I was back in med school seeing Phil through rose-colored glasses.

What was I doing? Phil could still draw me in after all he'd done to me? I looked at him and shook my head.

"What is it?" he asked again with that wry smile of his. "You noticing my receding hair line? I may shave my head since that's such an in thing to do these days. Your boyfriend looks good bald."

"You can leave Mason out of this," I said, "even though he *does* look good bald."

We arrived a little after one. Ryan jumped up to greet me. He'd aged in seven years, something I hadn't noticed on the battlefield after Carl's death. His thick brown hair had flecks of gray in it and his face had worry lines. Harper looked the same as when I'd last seen her in med school. Slim, blond, fashionable, with an angular set to her jaw. Everything about her screamed money and good taste. She remained seated and we hugged awkwardly.

"Mabel, it's so good to see you," she said.

I flinched a little. My good friends called me Ditie, from Aphrodite—the middle name my father had insisted on. People who didn't know me well stuck with Mabel—the name my mother gave me.

"Hey, Ditie," Ryan said. "You look great." He hugged me, and I remembered why I liked him so much. He was a warm, friendly guy.

"You haven't changed a bit," Harper said. I wasn't sure she meant that as a compliment.

We sat down at a small table toward the back of the restaurant.

"I remembered how much you liked food," Harper said. "Good food I mean, and this place has the best."

"How have you been?" Ryan asked me. He couldn't help looking at Phil.

"I've been great," I said.

I thought I might as well get the elephant out of the room.

"I'm sure you're both surprised to see Phil and me together after our breakup." I wondered what Phil had told them if anything. "I admit I was shocked to hear he was going to New York at the end of our residencies, but I got over it. It turned out to be a good thing for both of us."

I glanced at Phil to see how he was handling my version of the story. He had his face buried in the menu.

"I came back here a couple of years ago to be near my brother and my best friend. My life is really good now."

"Phil mentioned you have two foster children," Harper said. "How is that?"

"Wonderful. I'm in the process of adopting them."

"I'm sorry about your friend," Ryan said, "the one who was murdered. It must have been awful."

"It was, but we're all recovering. How are you two doing?"

"Good." Ryan nodded with a half-smile. "Work is plentiful in Buckhead."

"And lucrative," Harper added. "We're current with all the latest treatments—ahead of the game really. If you ever want a peel or Botox let me know. It'll be on the house."

We ordered lunch and caught up on our current lives. Harper and Ryan had no children, which surprised me. I actually thought Ryan might go into pediatrics the way he loved children.

"When did you two marry? I assumed it was right after graduation, but Phil said it was later than that."

Harper flashed Phil a cold look. "Have you been telling Mabel my life story?" She turned back to me. "It's no secret. Frank Peterson and I were together for a while and then…things just didn't work out. I couldn't see myself staying in New York, and he couldn't see himself moving South. You never met my father, but he was adamant I marry a Southerner."

"Lucky for me," Ryan said. "We married three years ago. Had a big wedding in Texas at the ranch."

"Do you go back to Texas much?" I asked. "It's the one state I've never really visited."

"My father died suddenly last year—a heart attack, so I don't go home as much as I used to. My mother and brother handle the ranch fine without me."

"I'm sorry about your dad," I said.

"Me too. I miss him, but he was a hard man to please. He was always pressuring me for grandchildren."

Harper was older than I was and I wondered if she felt her biological clock ticking.

She seemed to read my mind. "I won't have kids," she said.

"But we might adopt some day," Ryan said and squeezed Harper's hand.

She pulled her hand away. "If I don't have my own children, why would I want someone else's?"

This sounded like an old argument.

"No offense, Ditie," she said. "You were built to have kids—I mean, psychologically. I'm not surprised you took in strays and found a way to love them. It's great for you."

I felt my color rising. "They were never strays, Harper. Their mother Ellie was a childhood friend. She loved her kids, and *I* love them."

"I meant no offense, Mabel. We're just very different people, that's all."

This conversation was making me angry, so I turned my attention to Phil. He provided details about his new life. His research grants were booming. He made time for reenactments all over the country. He'd separated six months ago and hoped to be divorced by Christmas. He spoke about the divorce the way you might talk about getting rid of an old car.

"Are you sad about it, Phil?" I asked.

He was silent for a moment. "We were never a good match, Ditie. She always wanted to change me. I'm not sure I ever really loved her. She was getting desperate to have children and that's when I knew it was over."

"What's wrong with wanting children?" Ryan asked.

"Nothing. Not for other people, but my life is too busy. I don't have time for that right now."

We let the subject drop.

"So Phil got you involved with reenactments?" I asked.

"I grew up a tomboy," Harper said. "You might not know that, Ditie, from looking at me, but I could hunt and ride with the best of them. Daddy always made sure I could take care of myself in a man's world. So when Phil wrote about the joys of reenactments for the med school journal, I asked to join him. I've been doing it for a couple of years now."

Phil nodded. "You should see her on the field, Ditie. She's something else."

"It seemed time to get Ryan involved since so many reenactments are here in our backyard," Harper said.

"I could take them or leave them," Ryan said, "And after Saturday, I'll be happy to leave them."

Harper nudged him. "You'll grow to love them as much as I do."

"Are you going to participate in the next one, even after what happened?" I asked.

"Probably," Harper said. "What happened was dreadful, but it was just a terrible accident."

"I had no idea Carl was living in Atlanta," I said. "He always hated the South."

"We saw a lot of him and his wife," Ryan said. "Kathy grew up in South Carolina, down the street from Andy Morrison."

"How did they meet?" I asked.

"Carl came down with Sally looking for work," Harper said. "I think it was Sally's idea to come South."

"She and Carl stayed friends," I asked, "after she dropped out of school?"

"Yes," Harper said.

"Were they ever a couple?" I asked.

Harper shook her head. "I think maybe Carl would have liked that, but I don't think Sally was interested in Carl romantically. They worked together—Carl as a doc and Sally in the business end of things. I think they came South to see if Andy Morrison might have a job for both of them."

"Is Andy here in Atlanta also?" I asked.

"No," Ryan said. "He stayed in his home town in South Carolina."

Harper jumped in to finish her story. "Andy introduced Carl to Kathy, and as they say the rest is history." Harper gave me a funny look. "It was a shotgun wedding. Kathy got pregnant but later lost the baby."

"Do they have other children?"

"Nope. Lots of trying and miscarriages I think, but no kids," Harper said.

"Maybe that's for the best right now," Ryan said.

"Maybe so," I said, but I wasn't sure that's how I'd feel.

"Kathy's a teacher," Ryan said. "You'll like her. She's coming to the party."

I put my sandwich down. "I can't imagine she'd want to do that. She must be devastated."

"That's what we thought, but she insisted." Harper turned to Ryan. "She said anything would be better than sitting at home right now, didn't she, hon?"

Ryan nodded.

"When did Carl start working with your father?" I asked Phil.

Ryan looked at Phil. "You didn't give Ditie all the details?"

Phil continued to eat his shrimp po' boy and shook his head.

"I'd say a few months ago, wouldn't you, Phil?" Ryan seemed eager to tell the story.

Phil nodded.

"It was a shock to everyone," Ryan added. "We all heard Carl's tirades about Southerners, but something changed. Carl showed up here, and the next thing we all knew he had a job with Phil's dad. I guess *you* know all the details, Phil."

"First I knew of it was when I came here four months ago. Dad hadn't bothered to tell me before it happened. He said he owed Carl a favor."

"Owed him a favor?" I asked. "Whatever for? How did they even know each other?"

Phil ignored the first part of my question. "They met when we were second year students," Phil said, "My father seemed to like Carl a lot more than I did."

"Is Sally working for your father too?" I asked.

"No. My father discovered Sally didn't have a business degree and wasn't a CPA. She made that up, and no one bothered to check it out at the other places she worked."

"Why would she lie about that?" I asked.

"Good grief, Mabel. Even you can't be that naive," Harper said. "She lied for the reasons we all lie— to survive. What was the girl supposed to do? She dropped out of med school. Her father was a doctor and maybe he got fed up with her when she dropped out. Maybe he cut her off. Fathers don't like it when their daughters go against their wishes."

Harper's usual cool tone escalated.

"So, she did the only thing she could do—she lied and found a way to make money. She worked on Wall Street for a few years and then sold herself as a financial guru. She and Carl worked with Frank Peterson for a bit and then headed South for greener pastures."

"You kept up with her then, after med school?" I said. "I knew you were close in school."

"We weren't *that* close in school, but yeah, I stayed up with her," Harper said. "Why the third degree?"

Phil laughed. "Don't you remember, Harper? In med school, Ditie was the one who'd have to understand every last detail before she moved on. She hasn't changed."

"Speaking of details," I said turning to Phil. "Why was Carl at the reenactment?"

"Dad insisted I teach Carl some hands-on history. He said he couldn't have someone in his concierge business who didn't have a working knowledge of the Civil War."

I stared at Phil. "Did your dad know how much the two of you disliked each other?"

"I don't think so. Carl laid it on pretty thick about how close we'd become."

"I thought you were considering taking over your dad's practice."

"That was before I knew about Carl. I swear Dad thought he was a second son. I wasn't going to get involved with that."

"I guess now the door is open again for you to join the practice." I spoke before I thought about what those words might mean.

"What? Are you suggesting I might be happy Carl is dead, so I can take over my father's business?"

"No, of course not."

Harper patted Phil's hand. "Mabel didn't mean anything bad, I'm sure. She sometimes comes across a little harshly."

There are two things I really hate. People speaking for me and people who refer to me in the third person when I'm sitting in front of them.

I didn't respond, but Ryan did. "It's been a crazy week for all of us. The police swarming around. We all feel like suspects."

"I can't believe any of you want to go to another reenactment." I said.

"I'm here. I have my gear. I'm going," Phil said.

"I plan to sit on the hillside with Harper," Ryan smiled.

"No you don't," she responded. "I want to see my man in action. Besides I may bring my horse and be part of the cavalry."

A waitress arrived at that moment. "Can I interest you in dessert?"

I looked over at Phil. "I think I need to go."

He glanced at his pocket watch. "It's not even two thirty. Your boss said you didn't have to come back at all."

"Well, I do. I have paperwork."

"But you love dessert, Mabel," Harper said. "You've always loved dessert."

"We understand," Ryan said. I reached for my wallet, but he put a hand on my arm. "This is on us. It was great to see you, Ditie."

"I'll see you Wednesday?" I asked.

"We wouldn't miss it," Harper said. She stood up and gave me a peck on the cheek. She gave Phil a longer kiss on the lips. Ryan didn't look happy about that.

Chapter Six

Phil didn't speak to me for the first five minutes of the drive back to the clinic. It reminded me of the old days. If I did something that annoyed him, he'd give me the silent treatment. Usually, I'd beg him to tell me what I'd done wrong, but not this time.

Eventually he spoke up. "How could you have said that to me?"

I gave him a blank look.

"About how the door was open now for a reconciliation with my father."

"I never said anything about a reconciliation. Are you two estranged?"

"You know what I'm talking about, Ditie. You suggested I might have killed Carl to get him out of the way."

"I can see how you heard what I said as an accusation. I didn't mean it as one. Of course I was surprised Carl ended up working for your father. He hated the South, and you two stopped speaking in med school. You never told me why. Will you tell me now?"

"I don't think you want to hear this."

"Try me."

"It was over a girl."

"While you were dating me you were involved with someone else?"

"It's before we talked about being exclusive. I didn't do anything wrong."

"You never do, Phil." I sighed. "Okay, let me hear it."

"Carl and I got interested in the same girl at the end of first year."

"Someone from med school?"

"No names, just the story," Phil said.

"All right. Tell me the story."

"She didn't tell us she was dating both of us. It probably would have been okay with me. I didn't really want to get serious about anyone at that point. But Carl did. He found out about us and started spreading vicious rumors about me. Rumors that could have gotten me kicked out of school, like I was putting a scam together to help people cheat."

Phil didn't need to cheat. He was plenty smart in his own right. On the other hand, he cheated on me with his oncology nurse. Maybe that was the same thing.

"You're quiet, Ditie. Don't tell me you think I actually did cheat on exams. I was elected to AOA as a third year—you know how hard that is to do."

"I know, Phil. You never let me forget it."

"So if I'm in the medical honor society I didn't need to cheat."

"I heard about the cheating scandal, but I never knew any of the details, except that something was going on. The school managed to keep it hushed up."

"Well, you won't learn any details from me except to say Carl tried to convince the school and my father that I was the mastermind."

"Did he succeed?"

"My father is a proud man—concerned about the honor of the Brockton name. 'Never sullied in two hundred years,' that's his favorite quote. You can imagine what a scandal like this would have done to him."

Phil turned into the drive to the clinic and parked near the front entrance.

"So that's why I stopped talking to Carl—Carl claimed I'd engineered the whole thing when he was probably the one who did it."

I looked at Phil. Phil always liked to push the limits. He didn't need to cheat, but I wondered if he'd be curious to figure out how it could be done.

"I swear Carl accused me out of spite and to cover his own ass. I could only imagine the lies he was spreading to my dad."

"Why would your father believe Carl over you?"

"Carl claimed he'd overheard a conversation between me and Frank about cheating—a conversation he made up."

"That doesn't make sense, Phil. Your father knows you, and Carl was a complete stranger."

Phil was getting agitated. "What, you don't believe me either?"

"I'm not saying that."

"I'm not going to defend myself to you, Ditie. You know I had no reason to cheat. After a long conversation with my dad, Carl backed off his claims, and the school was able to keep the whole thing quiet. You know how much our school hates a scandal."

"I do."

"I found out about Carl working for my dad the last time I was here. Dad and I had a big blow up over him, but my father wouldn't budge. Carl had a job. If I wanted one I could have it. Let the best man win in terms of who might take over the practice. My father has always loved competition."

I'd need to go into the clinic in a minute, but I could see how distraught Phil was even now, and he wasn't done talking.

"I couldn't work in that environment. I hated the guy. He tried to ruin me at every turn."

It was a pretty good motive for murder. I didn't say that to Phil. "Are you and your dad speaking now?"

"A little. We're going to Carl's funeral together on Friday. Would you come with us?"

"No, Phil. I barely knew Carl and what I did know about him I didn't like. I'm sorry for his wife, but I'll see her at the reunion."

"I'm surprised she'd want to come to that," Phil said, "so soon after everything that's happened."

"Me too, but if it brings her some comfort, then I'm all for it."

Phil nodded, got out of the car, and walked around to open my door—always the Southern gentleman. He left me with a barely audible goodbye.

Vic caught me as I walked to my office. "I'm glad you came back. We're slammed. Did you have fun?" She didn't wait for my answer. She just looked at my face. "Was it really as bad as that?"

I nodded, and she handed me a couple of intake sheets. "New patients. They're yours."

"Thanks."

I found a young boy seated beside his mother. His intake sheet said he was ten, but he looked more like seven or eight. A nurse had recorded his vital signs. He had a low-grade fever and an increased respiratory rate. He looked sick and was struggling to get air. I introduced myself and the mother responded in Spanish. She said the boy had a sore throat and was having trouble breathing. They'd come as asylum seekers two days earlier from Venezuela. I motioned an interpreter to follow us to the examining room. I looked in the boy's mouth and saw a thick gray membrane partially covering the back of his throat.

I'd never seen a case of diphtheria, but this sure looked like one. I called in Vic, and she agreed. She also had never seen one and told me how rare they were in the US. She would notify the Georgia Department of Public Health about the suspected case.

We had one room in the clinic at the end of the hall, which we used for isolation, and that's where we took the boy and his mother. I put on a mask and gloves and hooked him up to oxygen along with an oximeter to check his oxygen level. I could see his effort to breathe ease and his respiratory rate decline as the oxygen filled his lungs.

Vic called the emergency room at the hospital, which was less than half a mile away, and spoke with a physician there. They would run the tests necessary to confirm the diagnosis and start the boy on antibiotics and diphtheria antitoxins obtained from the CDC. My nurse called for an ambulance.

I had the interpreter explain the situation to the mother including my assurances that we could treat her child in the hospital. I asked if she had other children at home and she said no. When I asked if she had any symptoms, she confirmed she was in good health.

The afternoon continued to be busy. I got home around six to find Lurleen, Lucie and Jason standing at the front door, full of news. Mason and Hermione stood behind them. The only creature who seemed indifferent to my arrival was Majestic. He was seated at the screen door observing two cardinals that had settled in my magnolia tree.

"Where's Danny?" I asked, once I managed to get in the door.

"He's with Phil," Lurleen said. "Phil wanted him to check out his hotel room for security issues and go over plans for the next weekend. If something bad is going to happen, that seems to be when Phil thinks it will occur."

"I've had about all of Phil I can take for the moment," I said.

Mason's face brightened and then soured again when I mentioned having lunch with Phil.

"Two classmates were eager to catch up with me. They insisted Phil bring me to lunch."

I sat on the sofa, took off my shoes and curled my feet under me. Lucie climbed up beside me, but Jason couldn't sit still.

"Wait 'til you see, Aunt Di," he said. "I'm a soldier in a war."

"You're a bugle boy," Lurleen corrected. "Show Ditie your bugle."

Jason ran out of the room and returned carrying a plastic bugle that looked like it was made of brass.

"Looks real, doesn't it," Lurleen said proudly. "I found it in a toy store."

Jason was busy blowing a single note.

Mason brought me a glass of white wine and sat on the other side of me.

"What about you, Lucie? Do you have a costume?" I asked.

"Lurleen said I can help her in her store, so I have a costume for a girl from a hundred years ago."

I looked up at Lurleen.

"You won't believe it, Ditie. You know that retro clothing store in Little Five Points. They had the perfect dress for Lucie and one for me. We'll show you after dinner."

"Dinner," I said. "I haven't even thought about dinner."

"No problem, I have," Lurleen said.

Lurleen didn't cook. "You're fixing dinner?" I asked.

"Not exactly. I thought we could go to the Varsity. Danny will meet us there in half an hour."

Mason patted his not so flat belly. "I don't know, Lurleen. I'm trying to eat a little healthier."

"What about you, Ditie?"

I took another sip of wine. "I do love their onion rings, but I'd rather eat in tonight. After my lunch out, I want to stay put."

Lurleen looked a bit ruffled. "But, *chérie*, I've already promised the kids, and Danny will be there." She brightened. "I'll take them and you two can have an hour to yourselves."

"That," Mason said, "sounds great."

"I'll bring you back some onion rings," Lurleen whispered to me.

I gave the kids a hug and tossed Lurleen the keys to my Toyota. "There's more room in my car."

They left in a rush and for a moment I didn't know what to do with the sudden calm.

"You look tired," Mason said to me. "Hard day at work?"

"Busy and one pretty sick child, but not bad. I hate to break my day up with a long lunch. And there was something about it that didn't sit well with me."

"Did it have to do with Phil Brockton?"

"No. Phil is the same person he's always been, although perhaps I'm seeing him more clearly now. No, it wasn't him. He did tell me about the split with Carl." I told Mason the abbreviated version.

Mason waited for me to continue.

"It was a funny feeling I got about Ryan and Harper Hudson. They seemed to be disconnected in some way—I don't know if I can explain it. Maybe after years of marriage that's what happens to a couple."

Mason shook his head. "If that's a way to say we shouldn't ever get married save your breath. We're getting married. Someday."

"Someday will be wonderful," I said. "Let's see if I can find us some healthy leftovers. Better yet I made Captain Sanderson's Boiled Pork and Bean Soup from an 1800s cookbook. We'll see if it's good enough for the party."

It was. We both agreed. I was not one for false modesty.

Mason and I talked a little about our work day. He was in the middle of a case involving the murder of a Buckhead socialite. It had made national news and was the kind of case Mason often got pulled in on. I asked him what the Gordon County investigator was making of the cannon explosion.

"Barden said the experts are only adding to the confusion. It's still possible it was an accident. It seems the inside of the barrel had a thinned area, maybe natural wear and tear or maybe man-made. The experts don't know for sure yet. Phil was the one who was supposed to inspect the cannons, wasn't he?"

"Yes, and he's a very meticulous guy," I said. "I can't imagine he'd miss something like that unless it was hard to detect."

"Given your story about Carl Thompson and Brockton's father, do you think maybe he didn't miss it?"

"You're asking me if I think Phil could have committed cold-blooded murder?"

"I am."

Chapter Seven

I didn't answer Mason right away. Did I think Phil could possibly be guilty of murder? He was outraged at Carl, that much was obvious. And to lose the respect of his father—that might be a blow Phil couldn't tolerate.

"I don't know, Mason. I dated Phil for six years. Could I date someone capable of murder?" I threw up my hands. "In the end, I felt as if I never really knew him. He didn't give me a clue he was leaving Atlanta, and then over dinner in a fancy restaurant, he told me he was walking out of my life."

"Are you sorry it didn't work out?" Mason asked.

"It's the best thing Phil ever did for me, although I didn't know it at the time." I squeezed Mason's hand. "I didn't realize I was waiting for you, but I was."

"So, do you believe Brockton could be a murderer?"

"Being self-centered doesn't necessarily make you capable of murder. I do know estrangement from his father might push him over the edge."

We heard the brief honking of my Toyota Corolla, followed by doors slamming, feet scrambling up the walk. Hermione whined until the door was opened and Lucie and Jason burst through it.

"What will you have?" Jason said, as if he'd been practicing in the car.

Danny came in and scooped him up. "Not, 'what will you have,' Jason. It's 'what'll ya have, what'll ya have?'"

Jason tried to take up the refrain, but before he could get the words out of his mouth, Danny was tickling him so hard all he could do was squeal.

Lucie was wide-eyed. "It's just like you said it would be. It's enormous! You can sit in your car and a waitress will come up to you to take your order, but Danny said we needed to go inside to get the real . . ."

"Atmosphere," Danny supplied.

"Everyone came up to the counter to order their hotdogs and hamburgers and French fries, " Lucie said, "and the people behind the counter kept asking us, 'What'll ya have? What'll ya have?' I want to eat there every day."

"Now look what you've done, Lurleen," I said.

"It was Danny's idea. You know me, *chérie*, I prefer a nice healthy salad. But Danny, *mon cher*, can't resist the French fries." She pulled out a Styrofoam container. "And for you the onion rings. Still hot. We raced home."

I looked at Mason. "We can't very well let these go to waste."

"No, we can't."

While Mason and I ate, Lurleen and Lucie left to put on their costumes. Lucie appeared first in a long cotton dress that buttoned up to her neck with a bonnet tied under her chin. She looked adorable. Lurleen followed two minutes later in a far more modest dress than I expected—long sleeves, high neck with multiple tucks and gathers in a checked burgundy.

"No belle-of-the-ball costume for you, Lurleen?" I asked.

Lurleen made a face. "Danny says I must be a store keeper, a sutler, and that means I must wear practical clothes."

"Well, you both look wonderful," I said and meant it. "But you're going to be very hot this weekend. It's supposed to be close to 90 degrees, and with all this humidity I don't envy you two."

"What are you talking about, Ditie? I got an outfit for you too. You have to help me in the shop."

All I could do was sigh and finish off the onion rings.

I helped Lucie out of her dress and got both children tucked in bed before nine. When I came back to the living room, Danny was in the middle of a long discussion about cannons used in Civil War reenactments.

"So, you see Mason, it could all have been done deliberately, but it may be difficult to prove. Phil swears he inspected each of the cannons the morning before the event started."

"Hmm," was all Mason would commit to. "You've told Officer Barden about this?"

"Didn't need to. He's the one who told me. I did talk to all of the reenactors near that particular cannon immediately after the explosion when I cordoned off the area. Seems friends stick together on the battlefield."

"And?" Mason asked.

"They appeared to be genuinely shocked. Maybe Sally Cutter most of all. They all swear Phil is the most competent organizer they've ever seen. That's both a compliment and damning, since they say to a man those cannons should have been in good working order."

"Did you learn anything useful, Danny?" Mason sounded irritated.

We all stared at him.

"No disrespect, Detective, but I didn't think this was your case," Danny said.

"It's not, but it seems you're all heavily involved, so I might as well be too. I know the Gordon County Sheriff. He wouldn't mind some help as long as we don't interfere with Barden doing his job. There will be a police presence at the Battle of Tunnel Hill on Saturday."

Picking up on Mason's train of thought, I pressed Danny a little. "Did anyone seem nervous about the investigation or especially relieved Carl was dead?"

"Not that they showed me. You were there, what did you think?"

"I told you what Sally said—that Phil hated Carl and that he made sure Carl was alone on one side of the cannon, the side that split apart. She seemed pretty anxious to put the focus on Phil."

Danny nodded. "That's the impression I got as well. Apparently, it's some kind of honor to pull the lanyard. Phil was supposed to do it, so why he let Carl do it is a mystery."

"According to Phil," I said, "he was trying to please his father, do the right thing, so when Carl asked to pull it, Phil agreed."

"Why would Carl ask to do that?" Danny said. "Carl had never been to a reenactment before. He knew nothing about how cannons worked. He was as ignorant about them as you are, Ditie."

"Thanks, Danny, but it's a good question. I wouldn't even know what a lanyard was if you hadn't explained it to me, so who explained it to Carl?"

"And why was he the only one on that side of the cannon?" Mason asked.

"Phil told me that was happenstance," I said. "He was a man or two short. The others knew to turn their backs when the lanyard was pulled and move back from the cannon. They just happened to be on the other side. Phil acknowledged he moved as far from Carl as he could get. He said he was furious about the whole thing."

"You got any more, Danny?" Mason asked.

Danny shook his head. "I know Investigator Barden and you know the Sheriff. We can keep on top of things."

I stood up.

"Good. Now, all of you need to let me do some baking tonight."

"Need any tasters?" Danny asked.

"I don't think so."

They left, and I went to the kitchen to sort through my recipes. What would sound good on a hot July evening? Soup wasn't the best idea, but Captain Sanderson's Boiled Pork and Bean Soup turned up more than once in my search for old recipes online. Mason and I both thought it was delicious, and I could certainly make it in big batches. Biscuits were easy, and Ozark Pudding sounded simple and tasty. I'd serve homemade ice cream, tea cakes and filled cookies. It would be a modest spread but if I knew this group they'd appreciate the attempt at authenticity. After they had a couple of beers, I expected they'd be pretty content. And who knew what Mason's mother would bring? Whatever it was, it would be delicious.

I made up a new batch of tea cakes, which gave me time to think. If Carl was murdered, was he the intended victim or was Phil the target as he claimed? Did Phil hire Danny because he really was afraid for his own safety or as a way to convince everyone he was innocent?

Lucie brought me out of my reverie. "Aunt Di, is something burning?"

I grabbed a batch of tea cakes out of the oven. They were a dark brown. I'd let them cool before I threw them away.

"What are you doing up?" I asked.

"I had a bad dream."

I sat down on a stool and took her onto my lap. She was too old for that usually but not when she was scared. "Tell me about it."

"Something bad happened in a war. A big explosion. I was all alone and someone was hurt."

I hugged Lucie. "You've been hearing too much about what happened this week. I'm sorry about that. You don't have to go on Saturday if you don't want to. The three of us could do something else."

Lucie shook her head. "Mommy said don't ever be scared. Face what you are afraid of and march straight ahead."

"We all get scared, Lucie. Sometimes being scared keeps us out of danger." I thought about Ellie. She always believed she was invincible—until she wasn't.

I watched the tears trickle down Lucie's cheeks. "I miss Mommy."

"I know you do, baby." I held her while she cried, and when she was done I got her a glass of milk and a tea cake from an earlier batch.

"You think about Saturday. If you want to go, we'll go, but if not we'll do something else."

"Jason wants to go, so I'll go. I'll wear my dress and I'll be very brave."

"You know it's just pretend, and it's supposed to be fun."

"That's what Lurleen says. I want to go, Aunt Di."

I took her back to bed and tucked her in. When I was sure she was asleep I went back into the kitchen and finished baking the tea cakes. Maybe the Saturday reenactment was a very bad idea. If I really thought Carl might have been murdered, how could I possibly take the children to what could be a dangerous battlefield?

The answer was I couldn't. I would need to come up with Plan B.

Chapter Eight

Tuesday was a blur. I woke up early to bake some filled cookies before I went to work. Lurleen offered to help, but some things, like baking, went better without her help. Besides the kids needed attention, and I needed a plan for what I would do with them on Saturday.

"They can't come to the reenactment?" Lurleen asked. "Jason will be so disappointed."

"Lurleen, if this was murder and not an accident, I can't possibly take them. Who knows what might happen? I need to find something that will be fun and keep them safe. Maybe dressing up for the party tomorrow night will be enough."

I went to the clinic, and the day passed quickly with many wellness checks and minor problems. I got home before six and demanded everyone go out to dinner for the second night in a row, so I could get some baking done. This time I said it had to be someplace healthy. Mason insisted on staying with me.

"Mom taught me a little about cooking," he said. "I'm good at chopping."

"Eddie called me to say she'd bring fried corn and turnip greens," I said. "I'm not a fan of turnip greens, but I know if your mom makes them they'll be delicious."

"They will be. If you plan on staying in the South, you'll need to get over that particular aversion."

I tied an apron around him and set him up to prepare the soup. We tripled everything. I'd soaked the beans overnight, so they were ready to go.

I put together the ingredients for the Ozark Pudding—apples and walnuts—while Mason dumped ingredients for the soup into the biggest pot I had. I told him about Lucie's nightmare and wondered where my head was. "Of course I can't let them go. Hopefully, nothing will happen, but the day will still be full of guns and cannons and people pretending to fall over dead."

"I agree with you, Ditie. I told the Sheriff I'd be there, so I'm committed, but you could do something else. You know what? After the day is over, we'll do our own reenactment in your backyard or maybe my mom's. She has a bigger backyard with lots of trees to hide behind. That should satisfy Jason and keep Lucie from being traumatized."

"You're a genius."

"Does that mean you'll marry me?"

"Someday."

The kids and Lurleen arrived home while the soup was still simmering. I got them to bed and had time to read each of them a story.

I'd forgotten Phil was going to come by with his guest list. Actually, I thought he might just email it to me in the end, but when I heard the doorbell ring and Hermione go berserk, I knew it had to be him.

Phil and Mason greeted each other like gladiators on the field of battle. They didn't exactly circle each other but they were definitely on guard.

Phil handed me the list. Ryan and Harper. Carl's wife Kathy. Sally, Frank and Andy. There were six more folks on the list who were complete strangers to me.

"You vouch for all these people?" I asked.

Phil shrugged. "You mean do I think one of them will try to kill me at your party? I don't think so, Ditie. If they want to see me dead, they'll make it look like an accident on the battlefield. Like what they did to Carl."

"You're convinced it wasn't an accident?"

"I don't know. I may not have told you this before, but that was an original Napoleon. Most of the cannons are reproductions with steel reinforced barrels. Only an original would have a barrel that could wear away and explode."

"Would you have seen the barrel was thinning during your inspection?" Mason asked.

Phil hesitated. "Probably not."

"You're saying it could have been done deliberately, and you might not have spotted it," I said.

"Yes," Phil said. "A person could have filed away a good portion of the bronze, and it might not have been obvious." He looked at me. "If it was done intentionally, then I was the target, not Carl."

"Maybe you should figure out who you've ticked off recently," I said. "Of course, whoever did this would have to know what he or she was doing."

"Yes, and that points to someone who knows about arms and ammunition—a Civil War mainstreamer," Phil said.

"Mainstreamer?" I asked.

"Someone like me who knows the details of how things are supposed to work at one of these reenactments."

"Then that narrows the field again," I said.

"If you're telling us the truth," Mason added.

"Look, Detective Garrett, I'm sure you're good at your job. I'm good at mine too as a physician and researcher. I wouldn't put all my years of hard work on the line to kill someone I disliked. I'd never do that."

We let the matter drop. We sat in the living room and went over the menu.

"Looks awesome." Phil turned to Mason. "I hope you know how lucky you are to have Ditie in your life. I didn't."

Mason said nothing.

"Where's Danny?" I asked to break the obvious tension. "I thought he was your bodyguard."

"He's in the car, keeping an eye on the neighborhood." He smiled at me. "You're the best."

He left after giving me a peck on the cheek.

"That guy really bugs me," Mason said. "He'd love to get you back."

I shook my head. "He might love to get my cooking back, and he'd probably like me to confess my undying devotion for him, but he doesn't want me. He never really did."

The rest of the evening was all about getting food ready for the party the next day. The batches of Ozark Pudding looked perfect if I did say so myself. I'd make the biscuits last thing Wednesday afternoon.

* * * *

Wednesday at work was normally reserved for paper work and walk-ins. We were busy, but I still managed to leave by one. When I got home, I saw that Lurleen had turned my house into a stunning pre-Civil War mansion with pictures of antebellum houses on every unused wall and Magnolia garlands wrapped along my staircase. The kids were in their outfits waiting for the party to start. Lurleen kept them occupied while I finished making the biscuits.

Phil and Danny were the first to arrive, in uniform, shortly before five.

"This isn't my actual uniform," Phil said. "I couldn't risk getting it dirty before Saturday. This is my back-up."

That would be Phil, planning for every possibility. Danny looked stunning in his borrowed Civil War outfit as an infantry man. He wore a slouch hat over his buzz cut and carried a haversack. I thought Lurleen might swoon when she saw him.

She sashayed down the stairs a moment later wearing a satin ball gown that Scarlett O'Hara would have been proud to call her own. The bright green fabric set off her eyes and her auburn hair. She twirled for Danny to approve. He did.

Eddie arrived a little before five carrying great pans of turnip greens and roasted corn. The pans were nearly as big as she was. Danny took them and then went to her car to get the rest of her supplies. I gave her a kiss on the cheek and thanked her.

"I came late, so the food would still be warm," Eddie said. She glanced over at Phil. "Mason didn't tell me it was a costume party."

"I'm sure he didn't, and it's a come-any-way-you-want gathering," I said. "I assume he told you what was going on."

"You mean about that unfortunate classmate and the exploding cannon?"

I nodded. Our conversation ended there as Lucie and Jason ran into the room from outside. Lurleen stood behind them.

"Grandma Eddie, you're here!" Lucie said, and Jason announced her arrival with his one-note bugle.

"I am." She gave each one of them a hug. "Don't you two look wonderful! And you, Lurleen, look stunning!"

Lurleen smiled appreciatively. "I have something for both of you." She swished her way upstairs and returned with two plaid aprons for us to wear.

"Pinner aprons," she said as she pinned them to our outfits. "Now you're of the right era."

Eddie, with her short white hair and small body, looked perfect, and she said the same about me.

Mason came at five thirty. He nodded approvingly at my outfit and his mom's. "You two look authentic."

He took the kids in hand and had them show him all the decorations. "You are my wards for the evening," he said.

"Wards?" Lucie asked.

"That means I need to know where you are and you need to do the same for me."

I saw Lucie open a notebook she was carrying and carefully write in it. Mason looked over her shoulder as she wrote.

That was the last I saw of them for most of the night.

Guests were prompt. Phil stood at my side to introduce them if they weren't old classmates. The day was so humid, everyone stayed inside for the first hour.

Ryan and Harper arrived a little before six. Harper gushed over my house and the food.

It *was* a perfect house for entertaining a small crowd—good flow as an architect friend told me for a bungalow built in the 1920s.

"Mabel, you are such a wonder," Harper said, "so into food and entertaining."

She wore a lovely blue outfit with a hoop skirt that highlighted her narrow waist and light blond hair. She batted her fan and gave me and Phil a hug before moving on. Phil followed her to the breakfast room where we'd set up the bar.

Hermione bounded in from outside with Jason at her heels. A moment later, I heard Harper scream. "Get that dog away from me!"

When I got to the room, Harper was crouched on the other side of the table, holding an unopened bottle of wine as a weapon. "Your dog tried to attack me!" she said.

Phil shook his head. He'd put Hermione in a down position, and Hermione didn't move. "She didn't do a thing," he said. "Look, she's good as gold."

I asked Jason to take Hermione to his room and leave her there, door closed.

Mason was nearby. "What did Hermione do?" he asked.

"Nothing," I said. "I don't think Harper likes dogs."

Sally Cutter arrived dressed in a Federal uniform. She looked a lot calmer than the last time I'd seen her. Her short dark hair accented her eyes and her outfit showed off her trim figure.

"How did Phil let you get away with that?" I asked.

"He needed a few more of the enemy," she laughed, "to make it a fair fight. I don't really care which side I'm on." She pulled me aside. "I hope you didn't take seriously what I said right after the accident. I was in a state of shock. Carl was the person who always stood by me. I can't imagine how it will be without him."

"I heard from other people how close you were. Were you ever more than friends?"

"Gosh, Ditie, you're so direct." Sally looked at me from under her thick dark lashes. "We were more like brother and sister—always had each other's back. The guy who's floating around here and available is Phil. He's told you about the divorce, I'm sure."

"Only a little."

"It leaves the field wide open," she said.

"I guess it does."

"You're really not interested?" she asked.

"I'm not. Are you?"

Sally shrugged. "Phil and I have stayed in touch. He's a great guy. I don't think his wife ever realized that."

"A few days ago you thought he might be a murderer."

"I was hysterical. I didn't know what I was saying. Phil couldn't hurt a fly."

Sally had me totally confused. Before I could ask her any more, other guests arrived. Frank and Andy came together, greeted me briefly and headed to the bar. They came back with a beer in hand and a biscuit.

"Nice house," Frank said. "Couldn't get something like this in New York for five million. Even around Ithaca, you'd spend a lot."

"You have a busy practice, Frank?" I asked.

"I'm doing the concierge thing like Phil's dad. I work mainly with university professors and their spouses. I can limit my number of patients and get very well paid for what I do. It's a good system. The nurse practitioners handle most of my workload."

Frank seemed more concerned about the money he made than the patients he saw. Lurleen would have pointed out my unfair bias—that somehow I thought it was wrong to get wealthy as a doctor or to ignore the poor people who needed care.

In any case, Andy Morrison was more my kind of doc. He'd always wanted to be a country doctor like his dad.

"Hey, Ditie," he said, planting a kiss on my cheek. "You still look like you're twenty-five."

"Thanks." Andy looked like the boy next door with his red hair and freckles. "You, too."

"Naw, you're just being nice. I eat too much and exercise too little." He patted his belly. "I've got two kids, wanna see some pictures? They're close in age to yours." He pulled out his cell. "The little one is Erin, she's six, and Elizabeth is ten."

There were no pictures of his wife. "How's Jenna?" I asked.

Andy's face darkened. "Long story. I'll tell you some other time."

"The kids are darling," I said. "You're still working with your dad?"

"Yes, in the small town I grew up in."

"How did Phil recruit you for his reenactments?"

"He didn't have to. I'm a stitch counter, like him."

"A stitch counter?"

"You know, the folks who have to get every last detail right."

Carl's wife came late. I didn't blame her. Frankly, I was surprised she came at all.

She introduced herself to me. "I'm Kathy Thompson. I thought I'd like to be here with Carl's friends, but now I'm not sure I can stay." Kathy was a slender woman with light brown hair in a shoulder length cut. Her face looked strained as if she were barely keeping it together. Her accent had the same lyrical Southern notes that Andy's had.

"I understand. I appreciate your coming."

"Could we talk privately for a moment?" she asked.

"Of course." I took her upstairs to my bedroom and closed the door.

"I have to tell someone. At first the police thought Carl's death was an accident, a terrible, horrible accident. I knew Carl didn't know one thing about the Civil War, and when he was going to a reenactment I couldn't believe it. He said a friend had urged him to go."

"What friend?"

"He didn't tell me, said I wouldn't know the person. His boss, Phil's father, also suggested it would be good for business."

"Phil told me Carl was working with him."

"That's right. Carl thought he'd be a partner soon, maybe take over the business."

She sighed and sank down on the bed.

"When I thought it was an accident, that was one thing. I thought I needed to be around people who cared about him. But now the police think it might have been murder."

Kathy started sobbing.

"Dr. Brown, if it was murder then someone downstairs in your house killed my husband. And if I had to guess who might have done it, I'd put my money on Phil Brockton."

I got her a glass of water from the sink in the bathroom and waited while she took a sip.

"Why do you say that?"

"Phil hated Carl. He blamed him for the rift with his father, but Carl had nothing to do with that. Nothing. That happened long before Carl was involved with the practice."

I thought about what Phil had told me. I wondered what Carl had told his wife.

"Did Carl tell you why Phil and his father were estranged?" I asked.

"Dr. Brockton found out Phil had developed a cheating scam at the school. He virtually disowned him at that point."

I wondered who was telling me the truth. Did Carl spin Kathy a tale or was Phil lying to me?

"Why did you come tonight?" I asked her.

"I heard about you from Phil's father—that you solved a murder at Sandler's Sodas. I'm asking you to do that for me."

"I'm not a detective."

"All the better. You know these people. If my husband was murdered, I want his killer brought to justice."

"Why do you think it wasn't an accident?" I asked.

"Because Carl warned me."

"What?"

"Before he died, he told me if anything happened to him I was to go to the police. He said someone was threatening him. He didn't know who it was, but the police needed to know his death was not an accident."

"I don't understand," I said. "Threatening him how?"

"He wouldn't tell me, but I think someone was trying to blackmail him."

"You've told the police all this."

"Yes, but I have no proof."

"You said blackmail. Was money disappearing?"

"Carl handled the money, so I don't know. He could be extravagant, buy me a diamond necklace or himself a vintage car. We always seemed to have enough money, so I never worried."

"If someone was trying to blackmail your husband, do you know why?"

"No." She stood up. "He was a good man. There was no reason why anyone would threaten him. I didn't mean blackmail. I meant more that someone was threatening his life. I have to go."

I followed her downstairs and out the door to her car. Andy came behind me. "Kathy, you decided to come. I'm really glad. I'll be at the service on Friday."

Kathy let Andy hug her and then burst into a new flood of tears. "I have to go," she said. She turned to me. "I did mean what I said to you upstairs, I do want your help."

Andy helped Kathy into her car, and then walked with me back to the house.

"She wants your help?" Andy asked me. He ran his fingers through his hair. "Why would she want your help?"

"I'm not really sure what she meant by that." I also wasn't sure what part of her story might be the truth.

Chapter Nine

When we got back to the house Danny was standing between Phil and Ryan, one arm pushed against Ryan and the other blocking Phil.

I looked around for the children and Mason. They and most of the guests were outside as the temperature had finally started to cool off.

"What in the world—?"

"I got it, Ditie," Danny said. "You should check on your other guests."

The handful of people who remained in the house weren't going anywhere, and I wasn't either.

"What's this all about?" I asked, looking at Phil and then Ryan.

"A misunderstanding," Phil said.

Were the two of them drunk? They didn't act like it.

"You two done?" Danny asked.

Phil turned away. "I am."

Ryan still looked angry. I remembered how quickly he lost his temper in med school. He was always insecure and got bent out of shape if he ever thought someone was making fun of him. So, had Phil humiliated him in some way?

Danny took Ryan by the arm and led him out to the front porch for some air. I followed behind. Danny made him sit on the swing.

"Cool off, man," Danny said.

Ryan looked up at me and colored. "I'm sorry, Ditie. I didn't mean to spoil your party."

I heard a burst a laughter from inside the house. "It doesn't sound like you did. What happened, Ryan?"

"Phil can't keep his hands to himself. I saw him outside, cornering Harper near your fish pond. I lost it. I'm sorry."

I looked at Danny.

"Later," was all he said.

"Let me get you some iced tea, Ryan. You want me to find Harper?'

"I'll take the tea. Harper can find me if she wants to."

Danny followed me into the kitchen. "If you want to know who was cornering whom, I'd say it was Harper all over Phil and not the other way around."

"Oh."

Harper had always been a tease. Ryan knew what she was like, but he'd married her anyway. I assumed they'd worked things out, but maybe not.

I brought the iced tea and sat beside him in the swing.

"I feel bad," Ryan said. "I'm not like this, honestly. I think what happened to Carl upset me more than I realized, and I can't talk to Harper about it. She says she doesn't want to hear."

"If you want, you can talk to me."

Ryan sighed. "I was standing across from Carl on the other side of the cannon when it happened. My back was turned when the gun exploded, but when I turned around, I saw more than I wanted to—Carl was down, and the cannon was lying in pieces. Smoke everywhere. One minute he's standing there smiling and the next minute he's...dead."

"I'm sorry, Ryan."

He sighed and rubbed his eyes as if he were trying to erase the image.

"Phil said he was supposed to be the one pulling the lanyard," I said.

"They did switch positions at the last minute. I didn't know why. I was the one tamping in the powder."

"And you didn't notice anything unusual about that?"

"Nothing. But I'd never done it before, and I assumed it was mostly for show."

I patted his arm, and at that moment Harper appeared.

"You two look cozy," she said.

I jumped up and offered her my seat. "I have to check on the rest of the guests. It sounds as if Saturday was pretty horrific for Ryan."

"For all of us, don't you think?" Harper said.

"Of course. But you weren't actually near the cannon at the time of the explosion."

"No. I was on the sidelines, but it was still ghastly."

"Did anything unusual happen before the battle started?" I asked Ryan.

"We were all milling around," Ryan said, "trying to find our station and get clear on what we were supposed to do."

"I planned to sit out the battle," Harper said, "once Phil told me I wasn't needed. On Saturday, I'll be part of the cavalry." She shook back her blond hair the way a horse might toss back its mane. "I've got my horse stabled north of the city."

"You can bet I'm not going," Ryan said.

"You can't let one horrible accident turn you into a coward," Harper said.

"You couldn't pay me to come."

"I know that's how you feel now, but you'll get over it. I've already told Phil that we'll be there."

"Is that what you were doing down by the fish pond—talking about the next reenactment?" Ryan couldn't hide his distress.

"I don't know what you thought you saw between me and Phil, but there was nothing to see." She said this more to me than Ryan. "We were having a laugh. I nearly fell into the pond and Phil caught me."

Ryan looked at her as if he wanted to believe her.

She took his hand. "Baby, you know me. I'm outgoing, not shy like you. You have to remember who I go home with. The reenactment next weekend will erase all these bad memories. I'll take Bullet and let him get some exercise. You could use a little exercise yourself."

"I got into this for your sake, you know that, Harper. You said it'd be great fun to relive the Civil War for a weekend or two. It's been anything but fun."

"Give it one more try. If you hate it, I won't ask you to come again."

Harper jumped up as I headed back into the house. "Let me help you, Mabel. I'm sure there's plenty to do inside."

I gave her the task of serving the Ozark Pudding while I brought out the ice cream. It didn't take long for the word to get out and a line to form around our dining room table. Lucie and Jason turned up beside me eager for a bowl of ice cream. Mason stood behind them. I sent the two of them off with ice cream and gave Mason a big bowl of the pudding.

"Maybe you could help them get settled into bed after you finish dessert," I whispered to him.

He nodded and led the kids upstairs to my bedroom away from the mayhem that was still going on downstairs.

Phil stopped by to say how great the party was. "I'm sorry you had to see that altercation with Ryan. He gets so strung out sometimes."

"He seemed to think something was going on between you and Harper."

"You know Harper. She'd flirt with anything on two feet."

"He's also really upset about Carl," I said.

"I know. It was a shock for all of us."

"What made you let Carl pull the lanyard?" I asked. "You hated the guy."

"I've already told you. He was so eager to do it—I let him."

Did he know how unbelievable that sounded? I looked at him, and he didn't meet my gaze.

"You said you wanted the party to end at eight thirty. It's past that now. You want me to get them out for you?" he asked.

"Sure."

Phil wandered to each small group, saying he was paying for a round at the Highland Pub in half an hour. That got their attention.

Frank was the first to leave. "You should open up a restaurant, Ditie, with good Southern food. Give up this pediatric stuff. You'd make a million."

I smiled. I wasn't a Southerner, but I'd learned the art of being gracious to guests. I wouldn't be seeing Frank again anytime soon, if it was up to me.

Andy came up behind Frank and hugged me goodbye.

"We have to get the kids together," he said. "We don't live that far apart. You could come for the weekend."

"I'd like that. The kids don't have any cousins, so you could be our Southern connection."

"Great." He handed me a card. "This has my email and cell. Be in touch."

Ryan and Harper were among the last to go. "Need any help cleaning up, Ditie? I'm good at that," Ryan said. "It would let me make amends for messing up your party."

"Thanks, Ryan. I've got it covered, and you didn't mess up anything."

The two of them left holding hands, so whatever tension they'd had earlier seemed to have blown over.

"I need to get a move on," Phil said, "or they'll beat me to the pub. Will you come, Ditie?"

I shook my head. "Kids tonight and work tomorrow."

Phil found Danny and they left together.

When the house was finally empty of guests, I grabbed a biscuit and a glass of wine and collapsed on the sofa. That's where Lurleen found me.

"I didn't see you all evening," I said.

"I know. I've been busy, listening in on conversations." She waited exactly five seconds. "I know who our murderer is, *chérie*."

Chapter Ten

I was too tired to bite.

Lurleen stared at me as she shook out her wavy hair from its braided chignon. "There, that's better. Did you hear what I said?"

"I did. Let me have another sip of wine, and then I'll be ready to hear all about it."

Mason came downstairs at that moment. "The kids are asleep on your bed. Do you mind?"

"Mind? No. You, Mason, are my hero."

He sat on the other side of me and gave me a long kiss. "Even out of uniform?"

"Especially out of uniform."

Lurleen dramatically raised her eyebrows. "Am I in the way here? I can leave."

"No." I turned to Mason. "Lurleen was about to announce the identity of the murderer."

She stood up. "You're making fun of me."

"Please sit down, Scarlett, and tell us what you know," I said.

Mason also stood. "Could you wait until I get one more helping of pudding with some ice cream? It really is delicious, Ditie. Shall I bring you some?"

I nodded. When I threw a party, there wasn't much opportunity for me to eat.

Lurleen tapped her foot impatiently. When Mason and I had settled back with our dessert, she asked if we were ready to hear.

"Yes," I said.

"You won't like this, Ditie, but Andy Morrison is your man."

"Andy? The nicest guy in the room with two young children and not one nasty bone in his body?"

"Precisely! Who in this gathering would you least expect to blow up a man with a faulty cannon?"

"Lurleen, the least likely suspect doesn't turn out to be the murderer in real life."

Lurleen looked hurt. I could see her lower lip beginning to protrude.

"You haven't even let me explain. I have evidence."

"We're listening," Mason said.

"I floated from group to group and got everyone talking about what happened and who might have tampered with the cannon. They all referred me to Andy. 'He's the expert,' they said. 'If anyone would know how to make a cannon explode, he's the one.' "

I turned to Mason. "To be fair, Andy is the one most into these games next to Phil, but that doesn't make him a murderer, Lurleen. What could possibly be his motive?"

"Ah, I am glad you asked me that, Dr. Watson. He hated Carl."

"I wouldn't be surprised if everyone at the party hated Carl—the ones who knew him from med school anyway. Carl was dismissive of all of us. He especially disliked Southerners. That's what makes it so hard to believe he was working for Phil's father."

"Maybe you'd like to know what Carl Thompson was doing before he joined Dr. Brockton's concierge business." She didn't wait for us to ask. "He worked with Andy for two years, and then Andy fired him."

Now she had my attention.

"How do you know this?"

"I was talking with Andy about Carl's wife and how awful it must be for her, and he mentioned that he knew Kathy Thompson well. They'd grown up together."

"So what happened to make Carl leave the practice with Dr. Morrison?" Mason asked.

"Andy was a bit vague about that. He said it was something about misappropriated funds. He wouldn't give me any more details no matter how hard I tried to get it out of him. He said it was all in the past and dealt with."

"Carl Thompson was embezzling money from Andy's practice?" Mason asked.

Lurleen nodded. "Andy implied there was more than just missing money. He said Carl was a man who destroyed everything he touched, but he refused to tell me what he meant by that."

I let this new information wash over me. Could Andy actually have had something to do with Carl's death? I knew people could hide their true selves, compartmentalize in a way even those closest to them might not see.

Could it be that Andy had been pushed to the limit by something Carl did to him? I tried to picture my friend Andy Morrison as a murderer. He had two children he clearly adored and a practice he loved. I couldn't wrap my head around that idea.

Mason followed me to the kitchen where I put on a pot of decaf coffee. "What are you thinking?" Mason asked.

"I can't see Andy as a murderer." I brought down three cups from the cupboard. "But I'd like to know exactly what Carl did to Andy. I'd also like to know who was threatening Carl." I told Mason about Kathy's brief visit and her accusation that someone might be blackmailing her husband.

"You have been busy," Mason said, "but if someone were blackmailing Carl, why would they kill him as long as he kept paying?"

"Maybe Carl had had enough and threatened to expose the blackmailer," I said. "But I wonder about that. I think Carl cared more about his status than money. I think he'd have done anything to protect his reputation."

We returned to the living room to start collecting empty glasses and plates. Lurleen was one step ahead of us. "I've got this," she said. "Why don't you put food away, Ditie, although I suspect there's not much left. Maybe you *should* open a Southern restaurant. You could make a killing."

"Not the best choice of words. I like what I do. Cooking like this every night would take the joy out of it."

Mason insisted on helping Lurleen clean up as I put away food for at least one more family meal.

When the coffee was ready, we all took a break and ate the last three tea cakes.

I turned to Mason. "I know you were entertaining the kids, but did you overhear anything of interest?"

"Hmm. Your Phil Brockton was glad-handing everyone. He didn't seem all that upset about what happened to Carl, and he didn't appear particularly frightened about his own welfare."

"He's not *my* Phil, but it is interesting. With me he pleads the case that he needs protection. He claims that if anything happens in the future, it's likely to be on the battlefield and made to look like an accident."

"I'm glad you're keeping the kids away on Saturday," Mason said.

"Me too. I'll have to tell them tomorrow." I sipped my coffee. "The person I wouldn't mind suspecting is Frank Peterson. He's all about money. He always wanted to be the coolest person in the room—that's how I remember him from med school. I'm surprised he and Phil stayed friends. They both wanted that particular title."

"You do know Harper almost married Frank before she married Ryan," Lurleen said.

"I heard that from Phil, but I didn't hear why the marriage plans broke up. Was Harper fooling around?"

"Maybe. But what I heard was that Harper had lied to Frank about one very important topic—the issue of children. She never told Frank she couldn't have them."

"Lurleen, how in the world could you have learned that at a party in the space of three hours? Maybe you really are a spy!"

Lurleen grinned from ear to ear. "You get people drinking and then it doesn't take much to get them talking. Most of it I heard from Sally Cutter."

"Go on," I said.

"According to Sally, she and Harper were close in med school. Harper fooled around a lot and got sick because of it. She had PID multiple times and ended up unable to have kids."

Mason looked at me. "PID?"

"Pelvic inflammatory disease. You can get it from multiple partners and unprotected sex."

"It left her infertile?" Mason asked.

"Sometimes you can harvest viable eggs and implant them in the uterus," I said.

"Well, it seems Harper didn't have that option," Lurleen said. "Her ovaries were too badly damaged to save any eggs. She couldn't have her own kids."

"Ryan, I assume, knows the truth," I said.

Lurleen nodded. "It's not a secret anymore. Maybe that's why Harper stays married to Ryan. He cares more about her than about having children."

"Ryan has always been devoted to her," I said, "from the time he first laid eyes on her."

Lurleen shook her head slowly. "If this evening is any indication, I wouldn't say the feeling was mutual. Phil and Harper seemed pretty intensely engaged with one another down by your pond."

"So Ryan wasn't exaggerating about what he saw when he picked the fight with Phil," I said.

"I can't say for sure," Lurleen said. "Ryan stormed in before I got close enough for a good look."

"Your pond is a very romantic spot, tucked away enough to be out of view from the deck," Mason said. "A good place for extracurricular activity."

"Poor Ryan," I said. "I won't be surprised if I hear they divorce soon. I think Ryan planned his life around Harper. He was interested in pediatrics until Harper decided on dermatology. Then he switched, and now they work in the same office. Maybe he thought that was the only way to keep an eye on her."

It was eleven before we finished putting my house back in order. Lurleen headed home with a container of soup and a bag of filled cookies.

Mason left empty-handed. "I may never eat again," he moaned.

I decided I would leave the kids upstairs and sleep on the sofa. I'd just gotten myself settled when the doorbell rang. Hermione was apparently dead to the world, so I was on my own. I peeked through the curtains.

It was Kathy Thompson. I opened the door and she practically fell into my arms.

"What is it? Are you hurt?"

She fainted without saying a word. I examined her. No obvious bleeding. Her pulse was strong. I looked her over more carefully. Her breathing was steady and slowly she came round.

"My purse," she said. "Someone left me the photo. I didn't know where else to go."

I helped her to the sofa and had her lie down again. Then I opened her purse. Inside was a picture of Carl after the blast.

Who would do such a thing?

Chapter Eleven

The picture was ghastly, taken from less than six feet away. I examined it closely. It was printed on good quality photo paper, the shot probably taken on an iPhone.

When I looked over at Kathy, she had her head turned away and her hand over her eyes.

"Why would anyone send this to me? He's dead. Why isn't that enough?"

Why indeed? What kind of person would kill a man and then send the photo to his wife? It was unimaginable, unless perhaps, it was the wife the person wanted to torture.

"We have to take this photo to the Gordon County investigator," I said.

Kathy nodded. "I don't want to ever see it again."

"Mason will know how to get it to him."

Kathy sat up slowly. "I don't understand who would do this?"

"Do you know anyone who might want to make you suffer like this?"

Kathy shook her head. "I told you about the threats."

"Were they ever written down in a letter or an email?"

"No."

She brushed her hair back from her face. "You may as well know the whole story. Carl and I were barely speaking to each other. We talked about divorce after I told him I wasn't sure I could go through another pregnancy. I'd had three miscarriages, and I thought maybe I wasn't meant to have children. To be honest, I wasn't sure I wanted them with Carl."

My head was spinning.

"Do you mind if we start at the beginning? But first, can I fix you a cup of tea, get you something to eat?"

Kathy surprised me. "I *would* like something to eat, if it's easy enough for you to do that."

"Very easy."

I took her to the kitchen and she sat on a stool at the marble island while I made tea, heated up some soup and brought out biscuits that were left over.

She ate as if she were starving.

"How long had you and Carl been having trouble?" I asked.

"Ever since I had my last miscarriage a year ago," she said. "I don't know if the miscarriage caused it, but suddenly everything I did was wrong. He accused me of not wanting the baby."

"Did you want the baby?" I asked.

She started to cry. "No," she said, "I'm not sure I did." She looked at me. "You must think I'm a terrible person, not wanting a child, especially when you have two you've taken in."

"I don't think that. Even last year I thought it might be that I'd never have children, and I decided I could live with that. I do feel incredibly fortunate to have Lucie and Jason, but I can understand women who feel differently."

She looked relieved.

"Why didn't you want a child?" I asked.

"It's more accurate to say I didn't want Carl's child. He wasn't the man I thought he was. When we met, he seemed different from anyone I'd ever known. He came down from New York with Sally Cutter to visit Andy. They were both looking for work—Carl in Andy's practice and Sally on the business end of things. Andy introduced us at a party. Everything happened so fast. Carl literally swept me off my feet."

"How did he do that?" I tried to imagine Carl charming anyone.

"Carl and I had a lot in common although you'd never know that from the outside. He came from a hard scrabble life in New Jersey and I had an affluent upbringing with an author-doctor for a father—Beau LeRoy."

"Beau LeRoy was your father?" I asked. "He came to talk to us in med school about his life as a country doc. He was a funny, charming man."

Kathy gave me a grim look. "That's what everyone says who didn't have to live with him. The man you saw at the front of the class was a fraud. I'm sorry to say it, but he was."

"What do you mean? He wasn't a doctor?"

"He was a doctor all right, but his best-selling books had nothing to do with his real life. He borrowed that history from Andy's father. Andy's dad was the real country doc, and Andy is following in his father's footsteps." She smiled at me. "They lived down the street from us. Andy and I were best friends growing up. He'd do anything for me. In fact, I think that's why he gave Carl and Sally a job in his practice. He didn't really need the help, but when he heard Carl and I were getting married—I think he did it as a wedding present for me."

"Andy cared that much about you even after what your father did?"

"The funny thing is neither Andy nor his father cared about the fact my dad used their lives in some best-selling books. They were happy to stay under the radar, and no one seemed to guess it wasn't my father's life."

I offered Kathy more soup. She nodded and took another biscuit as well. "It's delicious. Real Southern delicious. Most people could never make a biscuit as light as this. You're not Southern are you?"

"Nope. I grew up on a dairy farm in Iowa, but we did know how to eat well."

Kathy grinned and it changed the whole complexion of her face. It lost its drawn quality, but only for a moment.

"I was telling you about Carl—how he and I had a lot in common. You see while my father was out promoting his books, I was left at home to care for four younger siblings. I don't know why I'm telling you all this. Perhaps I just need to get it said."

I nodded and Kathy kept talking.

"My mother was an alcoholic, a bad one. She did nothing around the house. We couldn't get help because Dad was afraid it would ruin his reputation. So I got good at keeping secrets. I didn't even tell Andy much of what was going on, but I think he knew."

She took another spoonful of soup.

"Carl was the first person I could be honest with. He told me about his life with an alcoholic father and listened when I told him what I'd been through. For once, I didn't have to sugar-coat anything, and Carl listened. You have no idea what a relief that was!"

"I have some idea," I said. I thought about how I could say anything to Mason and he would never judge me. Phil always wanted to tell me how to fix my problems, and it always involved changing myself in some way.

"Things happened too quickly. I got pregnant after I'd been with Carl for a few months. My dad insisted on an immediate wedding, and Carl agreed. Carl was happy about the whole thing. I thought it was because he really loved me, but now I wonder if I was his ticket to respectability."

"Carl always said how much he hated the South," I said. "I don't understand why he came here."

"I'm pretty sure he was running away from something or someone. When the threats came I got the feeling it was about something in his past, something he'd done years ago."

"Were you happy together?" I asked.

Kathy paused. "At first. Until I lost the baby and started to see the other side of Carl—the driven side. Carl was insistent I get pregnant again right away."

"Why did you stay with him?"

"I thought he could change. If I loved him enough I thought I could help him heal. We were both troubled people, but I thought if we worked hard—or if I worked hard enough for both of us—I could make Carl into a good and loving man."

Kathy started to cry.

"I didn't know he was troubled beyond repair until I saw what he did to Andy."

"He stole money from him?"

"How did you know that?"

"My friend Lurleen has a way of getting people to talk."

"You two make quite a pair," Kathy said. "Carl denied he stole the money, but I promised Andy I would pay back every cent. I couldn't fix the other thing Carl did. I think he broke up Andy's marriage. Jenna worked in the front office. Andy never told me what happened, but he and Jenna divorced three months after Carl left the practice.

"You think Carl was having an affair with Jenna?"

"Yes. I know how sordid that sounds."

"You didn't leave him then, why?"

"I've asked myself that a hundred times. I think I was still the good Southern girl who could keep secrets and do what was expected. Divorce in my family was unacceptable. Maybe I believed Carl when he said he really would change."

I poured Kathy more tea and myself a glass of wine. "Would you like something stronger?"

"I would, but I can't. I'm pregnant again."

"Did Carl know this?"

"He did, and he seemed excited. I thought maybe things could finally get better between us."

"How do you feel about this pregnancy?"

"I want to keep this baby." Her look didn't match her words. Maybe she feared this pregnancy would end in a miscarriage like the others, or maybe she didn't want to be carrying the baby of a dead husband.

She stood up. "It's very late. I'm sorry. I didn't know where else to go. I'm sure you have work tomorrow. I'll leave."

"Do you have family staying with you?"

"No," she said.

"Then why don't you stay here for the night. I'll change the sheets, and we can both get to bed."

"You don't even know me," Kathy said, "why would you do that?"

"One, because it's no trouble, and two, because sometimes you just need people around. I promise you the kids and my friend Lurleen will keep you busy. You can leave anytime you want tomorrow. I'll be going to work at nine."

I made up the bed in Lucie's room for Kathy, and settled myself once more on the sofa in the living room. It was lights out around midnight.

I had more questions than answers. The main one centered on who would have been cruel enough, or vindictive enough, to send the photo to Kathy. Despite my troubled mind, I was asleep in half an hour and woke up to the sound of two children shushing each other, so they wouldn't wake me. I looked at the clock. Almost seven.

"You beat my alarm by eight minutes. I'm awake and need to get going."

I told the kids about our house guest and asked them to be quiet and not wake her. That meant we had to find clean clothes for Lucie in the dryer.

Lurleen came at eight. The four of us sat in the breakfast room eating cereal and fruit and revisiting the best parts of the party.

Jason went first. "I played my bugle for everybody!"

Lucie was thoughtful. "Lurleen took me around with her and everyone said they liked my dress. And Uncle Mason played with us the whole time."

Before we had a chance to talk more, Kathy came out of Lucie's bedroom. She looked better, more rested. I introduced her to Lurleen and left them to it while I got ready for work. When I returned I heard Lurleen speaking about her brief stint as a math teacher, and Lucie was enthralled to learn Kathy taught fourth grade, the grade she'd be entering in the fall. Lucie offered to make Kathy some toast—little did she know that was probably the perfect choice to settle Kathy's stomach.

"Stay as long as you like," I said to Kathy. "I have fresh towels in my bathroom upstairs."

I could hear Lurleen as I left, urging Kathy to spend the day with them. I knew if she did there'd be no talk of death.

I called Mason on the way to work and told him about the photograph. He said he'd meet me at work to pick it up. He'd get it dusted for fingerprints although we both knew that was unlikely to turn up anything useful.

Chapter Twelve

Mason arrived at the clinic just as I did. We exchanged a kiss in the parking lot, and I told him how much I appreciated the time he spent with the kids during the party.

He looked at me with a strange expression on his face. "I love those kids. You know that. They were a lot more entertaining than conversations about the Battle of Tunnel Hill or where people got their authentic South Carolina belt buckles. Have you told the kids they're not going on Saturday?"

"I didn't have a chance, but I will tonight."

"I'm thinking Mom would love to get involved with a reenactment on Saturday in her backyard. Maybe your brother could come."

I sighed. "I can see your mom being a good sport about all of this, but it's a little hard for me to imagine Tommy taking part in the activities."

"I thought you two were much closer these days."

"We are, but he still likes his privacy. He loves the kids, so I'll ask. Just don't count on him."

I wondered if I was being too hard on Tommy. He really had changed. His boyfriend Josh had a lot to do with the new, happier Tommy. That and the fact he felt he no longer had to hide his relationships from me.

Work consumed me for three and a half hours. When I looked at my watch it was twelve thirty and time for a lunch break.

I called Tommy and explained the situation to him.

"I heard about the accident in Resaca—I hadn't heard they were officially calling it murder."

"I'm not sure it's official, but that may be what it was."

"And I bet you're in the middle of it if that old boyfriend of yours is involved. He dragged you into it, didn't he?"

I didn't get a chance to respond.

"Not that he'd have to work hard to do that. You still have your rescue complex. If you need a good therapist, I know one."

"Thanks." I decided not to pick a fight. "You can see why we can't take the kids on Saturday—in case something else happens."

"Got it. Amazingly, I think I'm free to help out, and I haven't seen the kids in a month. Are you going to tell me to rent a uniform?"

I had to laugh. The idea of Tommy in a Confederate uniform was more than I could imagine. Getting him out of Armani was work enough. "With your blond hair and blue eyes, you would look very handsome in gray."

"I have a better idea. We'll actually teach the kids something. We'll see the Civil War exhibit at the Atlanta History Center. You think Jason is too young for that?"

"He might be, but I love the idea."

"There's a room devoted to Civil War guns—he'll think that's cool for at least five minutes," Tommy said.

I got off the phone amazed at Tommy's transformation and perhaps mine as well. I never expected much from Tommy, so that I'd never be disappointed. I needed to begin to see him for the man he was now. I hadn't known how miserable he'd been as a child or why Mother sent him away to boarding school. When he didn't write I assumed he cared nothing for me. I didn't realize Mother intercepted our letters, so we wouldn't communicate—all because she couldn't accept the fact that Tommy might be gay.

Lurleen called as I finished my sandwich. She never called me at work unless it was an emergency.

"No, no," she assured me. "The kids are fine. It's Kathy. She's fine too or as fine as she can be. The service for Carl is tomorrow, and she hopes you can come. It starts at one, and I can watch the kids."

"I'm off then, so that'll work. Thanks."

"Kathy thought you might have a few more questions for her since you agreed to help find Carl's murderer."

"Whoa," I said. "I never made any agreement like that. My first priority is the kids. I can't get involved in anything that might put them at risk."

"*Chérie,* you and I both know you are like *l'eau bouillante* when it comes to a mystery."

"Boiling water?"

"*Bien sûr.* You can't let it go. It just bubbles inside you until you find all the answers. Kathy isn't asking you to go on the battlefield. Danny and

I will handle that part. She just wants you to use your head, figure some things out. She went on and on about how smart you are."

"Enough, Lurleen. Kathy barely knows me. I can hear when I'm being manipulated."

"She wondered if you might come by her house on your way home from work. I'll stay with the kids until you get home. No problem."

I agreed, and she gave me the address. Truth be told, I did want to hear the rest of what Kathy might have to tell me.

The afternoon at work was busier than the morning. Several children in one family from Bhutan needed to be checked for tuberculosis. A child from Ethiopia had chronic hepatitis B and I knew him from a previous visit. He was there for a six-month follow-up with labs to make sure the virus was remaining inactive. Two children and their mother from Indonesia had influenza. By six my paper work was done and the clinic was empty.

Vic took a minute to ask how things were going. She'd read the paper like the rest of us.

I told her my plans to spend the day with the children on Saturday. She and I worked out a schedule that would leave me free to do that.

"And Phil Brockton? How are you doing with him? Any old sparks flying?"

I shook my head. "Unfortunately, Mason's not as sure about that as I am."

I hurried off to see Kathy. She lived in a high rise on Peachtree. A doorman called her when I arrived and then walked me to the elevator. Kathy greeted me at the elevator door down the hall from her apartment. She looked even more drawn than the last time I'd seen her.

The apartment was elegant and spacious.

"These were supposed to be temporary quarters," she said, "while we searched for a house, but we never seemed to find one we could both agree on."

She led me to the living room, done in black and white with framed photographs along the walls. The chairs and couch were covered in soft white leather, midcentury sleek on brass legs. It was all tasteful, and none of it looked like what I imagined would be her taste.

She offered me a glass of wine and poured one for herself. I looked at her.

"I lost the baby," she said, "so I'm free to have a glass of wine." She spoke in a monotone. "After I left Lurleen, I started to cramp. I went to the Emergency Room, but I knew what was happening. It was the picture! I'm sure it was the picture that did it."

"I'm so sorry," I said.

"I think it's for the best. How could I cope with another life? I can barely take care of myself right now. I got pregnant to please Carl, and he was pleased. I suppose I have that to hang on to."

She sounded so calm, it was unnerving. I wondered if the doctor had given her something.

I looked around the room.

"You're wondering what I'm doing in a place like this. Carl insisted on using a decorator. He said he didn't have time to pick out fabric and furniture and that we needed a professional to do it correctly. It's not my taste at all."

"Did you protest?"

"When Carl wanted something, he went after it and got it. It took me a while to figure out why he wanted me."

She took a sip of wine.

"I had a small trust fund from my father, and I had good Southern credentials. My father knew Phil's father. They'd worked together for a while."

"Carl cared about your Southern connection?"

"More than anything. Carl badmouthed the South because it seemed like a society closed to him. When he saw his chance to belong through me he was ecstatic. He saw children as securing his place and his standing. I do think Carl genuinely wanted to make a better life for his children than the one he had."

"I never really knew Carl," I said. "I mostly knew what Phil said about him."

"Carl could be charming. A lot like my dad. Strangers thought my father was the epitome of the Southern gentleman. To my mom, he'd say terrible things, and she'd just put up with it. When I asked why, she said that's what women did. It was as if my mother were living in another century."

Kathy tucked a strand of hair behind her ear. Her hair was the color of wheat, a light brown and perfectly straight. For the first time, I realized what a pretty woman she was. She was someone who kept her looks and her secrets under wraps.

"The irony is that I turned out just like her. They say you marry your mother. I married my father."

"How did Carl come to work for Phil's dad?"

"They met years ago. Carl spoke as if Phil's dad owed him a favor. It was odd. He said something about cashing in at last. He was also happy to make Phil miserable, and he knew he could do that by joining the practice."

"Do you know why Carl hated Phil so much?" I asked.

"I have a theory about that," Kathy said. "Phil's Southern lineage went back generations. It was a club Carl was shut out of, and I think that made him furious. By joining the practice Carl could turn the tables—make Phil as miserable as Carl had been in med school."

"That all makes sense, but I think something more happened second year, something to do with the cheating scandal. They stopped speaking completely after that."

"Yes. Carl told me Phil came up with a plan to beat the testing system. Sally Cutter got caught in the middle of it and was expelled. Carl thought she got a raw deal while Phil got off scot-free. That's one reason he was so protective of Sally. Carl vowed he'd get even with Phil if it took him the rest of his life."

"So that's what happened," I said. "Phil denied having anything to do with that scandal."

"According to Carl, Phil threw Sally under the bus to save his own skin."

"It's odd about Sally," I said. "One minute she's telling me Phil probably killed Carl, and the next minute she's telling me he's a guy who couldn't hurt a fly."

"I don't really know any more about her than you do. She seems to say what she thinks people want to hear."

"You never worried about how close she and Carl were?"

Kathy shook her head. "She acted more like a kid sister to Carl than anything else."

I'd finished my glass of wine. It was almost seven, and I needed to get home.

"Just one more question. Have you thought more about who might have been threatening your husband and why?"

"I don't know any more than I told you before. Carl was scared. He thought someone might bring an end to his career plans and his chance to belong somewhere."

Kathy took my glass. "You'll come tomorrow to the service?"

"I'll come."

"And you'll help me find out what happened to Carl?"

"I make no promises about that. My first priority is the safety and security of my children. You can understand that. According to Mason both the Sheriff and the county investigator are competent people."

"They may be, and I don't want to put you or the children in harm's way, but please help me, Dr. Brown. You know everyone involved. You went to school with them. That picture was meant to hurt me—or to threaten me."

"Why would anyone want to threaten *you*?" I asked.

"I can't answer that. Perhaps someone thought Carl confided in me, told me something the murderer didn't want me to know."

"Like their identity. Carl must have known the blackmailer."

"He denied that to me and said it was all done anonymously through text messages from an untraceable phone. I did wonder if he was lying to me."

"Did you think he might have been trying to protect you?" I asked.

"I never considered that. He did say the less I knew about the whole thing the better."

I hugged Kathy and left her standing at her open door.

She called after me as I walked down the corridor. "Thank you, Ditie. You've given me something to hang onto. Perhaps Carl was trying to protect me in the end."

Chapter Thirteen

I left Kathy's apartment and focused on the fact I had to tell two children about the change in plans for Saturday. One of them would be very disappointed. Mason and Lurleen were waiting for me on the porch. Lucie, Jason, and Hermione ran down the steps to greet me. Even Majestic sauntered by to say hello.

Jason grabbed my hand and pulled me toward the house. "Surprise! Surprise!" he said.

"May I get a kiss first?"

Jason stopped and allowed me to plant a small kiss on the top of his head.

Lucie took my hand and walked beside me up the steps.

Jason raced ahead. "Look," he said when I finally got inside. "Look what Uncle Danny brought me!"

I saw it lying on the sofa, and I was not happy. It looked like a child-sized wooden musket.

Lucie must have seen the look on my face. "It's not real, Aunt Di," she whispered. "It's just a toy."

Obviously, Danny hadn't gotten the word on Saturday.

I moved the gun to the mantle. "You two need to sit down, we have to talk."

"Did we do something wrong, Aunt Di?" Lucie asked.

"No, I did."

Lucie sat on one side and Jason on the other.

"I'm sorry to tell you this, but we are not going to the Civil War reenactment on Saturday. I forgot how much noise and confusion there would be. It's really for adults and not for children, but we're going to do something just as fun, maybe more fun."

Lucie looked relieved, and as I expected Jason looked crushed. "But I want to go! Danny said we are going and I can shoot the gun. Like a real soldier."

He jumped off the sofa and tried to reach for the musket, but he wasn't tall enough. I got it down, took a look at it, and handed it to him. "No playing with this inside, but you can play with it in the yard."

Years ago I would have been all about gender neutral toys, but I'd learned a little in the last seven years. Boys will make guns out of whatever is at hand—a stick, a broom, it didn't matter. Not all boys, but most of the ones I'd seen.

"I want to go to the 'actment!" Jason stamped his feet. He was a little old for a full-blown temper tantrum, but this was close enough.

I waited a moment, and when he was quiet, I asked if he wanted to hear our new plans.

"I do, Aunt Di," Lucie said.

Jason still had his back to me.

"When you are both ready to listen, I'll tell you."

Lucie turned Jason around to face me.

"You may both wear your costumes—all day if you like. Here's the plan. The three of us will meet Uncle Tommy at the Atlanta History Museum. We'll get to see real Civil War uniforms and muskets and cannons. Everything! Then we'll look at an old farm and a grand mansion and eat in a tea room. After that we'll go to Eddie's house, and Mason will join us there. We'll have our own reenactment in her backyard. You haven't seen Eddie much lately or Uncle Tommy."

Lucie's eyes lit up. "Will we see her new dog? Can we take Hermione?"

"You will get to see her new dog, but Hermione will have to wait to visit another time."

Hermione heard her name mentioned twice, sauntered up to us, and started wagging her tail in hopes of some new adventure. Instead she got a good rub from me and Lucie.

Jason couldn't seem to make up his mind about whether he should be excited or stay mad. Sometimes it's hard to be a five-year-old. "Can I take my musket?"

"You can," I said. "They might not let you take it into the museum, but Eddie will let you have it, that's for sure."

"Okay." He pulled on Mason's hand. "Can we go outside and play with my musket, Uncle Mason?"

"You bet." Mason took Jason's free hand and they went into the backyard, leaving us three girls to work on dinner.

"Aunt Di, why did you change your mind about Saturday? Was it because I wasn't brave enough?"

"Sweet girl, you are plenty brave. I changed my mind because—well—to be honest, you and Jason have seen too much that's been scary. You don't need to see anymore right now, and I don't either."

Lurleen had been silent the whole time. She gave Lucie a hug. "I'll come over after the other reenactment and tell you all about it. You and Jason won't miss anything but the smoke and noise. Okay?"

Lucie nodded.

Then Lurleen turned to me. "If I'm supposed to be selling things, could we make it a bake shop and could you supply me with something to sell?"

"How about tea cakes, filled cookies, and iced tea, and how 'bout you just give it away?"

"Perfect."

I breathed a great sigh of relief and made a quick dinner of leftover soup and fresh salad. That seemed to even out everyone's temper. After dinner, the kids took their baths and got into their own beds on time. Lurleen went home and promised to be back around noon the next day, so I could get to the service.

Mason and I spent a quiet hour together. I asked him if he'd had any luck tracing the photo.

None, he told me. It was probably taken on a cell phone, and anyone on the field might have had one with them.

I wondered how someone had taken a photo and none of us had noticed.

"Inspector Barden interviewed everyone about that. He's convinced no one got near the body other than the people you saw—Phil Brockton, Ryan and Harper Hudson, Andy Morrison, Frank Peterson, Sally Cutter."

"I didn't see anyone take a picture," I said. "I would have remembered that."

"You were sent away by the investigator. The photo could have been taken anytime, before you arrived, in the midst of the dust settling, or long after," Mason said.

I nodded and searched my memory for anything I might have missed. Sally was the one staring at the body when I came over. She could have taken a photo before I talked to her.

"What is unusual is that the cannon was an original Napoleon," Mason said. "The investigator said that was very rare to see at a reenactment."

"Phil told me it was an original," I said.

"Did he mention who owned that gun?" Mason asked.

I could feel my face drain of color.

"It was Phil's, wasn't it?" I said. "He brought it because he wanted everything to be as authentic as possible."

"You got it. He had it hauled on site. He keeps it in Atlanta."

"Why would Phil fail to tell me that?" I asked, although I knew the answer.

"Phil didn't want you to suspect the obvious—that he was the one who shaved the bore," Mason said.

"But he'd know the investigator would figure out it belonged to him," I said.

"I guess he was buying time or praying for a miracle," Mason said. "He came clean once Barden confronted him with the information. It seems Brockton has a storage unit in Atlanta where he keeps his precious artifacts, including the cannon. It's climate controlled with security cameras. Most of the reenactments are in the South, so Dr. Brockton just ships the gun to wherever the next reenactment is. An expensive operation I'll bet."

"Phil must have loved that gun, and if he did how could he bear to blow it apart?" I asked.

"Phil said he cleaned it carefully once a year. Last time was in the Spring. It seemed fine then. He claims he might not have seen the thinning if it was subtle—he wasn't measuring the inside width of the bronze barrel. It could have worn away naturally over time."

"Did other people have access to the storage unit?" I asked.

"Yes, according to Phil, but only people he trusted. He let his med school friends keep their guns and uniforms in it and had spare uniforms for people to use."

"I assume Inspector Barden is looking over the security tapes to see who came and went to the unit, maybe who spent a long time inside it."

"He is, but he's discovered the surveillance camera was covered for twenty-four hours—two days before the reenactment."

"So someone knew not only how to make a cannon explode but where the security camera was located as well," I said. "Surely the experts will be able to see if the thinning was freshly made and not normal wear and tear."

"Maybe," Mason said. "Barden says they're working with fragments."

Mason could see how disturbed I was. "It's still possible it was a hairline fracture that wasn't man-made and just got missed."

"You don't really believe that," I said, "and I don't either. Not with the blocked surveillance camera."

Mason nodded his agreement. "The Georgia Bureau of Investigation did say it wasn't a bomb, which is what a lot of people thought at first."

"Someone made that cannon explode," I said, "and then had the audacity or cruelty to photograph Carl's body and deliver the picture to his wife. Who would do that?"

"You're assuming that the person who took the photo also killed Carl," Mason said. "Maybe someone took advantage of a horrible situation and hated Carl or Kathy enough to want to make Kathy suffer even after Carl's death."

"I can't imagine what Kathy could have done to make someone hate her enough to do that. I could imagine a lot of people might feel sorry for her, both for marrying Carl and then for the horrible way he died."

"I had another thought," Mason said. "What if someone was supposed to provide proof of his death to Kathy?" Then he answered his own question. "If that were true, she'd never have come running to you, unless she was shocked by what she had done."

"You're suggesting it could have been a murder for hire—'among friends'. Most of the people in that group had no love for Carl, that's for sure. But if Kathy hired someone to kill her husband why would she ask me to look into his murder? And why would she need proof of a murder that everyone witnessed?"

Mason took my hand. "Maybe she hated Carl as much as everyone else seemed to. Perhaps she wanted to literally see him dead. And maybe she thought if she asked for help you'd defend her just the way you're doing now."

I let this sink in. I didn't know Kathy well, and I tended to take people at face value until I had proof they were not what they seemed to be.

"It's possible," I said. "Carl was using her to get ahead and certainly didn't care much about her feelings."

I sighed. No matter how you sliced it, someone I knew was a murderer.

"Kathy was pregnant. She'd told Carl, and he was pleased. She thought the baby might offer them a new beginning. What motive would she have to kill the father of her baby?"

"None," Mason said, "if what you're describing is actually true."

"You're right. She told me she'd lost the baby this afternoon and said it was because of the photo. She seemed so calm about the loss, it unnerved me. I wondered if it was simply one more shock, or—"

"Maybe she hadn't been pregnant in the first place." Mason finished my sentence for me.

Chapter Fourteen

The service for Carl was held at a large Episcopal church on Peachtree. More than a hundred people were in attendance. It was a formal service, and it didn't tell me any more about Carl than I already knew. There was a reception after the service but nothing graveside. His body would be cremated after it was released by the medical examiner.

I greeted Kathy at the reception in a large room in an adjoining building. She stood beside her mother and four siblings. I remembered then that her father had died some years before, shortly after he'd given his lectures to us in school. I could still remember how he'd stopped in the middle of his talk and looked at the sixty or so of us sitting in the classroom.

"Put that newspaper away," he'd said to a student in the back row. "And you, you there, wake up. What do you think y'all are doing? You're going to be doctors, at least most of you are."

We snapped to attention. Even my more cynical classmates responded. It was quite a show.

Kathy brought me back to the present. She thanked me for coming and introduced her mother and siblings.

"Are you living in Atlanta now?" I asked her mother.

"No. I still have our family home in South Carolina. You must visit sometime."

"Andy Morrison gave me the same invitation, so you may see me on your doorstep one day."

"That would be lovely," Mrs. LeRoy said graciously. "I haven't seen much of Andy for a couple of years. He's a fine man, don't you think, Kathy?"

Kathy blushed slightly. "Of course, Mother."

Kathy turned away from her to introduce me to Carl's mother, a woman who looked distinctly out of place in the crowd of well-dressed, well-moneyed Buckhead people.

"Mama Beatrice, this is a friend, Dr. Brown. She knew your son in medical school."

She smiled. "You knew my Carl? It's so nice to meet you."

I shook her hand and talked about how smart he was.

She nodded. "I always knew Carl would go far. He was smart and honest and determined to get out of our town. I missed him when he left, but I knew it was for his own good."

I nodded and she kept talking.

"He was a good boy. I know he rubbed some people the wrong way, but that was only because he had such a drive to make something of himself. He never forgot his mother. Never. After his father died, it was hard to make ends meet. Carl sent me money every month."

Again I nodded. This was a side of Carl I knew nothing about. Was it a mother's wishful thinking or was it the truth? I doubted she made up the story about the money, but was she right or wrong about his honesty?

Kathy intervened, perhaps afraid Carl's mother would never stop talking in her grief. "The med school crowd is by the punch bowl. And I assume you know Phil's father."

"I'm very sorry about Carl," I said to Mrs. Thompson. "I wish I'd known him better."

"He was a scrapper," she said. "He had to be in our neighborhood. Not many people saw his soft side—except Kathy and his friend Sally. Kathy was the best thing that ever happened to Carl."

Kathy heard that and gave her mother-in-law a hug.

I walked slowly to the gathering by the punch bowl. Had we all misjudged Carl or was it a mother's love speaking?

Phil's father nodded at me as I approached. I wasn't eager to see him again. He'd never considered me a fit partner for his son. His disdain was never spoken out loud—that is not part of Southern tradition—but I had no trouble getting the message. I didn't come from money like all the people who lived in Dr. Brockton's upscale Buckhead neighborhood, and I had no interest in climbing the social ranks of Southern society. He didn't say he disapproved of my becoming a doctor, but he did express his hope that I would not work when our children were small. I guess he took our relationship more seriously than Phil did.

Danny was standing a few feet away, trying to be invisible perhaps. That was never going to happen with a man built like Danny who towered over everyone else in the room.

Phil greeted me warmly. "Hi Ditie, I'm so glad you came. Dad, you remember Dr. Brown."

"Of course, I remember Mabel," he said. "I never had a chance to compliment you on how you handled that unfortunate Sandler situation in the spring."

We shook hands.

"Thank you." I was careful not to prick any sore points by asking how it came to be that Carl was working for him.

As I left him, Phil looked over at me and smiled. He brought me a cup of punch. "Thanks, Ditie, for not saying anything...provocative."

I nodded. "You and your dad seem to be getting on well. Has the atmosphere warmed?"

Phil shook his head. "Not really. Dad has always known how to behave in public."

Together we joined the rest of the group. I remembered in med school, Phil had his tight circle of friends. Here they were clustered together as if they were the only people on earth—Andy, Frank, Ryan, Harper, and Sally.

Agatha Christie would have loved this gathering. A small clutch of people with one murderer in the mix.

I must have shuddered because Andy asked if I were cold. "It's the air conditioning in here," he said. "They've got it going full blast. You want my jacket?"

I shook my head. "I'm fine. I feel a little odd about being here. I was never close to Carl."

"I know the feeling," Andy said. He moved away from the rest of the group and lowered his voice. "Makes me feel like a hypocrite. I was ready to sue the guy and now he's dead. I guess you know what he did to me. Phil probably told you."

"Actually, Kathy did. She said she was intent on paying back every cent he embezzled."

"Yeah. I didn't want her to. She's not responsible for what he did, but she insisted."

"Was Sally involved?"

"I mean no offense, but Sally isn't the brightest bulb. She may have her degrees in business and financial planning, but I never knew for sure if she was actually competent at what she was doing."

"Phil told me she didn't have any financial degrees—that's why she isn't working for his dad."

Andy shook his head. "That's news to me. Frankly, I was happy to get them both out of my practice."

"Did you bury the hatchet with Carl? Sorry, bad choice of terms."

"What's done is done, but I couldn't believe it when Phil told me his father took Carl on as a partner. Carl never asked me for a reference and I never gave one."

Our conversation ended abruptly when Ryan and Harper joined us.

"You have to try these canapés, Mabel. Tell me what you think?" She practically stuffed a cracker with shrimp and avocado into my mouth. I took it from her and tasted it. "Delicious."

Sally walked up and looked as if she'd been crying.

"Are you all right?" I asked.

She nodded and headed for the ladies' room. I followed.

"Carl's mother told me how close you were to Carl," I said, once we were alone inside the restroom.

She stood at the sink dabbing at her mascara.

"People misunderstood him. They thought his bluster was who he really was, but I knew him as a friend. It's heartbreaking—he was getting a fresh start, making amends."

"Making amends to Andy?" I asked. "Or Phil?"

"Not Phil. Phil can be really pig-headed. All this talk about how his father threw him over for Carl—that's all nonsense. Phil made a mess of his relationship with his dad. He didn't need any help from Carl to do that, and Carl never said a bad word about Phil to his father."

"How would you know that?"

"I thought about working with Phil's dad on the financial end of things. But the whole concierge thing—I'm not sure I really want that. It seems so Buckhead, and I grew up in a small town."

I decided not to confront Sally with Phil's version of events—that she had no financial degrees.

"I spent some time talking to Phil's dad," Sally continued. "He was crushed that Phil wouldn't join the practice. That was Phil's choice, not his father's."

Sally finished putting on new make-up. She patted my arm as she turned to leave the room.

I thought she might break down again, but she sniffed, put her head back and walked ahead of me. "I'll see you at the reenactment?" she asked.

"No, I can't bring the kids to that. They've been through too much."

"Then how about we have a drink sometime soon? I've missed you, girl, I have." She handed me her card. It stated she was a financial planner. She wrote down her cell number on the card. "If you know anyone who's looking for help with their investments, let me know." She looked at me with her pixie smile. "You remember the times we had in Anatomy Lab? We were the only ones willing to do certain dissections. I thought the boys would pass out when we got to those parts."

Sally was laughing, and I had to smile. It was the one time our more cocky colleagues let us step forward.

I watched Sally walk over to Kathy, give her a hug and leave. I stood alone, trying to figure out where to go next, when Danny came up beside me.

"You look lost," he said.

"I'm feeling that way. How's it going with Phil?"

"Piece of cake, so far. We go out to eat at expensive restaurants. I sleep in the spare bedroom."

"Does Phil seem nervous about tomorrow?"

"Eager, I'd say. Not exactly like someone who had a near-death experience."

"So you don't think he really believes someone meant to kill him?"

Danny made a face. "I don't know. He's talked to me a lot about the cannon. You want to hear this?"

"You bet I do. I know the cannon was an original and belonged to Phil."

Danny smiled at me. "You're stealing my thunder. Phil claims the cannon was the most priceless possession he owned. He claims he's devastated it's destroyed, and I kind of believe him."

"You believe someone else may have damaged the cannon?" I asked.

"Or it was truly an accident. Phil says it would be impossible to know precisely how the cannon would explode or who would get hurt. If it wasn't an accident, he tells me someone meant to kill him—or frame him for murder."

"Are the police calling this murder?" I asked.

"Not yet."

"The picture was no accident. You and Phil are sure no one could have wandered on the field and taken that photo after it happened?"

"Phil was there when the gun exploded, and I got to the spot maybe thirty seconds later. No one else came near the body before the police arrived. You saw that as clearly as I did. Phil was very precise about the events and about who was where at the time, and he never mentioned anyone using a cell phone to take a picture."

"He is precise. I'm just no longer sure how truthful he is," I said.

"You think he could have killed Thompson?" Danny asked me. "And then taken a picture of the body? Why would he do that?"

"I have no idea, and I find it hard to believe he would blow up his precious cannon to kill a man. Still, he hated Carl with a passion, and Carl was worming his way into his father's good graces."

"You dated the guy for what—six years? You think you dated a murderer?"

"Don't rub it in, Danny. I am beginning to think it's possible. The part that makes no sense is why he'd take a picture of the man he'd just killed."

Chapter Fifteen

Most of the people who'd come to the service had left by the time Danny glanced at his watch. "I've got to go. Phil will be having a fit. It's after three and he wanted to be out of here by then, so we could go over last minute arrangements for tomorrow. You're not coming, right?"

"Right."

"And Mason?"

"Mason will be there."

"Then I guess Mason, Lurleen, and I will hold down the fort so to speak." Danny said.

"Do you expect trouble?" I asked.

"If Phil really was the intended victim, then who's to say the murderer won't try again. You can bet the cannons will be guarded, but a lot can happen on a field amid the smoke and gunfire."

"Maybe Lurleen shouldn't go either," I said.

"She's a sutler. She'll be selling things, so she won't be on the battlefield. I made her promise that. There will be a beefed up police presence, and that may deter anyone who'd like to make mischief."

"You take care, Danny," I said. "I know this is your profession, but don't do anything foolish."

"I have one job tomorrow, and that's to keep Phil Brockton safe. That's what I'll do."

Phil came up, a pocket watch in his hand. "I thought I said three and it's already three fifteen."

"Are you kidding, Phil?" I looked at his watch. "It's circa Civil War, isn't it?"

"You bet it is, and the time is accurate to two seconds."

"Sorry, boss," Danny said.

"It's my fault, Phil. I cornered Danny."

Phil looked at me a little warily, or so it seemed to me. "I saw you talking a long time to Sally. What was that all about?" he asked.

I wasn't sure how to answer him, and he saw me hesitate.

"Sally told you some story, didn't she, about how it was all my fault and my decision that I'm not working for my dad. You should know she had a thing for Carl. He could do no wrong in her eyes, so whatever story he fed her, she believed."

My head was starting to hurt. Had I gone to school with a pack of liars?

"Are you scared about tomorrow?" I asked.

"Scared? No, I'm excited. It's going to be a great show, and I'm sorry you won't be there."

"You were so sure someone meant to kill you. You're not worried they'll try again?"

"That's why I've got my protection." He nodded at Danny. "Who would mess with him?"

Phil either had a lot of bravado, or he knew he was in no danger. I turned and headed to Kathy and Carl's mother to say good bye. Only a few people lingered around the refreshment tables. The great hall looked as sad and lonely as those two women did. Ryan and Harper were standing next to Kathy.

Mrs. Thompson greeted me like an old friend. "Thank you so much for coming."

I told her how glad I was to meet her and how sorry I was for what she was going through.

Kathy smiled at me. "Thank you for taking the time to come. Can I call you tonight?"

"Of course. I get the kids in bed by nine. If you're not too tired you can call me then."

"We're just leaving," Ryan said. "We'll walk you out."

When we'd left the church, Ryan turned to me. "What was that all about? I didn't know you and Kathy were friends."

"We're not exactly. I've just met her, but she needed some support, and I offered to provide it."

Ryan and Harper exchanged a look and left me in the parking lot.

I got in my car and called Lurleen. All was well with the children. They were in the backyard eating watermelon, and Lurleen had just told them about how she used to pick melons in the south of France with her farmer boyfriend Valentin, a boyfriend she'd never mentioned to me.

I got home as Mason pulled up.

He kissed me, and we walked together around the side of the house to say hello to the kids in the backyard.

"I can't stay," he said as we walked through the side gate. "I have work to do at the office, but I wanted to see you after the service. How'd it go?"

"Everyone is telling me a different story. I have no idea who's telling me the truth."

"If any of them are," Mason said. "People lie, sometimes for stupid reasons, and it never gets them far. Barden is hammering away at your classmates. And the crime lab has a few more facts. You want to hear them?"

"Absolutely."

"According to the Sheriff, the lab found a hairline crack in the barrel fragments, which isn't uncommon in those old cannons. But they also found that a section of the crack had been deepened, and they don't think that occurred naturally."

"So it was murder!" I said.

"Looks like it."

We got to the backyard in time to see Lurleen placing watermelon rind in a trash bag. The kids ran up with sticky fingers and I warded them off with a kiss on their heads and urged them to run inside and wash their hands.

That gave me a minute to tell Lurleen the latest news. Before I started I looked at Mason.

"Is this confidential?" I asked.

He shook his head. "The Sheriff doesn't seem to think it needs to be kept quiet. He's more anxious to see how everyone reacts to the information."

"Okay then." I told Lurleen it looked like murder.

"Someone damaged the cannon to make it explode?" Lurleen asked. "How could you do that without killing everyone in sight."

That seemed like a very good question. "Somehow, Carl was the only one on the left side of the cannon," I said. "The others stepped away and turned their backs. I assume the weakness in the cannon was on the left side."

"It was," Mason said, "and it appears Phil was in charge of where people stood."

"He was. We watched them practice their roles. Danny explained to me what was going on. Phil placed Carl in the number two position to the left of the cannon. He was behind him and then backed away altogether when Carl pulled the lanyard."

"It's not looking good for your former boyfriend," Mason said.

"No it's not," I said. "Normally, two people would be to the left of the cannon. The gunner—Phil—would be directing the show, standing well behind the cannon. However, according to Phil, they were a couple people short, so he filled in. Originally, he was going to pull the lanyard, but when Carl asked to do it, he stepped away."

I thought about the picture in my mind. Andy was to the right front of the cannon. Sally was behind him. Ryan stood behind both of them. Carl was to the left side, initially in front of Phil. Frank was in charge of the powder and standing a few feet away from the cannon near the ammunition wagon. Phil was in charge and held the lanyard in his hand. After a conversation with Carl, he gave the lanyard to him and backed away.

"In the end, Phil was several feet behind the cannon," I said.

"Where was Harper?" Lurleen asked.

"Harper wasn't there.," I said. "Phil had assigned her to be a Yankee and then at the last minute they didn't need her for that. After the explosion she came running over from the sidelines."

"Dommage," Lurleen said. "So she couldn't have orchestrated where people stood. Looks like we have one less suspect. I must say I'm sorry to take Harper off the list."

We stopped talking when we saw the kids reappear on the deck. Together we went into the house, and I gave them a proper hug and kiss.

"Hungry for dinner?" I asked.

Lucie groaned. "Lurleen made us eat the whole watermelon."

"What a storyteller," Lurleen said. "I brought home half a small watermelon, and they kept eating. You can't blame this on me, Lucie."

"Never mind," I said. "My brother, father, and I used to do exactly the same thing in Iowa, only we'd eat a giant watermelon out in the field behind the house and do our best to keep the bees away."

That was a fond memory of Tommy and my dad—before Tommy left for boarding school and my father got sick with cancer.

"We'll wait a bit and then have a light dinner. You two can take your baths and find a movie to watch." I glanced over at Mason. "Do you need to go?"

"Shortly. I can stay for dinner."

"I'll help with Jason's bath," Lurleen said.

"Good. I need to call Phil."

Mason stopped smiling.

I went upstairs to call. Phil was annoyed to hear from me.

"Ditie, it's twelve hours before the reenactment. This better be important."

I almost hung up on him.

"Phil, I've just heard the police think the cannon was deliberately tampered with to make it explode. Have the police talked to you?"

Phil sighed audibly into the phone. "Yes. For over an hour. It sure as hell wasn't me who damaged it. That gun was a classic—it belonged in a museum, and I was going to put it there someday. You can't believe I'd destroy that."

"Why did you put Carl on the left side of the cannon?"

"Carl knew nothing about reenactments. It was the only position he could handle. He just had to receive an imaginary cannon ball and pretend to put it in the cannon. It was actually the position he wanted. Someone told him it would keep him close to the action."

"Someone told him that?"

"I don't have time for your interrogation. Someone told him that. I don't know who, and I didn't argue."

"It turned out to be the right position to get him killed," I said.

"Look, I'm busy, and if all you want to do is accuse me of murder, I don't need that right now."

"Okay." This time I did hang up.

I came downstairs to find Mason and Lurleen in the kitchen. "Phil is impossible," I said.

Mason looked pleased. Lurleen gave me a sly look.

"What's that look about, Lurleen?"

"He's always been impossible, *chérie*. You just didn't recognize it—you were blinded by his good looks, and you were used to being ordered around by your mother."

"Well, I'm done trying to protect him. I'll get dinner started."

"I've got it covered," Mason said. "I'm a one-dish wonder and I'm working on my world-famous spaghetti, actually my mother's world famous spaghetti—Spaghetti à la Eddie."

"Great. I'll make the salad."

"I've got it, *chérie*," Lurleen said, pushing her sunset red hair away from her face with the back of her hand. She pulled a store-bought bag of salad greens from the refrigerator and ripped it open. "Have a glass of wine and enjoy the kids."

I heard the kids in the living room. Jason was apparently following Lucie around with his bugle.

"I'll wait with the wine," I said.

I gathered both children on the sofa with me and asked about their day.

Lucie went first. "Mrs. Foster made us write a story, so I wrote one about Lurleen and her old boyfriend Antoine, but I called him Tony because that's what Lurleen called him."

"What did this boyfriend do for a living?" I was almost afraid to ask.

"He worked in a zoo in Paris with the parrots and taught them to talk," Lucie said.

"How did Mrs. Foster like your story?"

"She said I had a very good imagination, and she asked if Lurleen was my imaginary friend. I told her I was too old for an imaginary friend, but I'm not sure she believed me."

I was sorry Lurleen had missed this.

"How 'bout you big guy?"

"Oh, Mommy, I'm not a big guy." Jason stopped and looked stricken.

"Jason, it's okay to call me Mommy. That's how I think about you. Both of you. I feel like your second mom, and if that's all right with you, it's good with me. Your first mom wouldn't mind. In fact she'd be happy to know someone loves you as much as she did."

Chapter Sixteen

We all woke early on Saturday. The kids were excited and didn't make a peep about not going to the real reenactment. Instead, they asked about when they would see their Uncle Tommy and would he be in a costume. I assured them he would not.

They dressed in theirs, and I insisted on pictures before we headed out.

We met Tommy at ten outside the Atlanta History Center. He looked great, but then Tommy always looked great— blond hair, buff body. He spent an hour a day in the gym regardless of what else was going on in his life, but the big difference in him was that now he was really happy. He had a serious boyfriend, a doctor not a lawyer, which meant they couldn't talk shop when we had them over for dinner. Of course, Josh, the boyfriend, and I could do that, but we tried not to. Actually, we did it occasionally just to get a rise out of Tommy. Tommy was still used to being the center of attention—that hadn't changed. He liked seeing himself on TV handling the most sensational cases he could find.

Today, however, he was all about the kids.

"Look at you, Jason," Tommy said. "You look like a real Confederate soldier!"

"I am a soldier! Will you come to the 'actment later at Eddie's house?"

"Wouldn't miss it. I think Josh will come too. And you Miss Lucie, you look divine. Does that dress twirl by any chance?"

Lucie giggled and twirled under Tommy's arm.

"Indeed it does," Tommy said and planted a kiss on her cheek.

"You get one too, my little man." He gave Jason a kiss and ruffled his dark hair.

Jason glanced at me and hesitated.

"What is it, Jason?" I asked.

"Is it okay?"

I wasn't sure what he meant but I nodded my head anyway.

Jason looked at Tommy. "Mommy said I'm a big boy."

Tommy shot me a look and smiled.

"He is a big boy, don't you think, Tommy?" I asked.

"I hardly recognize him."

Tommy took Jason's hand. I took Lucie's. We entered the Atlanta History Museum's main building, and Tommy showed his pass. It seemed he'd done some pro bono work for them and had a lifetime pass for himself and anyone he cared to bring with him.

We had an amazing time. When I looked at my watch we'd been inside for an hour, and Jason showed no signs of getting restless. I begged for a break, and we went to the museum cafe for something to drink.

"You haven't even seen the room with all the Civil War guns," Tommy said to Jason.

Jason couldn't stay in his seat. "Let's go now, Uncle Tommy!"

I smiled at Lucie. "What do you say, Lucie? Have we seen enough? If so, we'll leave the boys to it, and we'll go to the mansion up the hill. I don't think Jason will want to see that."

Lucie nodded enthusiastically.

"How 'bout we meet up again in an hour at the Swan Coach House for lunch?"

"Perfect," Tommy said.

Lucie and I headed up the hill. She took my hand and stopped walking. "Aunt Di, is it okay for Jason to call you Mommy?" she asked. "Do you think it makes Mommy feel sad?"

I hugged Lucie. "If you had a little girl and a little boy and you couldn't be with them, would it make you sad if someone else loved them?"

"No," Lucie said. "I'd be happy about that."

"Well, that's what I think your mom must feel. She and I were friends for a very long time."

"When you were little kids," Lucie said. "Mommy told me."

"Yes. We met when I was younger than you are now." I looked at Lucie with her white blond hair and sapphire eyes and for a moment all I saw was her mother. "You look just like her."

Lucie beamed at that. "I do? Mommy is beautiful."

I nodded, and I could see Lucie was close to tears. "Want to sit for a while?" I asked.

Lucie nodded. We found a large oak tree with a circular bench around it. From where we sat we could see a glimpse of the Swan House, a beautiful mansion built in the late 1920s.

"Do you want to talk about your mom, Lucie?"

"Yes," she said.

"I do too."

Lucie looked at me and burst into tears. I wasn't far behind. We cried and we talked.

"You know, I think your mom would have loved to live in a house like the Swan House. You'll see when we get inside. The rooms are big and elegant and we'll look for swans—the architect loved them. That's how it got its name."

Lucie nodded. "Mommy said someday we'd live in a mansion. But you know, Aunt Di, I never want to live in a mansion. I want to live in a house just like yours."

"I'm with you, Lucie. When we were little your mom and I would play house all the time. She'd be the mom and I'd be the dad."

That made Lucie smile. "You'd be the dad? But you don't even look like a dad."

"Thanks. I didn't think so either, but whatever your mom said to do, I pretty much did."

"Like me," Lucie said.

"Yes. One time your mom said she was so hungry for an apple and would I climb up a tree and get her one. I did, and then on the way down I slipped and landed on my back. I wasn't hurt but the apple was smashed. Your mom picked me up and dusted me off and made sure I was okay. Then she asked me if I'd climb up and get her one that wasn't smashed."

"Did you, Aunt Di?"

"What do you think?"

"I think you did."

We both laughed at that, and then for some reason we couldn't stop laughing. People stared at us as they walked by.

Finally, we headed up the road to the grand front steps of the Swan House. Lucie stopped on the second step and put a hand over her mouth.

"Oh, Aunt Di, I saw this in a movie."

"A movie?" I asked.

"*The Hunger Games.* Lurleen let me watch it when Jason had a play date."

"Lurleen let you see *The Hunger Games?* All three of them?"

"She said not to tell you because you'd get upset," Lucie said. "She covered my eyes when something scary happened."

All I could do was shake my head.

"It wasn't bad, Aunt Di. It was wonderful. I'm going to grow up and be just like Katniss."

"I bet you are."

"Lurleen said when I turn eleven, and if it's okay with you, I can read the books."

"We'll see."

We entered the house. A beautiful curved staircase led up from the marbled black and white floor. Lucie could barely contain herself when she entered a room she'd seen in the movie. "That's where they sat around a huge round table," she whispered when we entered the dining room. "That's where President Snow sat," when we saw a desk and later a period sofa in an elegantly furnished room."

We left the house by the back entrance, and Lucie looked at me, eyes sparkling. "That was wonderful, Aunt Di. Wait till I tell the kids at school!"

We walked up the hill to the Swan Coach House restaurant where we found Jason and Tommy waiting for us.

"They let me hold a musket, a real musket," Jason said.

"It was taller than he was," Tommy said, "and heavier." He took Jason's hand and headed for the entrance. "I'm starving. Can we eat now?"

"Yes." I said.

Jason wasn't happy once we got inside. It was very froufrou, and that was not something Jason had time for. He did finally agree to eat a tuna salad sandwich while the rest of us had our dainty salads and cheese straws.

After we ate, we spent a few minutes at the old farm. The kids enjoyed the animals, but they'd had enough of museums and old buildings. They wanted some action.

We arrived at Eddie's a little after two. It was only then I thought to call Mason.

He didn't pick up, so I left him a message.

When we entered the gate to Eddie's front yard, we were greeted by her one-year-old poodle mix—the cutest dog you'd ever want to see. We'd helped Eddie pick him out at the pound, and I swear he remembered us. He couldn't get enough of the kids and bounced all over them in the yard.

I always felt as if we were coming home when we arrived at Eddie's, and she treated us the same way. She gave me a giant hug, and together we watched the kids tumbling on the grass with Schnitzel. Schnitzel Doodle was his full name.

Eddie hugged Tommy the same way she hugged me. It used to be Tommy would freeze if anyone tried to hug or kiss him. Not anymore. He gave Eddie a warm kiss on the cheek and asked if she'd heard from Josh.

"He said he'd be here between three and four in uniform."

"That figures."

"And Mason?" Eddie asked me.

"I left him a message, but he didn't pick up." Just then my cell rang. It was Mason.

"Everything okay there?" I asked.

"Yes. Lots of smoke and gunfire, but no accidents or surprises. We're done for the day."

"Thank goodness. Is Lurleen with you?" I asked.

"She's going to spend a night out with Danny. Phil apparently gave him the evening off."

It was a long drive for Mason, and he didn't think he could get there until five, so we carried on without him. Josh arrived as Eddie was explaining the ground rules for our reenactment.

Eddie must have been studying the tactics of war because she laid out a battle in her backyard that even Phil would have admired. We had to make the sounds of guns firing and cannons booming, but Josh and Tommy did that admirably. Jason got to use his wooden gun and hide behind trees. We all fell over when he yelled, "Got you!"

Then Jason would demand the whole thing start over again.

Those of us who were Yankees surrendered for the final time a little before five. Eddie started the grill while I took the kids inside to help them clean up for dinner. Josh and Tommy followed.

"That was the best 'actment ever," Jason said. "Wait 'til I tell Uncle Mason. I killed you three times, Uncle Tommy."

"Only three?" Tommy asked. "Then why am I so sore?"

"Getting old," Josh said.

Josh and Tommy were a good pair but they were nothing alike—Tommy, meticulous in all things and Josh, casual. They'd known each other for years but had only gotten serious in the last three months. Already Josh had softened some of Tommy's uptight edges. I think for the first time in his life, Tommy felt someone knew him inside and out and loved him for the man he was. That's all it took to make me love Josh.

Mason arrived hungry and thirsty. Over dinner he described the day in glorious detail. I asked Josh if he knew any of the players involved. He was an internist in Buckhead.

"I know the Hudsons," he said. "I refer to them often. And of course I know Phil Brockton's father. Everyone in Buckhead knows him. I also met Carl Thompson and his wife—what's her name?"

"Kathy," I supplied.

"That's right. She had the famous dad who wrote those books."

"Yes."

"I met Carl and Kathy at a party at Brockton's house a couple of months ago. Phil was there and Sally Cutter."

"What did you think of them?" I asked.

Josh hesitated. He was not one to speak ill of the dead—or the living for that matter.

"Maybe we'll finish this another time," I said. "I need to get the kids home to bed."

"I was wondering if you might let them spend the night?" Eddie asked. "I've got their beds made up, and you know I still have some of their clothes from when they stayed here the last time. We could spend the day together tomorrow. I haven't seen them in a while."

"Could we?" Lucie asked.

"Can we play with my musket tomorrow?" Jason asked.

"Of course," Eddie said.

This was an opportunity I was not about to pass up.

"Sounds good to me," I said.

Eddie shooed us out of the house and ordered the four of us to enjoy the rest of our evening.

Tommy suggested Josh change out of his Federal uniform but Josh just shrugged.

"Don't have anything else," he said, "and I kind of like the authority it gives me. Guess you'll have to take me as I am."

"You're going to stir up all kinds of trouble in that outfit," Tommy said.

"You're afraid I'll embarrass you," Josh said and smiled. "Consider this a growth experience for you. How about you two? Are you embarrassed to be seen with me?"

Mason and I shook our heads.

We headed for a favorite Buckhead bar and then huddled together at a table in the back where we could almost hear one another if we shouted.

I leaned toward Josh. "Now I want to hear the rest of the story about that party you attended."

Josh glanced at Tommy.

"Don't look at me. If my sister wants to know something she'll get it out of you one way or another. You might as well get it over with."

"It was almost as lively as our reenactment today," Josh said. "Fortunately, no one was armed."

Chapter Seventeen

The crowd at the bar showed no signs of thinning out. It was after ten and about the time when the Buckhead party crowd got started.

"Okay, Ditie," Josh said, "let me get another scotch, and I'll give you every last detail."

He raised his hand and waited for our waitress to see us. She didn't look pleased when Josh was the only one ordering a second drink.

While we waited, I asked Mason if everyone came to the reenactment.

"Yes."

"Even Ryan? I thought he was pretty shaken by Carl's death."

"Ryan came as a Federal and Harper was part of the Confederate cavalry," Mason said. "She said she brought her horse to Atlanta after her father died last year and was anxious to give him some exercise."

"I tend to forget Harper grew up on a ranch," I said. "She told me she was a tomboy, but it's hard to imagine that."

"It wasn't just any ranch," Josh said. "It was one of the three biggest cattle ranches in Texas."

"I heard that as well, but how would *you* know that?" I asked.

"Straight from the horse's mouth—make that Harper's mouth," Josh said. "We tend to run in the same circles, and I heard about her life on the ranch—how she loved to hunt, ride horses. She even branded some of the cattle."

"It sounds as if you two talked a lot," I said.

"Josh is like you, Ditie," Tommy said. "People open up to him, especially after a few drinks. Harper couldn't help herself. Even I heard her life story after her father died last year. It's like a dam broke."

I remembered how I felt when my own father died.

"I guess they were very close," I said.

"Yeah," Josh said, "I think she worshipped her dad, although she did say something funny to me. She said she was now free to live her own life, not the one her father had planned for her."

"And she seemed happy about that?" I asked.

"Hard to tell, but I think so."

"I'm coming to the reenactment tomorrow, so I guess I'll see her on horseback," I said.

"Maybe," Mason said. "I heard her say one day on the battlefield might be enough. Her husband didn't seem to like that. He quizzed her about where she would be and what she would do on Sunday. Then he begged her to come."

"I don't think Ryan trusts her out of his sight," I said.

"It also sounded like he wanted her to see him in action, admire him," Mason said. "It was a little odd, I have to say."

"I'm beginning to think their whole relationship is a little odd," I said.

"I can add to that," Josh said, "but not until I get my second scotch."

Mercifully, it arrived before he'd finished his sentence. He took a sip.

"Ah, this is good. Speaking of scotch, Dr. Brockton had a Macallan twenty-five-year-old single malt and didn't mind sharing it."

I gave Josh a look. "Should we be worried about your drinking?" I asked.

"Two's my limit I swear, and Tommy'll drive us home. I'll get my car tomorrow."

"Very responsible," I said. "Now, what is it you have to add?"

"Every time I see Harper and Ryan together, he's all over her," Josh said, "and she seems anxious to get away. I feel sorry for both of them really. Ryan's like a dog with a bone, and I don't think Harper likes being the bone."

"Nice way with words, Josh," I said.

"I should have been a poet."

Tommy put one arm around Josh. "Don't give up your day job."

"Now about the party at Dr. Brockton's house," I said. "When was it and who was there?"

"Let's see. It was six or seven weeks ago, right Tommy?"

Tommy nodded.

"Tommy came as my lawyer and partner. I'm not sure Mrs. Brockton was too happy about that once she figured out our relationship, but she was polite."

"She was never all that happy about my relationship with Phil either," I said. "I think she hoped Phil would get serious about someone a bit more gorgeous and a lot more Southern. There was probably a small celebration when he broke it off."

"Besides the two of us, there were eight or so others. Phil came down from New York just for the meeting. Carl and Kathy Thompson were there, Sally, Harper and Ryan, and a couple of other docs."

"Why was Sally there?" I asked.

"I think she came as a package with Carl, and the senior Dr. Brockton mentioned an open position in his financial department."

"Phil told me his dad wouldn't hire her because she didn't actually have any business degrees despite what she claimed."

"Maybe no one knew that at the time," Tommy said. "You don't check references until you're about to make an offer."

Josh continued his story. "It was a small gathering for the Brocktons. I've been to their Christmas parties and those are for hundreds. Dr. Brockton lives in one of those modest cottages on Tuxedo Road—I'd guess 10,000 square feet, newly renovated."

"I know the house," I said.

"Enough reminiscing," Mason said. "What did you think of the people there, Josh? Did any one of them seem especially angry at Phil?"

Josh laughed. "Funny you should say that. The person who seemed most angry *was* Phil. I don't think the free-flowing alcohol helped much, or the discussion of how Dr. Brockton had plans to expand his business."

"It wasn't really a party," Tommy said. "More a business meeting with Southern hospitality. There was a fairly elaborate dinner—you'd have loved it, Ditie. You know that new Atlanta chef— Boone Babbitt—he served us the best southern fried chicken you'd ever hope to eat, outside of yours of course, followed by lemon meringue pie for dessert."

"You are making my mouth water, but I really want to hear about the party. Then I need to get home and get some sleep before tomorrow's reenactment. I plan to go, so I can help Lurleen."

"I'll cut to the chase," Josh said. "After dinner, we settled in Dr. Brockton's den. Mrs. Brockton excused herself, but everyone else stayed. Brockton said that he wanted each of us to seriously consider being a part of his new venture. He'd continue as the nominal head of his concierge business but hoped the rest of us would bring on board our current patients."

"Did he include Harper and Ryan in his offer?" I asked. "They're dermatologists, not internists."

"Brockton said he wanted to work out something with them—exclusive referrals, that kind of thing," Josh said. "The rest of us were internists or family docs, and Brockton described how great it was to give patients the time they wanted for an annual fee to ensure our availability."

"Nothing sounds unusual about that," I said.

"I agree. It didn't interest me, but I could see Carl Thompson practically salivating. He said he'd really enjoyed his work with Dr. Brockton and looked forward to helping him manage the new corporation. He said it as if he'd be the managing partner." Josh savored his drink and a moment of silence before he continued. "That flew all over your ex. Phil stood up, yelled at his dad. 'I am supposed to take over when you retire.' His father didn't bat an eye. 'I'll see who does the best job and then I'll make my decision.'"

"Things went from bad to worse," Tommy said. "Carl made some comment about letting the best man win, and Phil grabbed the nearest thing to him, a half-full decanter of whiskey. He looked as it he were going to smash it over Carl's head, when Ryan, Josh and I jumped in to restrain him."

Josh took a last sip of his scotch. "Never allow a person to waste perfectly good whiskey. Phil cooled off and left, but not before he told Carl he'd never be the managing partner of his father's business."

"That sounds incriminating," Mason said.

"The party broke up at that point," Josh said. "I spoke to Dr. Brockton on my way out saying I was flattered to be asked but was very happy with my present situation. Truth is I had no desire to work with a bunch of hot heads fighting to be in charge."

Tommy patted Josh on the shoulder. "We only need one prima donna in this family."

Amen to that, I thought.

"How did Sally Cutter react?" I asked.

"She seemed pleased," Josh said. "She told Carl not to worry about Phil—that he was finally getting what he deserved. Then she made another comment about how they were about to climb on the gravy train at last."

"That she said under her breath," Tommy said. "We only heard it because we were standing behind them while we waited for our cars. Funny thing was Kathy Thompson didn't seem all that happy. She looked at Carl, and Carl told her it was just a figure of speech, nothing to worry about."

"Odd," I said. "You do know that Andy Morrison fired Carl for 'missing money' from the practice. Sally was working for him at the time."

"Interesting," Tommy said.

"Yes. And then Sally isn't hired according to Phil because she didn't have the credentials she claimed. Sally told me it was her decision not to work with Dr. Brockton, not the other way around."

"Well, she was certainly eager to do it that night," Josh said.

It was almost midnight when our party broke up. Mason followed me home and spent the night. We didn't get to do that very often, so we made the most of it.

* * * *

In the morning, Mason asked if I really intended to go to the reenactment.

"Yes. I won't be on the battlefield. I'll just offer the weary warriors iced tea and cookies. I'll get to see that famous railroad tunnel everyone has mentioned—Danny's version of living history."

Lurleen arrived, and we decided we could all go together in my car. It was a two hour drive to the Battle of Tunnel Hill. When we arrived we saw a hundred reenactors already on the field. Some were on horses.

"This should be quite a show," I said, as we walked toward the tent that housed Lurleen's store along with another woman serving hot tea and biscuits. The woman greeted us warmly. Danny showed up as we were getting supplies arranged in the tent.

"I thought you had to guard Phil," I said.

"He gave me a fifteen minute break to say hi to you. Everything went like clockwork yesterday, and I think he's feeling good about that. Today is the day when the Confederates get to win. It's a two-day affair, so both sides can be victorious. Phil's even more pumped about today."

We saw Phil walking across the field. Then we heard a stray shot or a car backfiring. Phil clutched his chest and fell to the ground. We all started running towards him when he jumped up and waved us off.

Danny reached him first. "Don't ever do that again, man."

The rest of us arrived seconds after Danny.

Phil looked at our faces. "Hey, lighten up. I think the whole mess last week was an accident. Had to be."

"That isn't what the police think, and that doesn't explain the photo Kathy received showing Carl's body," Mason said.

"What are you talking about?" Phil asked.

Mason described the photo in detail.

I looked at Mason. Was he trying to make Phil nervous?

It did the trick.

Phil grew serious. "I can't explain the photograph."

"We know about your threat that Carl would never manage your father's business," Mason said, "from an eyewitness."

"It's that brother of yours, right, Ditie? He never liked me when we were dating. Yeah, everyone knows I hated Carl. He fed Dad lies about my involvement in the cheating scandal and then backed off when my father asked him to."

"In return for something?" I asked.

"I'm sure my dad offered him a job or a reference in the future if he needed it."

I nodded.

"You give yourself a good motive for murder," Mason said.

"If I were going to kill Thompson, you think I'd blow up my own cannon to do it? Believe me, I'd find a better way. That cannon was priceless."

Mason didn't answer. He turned and walked off the field towards Lurleen's store.

"You need to do something about that boyfriend of yours," Phil said. "I think he'd be happy to see me brought up on charges."

"He's not working on your case in any official capacity," I said, and then I followed Mason across the field. We found Lurleen chatting with Sally and drinking iced tea. Sally didn't look happy to see me.

"What are you doing here?" she asked. "I thought you were keeping the kids away."

"The kids are with their adopted grandmother," I said, "so I thought I'd see what was going on. People claim this is a special place with the original tunnel and the house Sherman used to plan his Atlanta campaign.

Sally did one of her quick turn arounds. "It's great you could come. You should see the tunnel and the house—they're awesome." She looked at her Rolex. "I'm late for some pre-battle planning. I have to run."

It would be a few hours before the reenactment started. Mason said he wanted to talk to the officers he knew. Lurleen didn't need me, but she couldn't leave the store, so I decided to go exploring on my own. Andy and Frank caught up with me as I was wandering from tent to tent.

"We didn't expect to see you here," Frank said. "God knows I wouldn't be here if I hadn't made a commitment to Phil."

"Relax, Frank," Andy said. "You had a good time yesterday, you know you did."

"Your idea of a good time and mine are different. I just can't imagine why Ditie would choose to come to another reenactment."

I suddenly got the feeling I was crashing a private party.

"I for one, am glad you're here," Andy said. "I guess you know about the Clisby Austin house Sherman used as his headquarters."

"And the tunnel," I said. "Everyone tells me I must see the tunnel."

"Absolutely," Andy said. "It's up the road. I'd go with you but we have to report for an artillery drill. You coming, Frank?"

"I'll be along. I need something to eat. The whole thing doesn't start for hours."

He headed towards a stand that offered fried corn on the cob and barbecued chicken.

I continued to meander among the sutler tents. All the women I saw were in period costumes and quite willing to talk about the Civil War—from their perspective. One woman claimed the war was the result of outside agitators from Europe. I let that pass.

I saw Harper from a distance on a beautiful white stallion. She waved in my direction. I saw no sign of Ryan.

Phil and Danny joined me.

"Isn't this fantastic?" Danny said. "Been to the tunnel yet? The track's paved over now, but the walls are the original ones that surrounded the railroad. It was quite an achievement at the time."

Phil continued where Danny left off. "Tunnel Hill was named for the Western and Atlanta Railroad tunnel built through the hillside in 1850. The fight in 1864 was over who could control the tunnel and the railroads going into and out of Atlanta."

"Thanks for the history lesson," I said.

Phil pointed to the road behind us.

"It's just up there. Don't miss it."

They took off in the direction of the battlefield, and I was once more on my own. It was a hot summer day, and the heat was oppressive. I stopped in one's sutler's tent and bought some sassafras root beer, which I drank before I headed up the road toward the tunnel.

The entrance was dark. The tunnel itself was much smaller than I expected. I wondered how a train could actually have traveled through the space. Trains must have been a lot smaller then.

Inside, it was wonderfully cool. I stopped for a moment to appreciate the drop in temperature and let my eyes adjust to the low light. It was easy to imagine how it must have looked at the time of the Civil War. Ground lights barely illuminated portions of the walls and paved ground.

I enjoyed the quiet, the dank smell, the darkness. It was a world in which time stood still. I walked slowly and stopped to feel the wall beside me. It was moist and roughhewn, chiseled more than one hundred fifty years ago. I tried to imagine Confederates and Union soldiers fighting over this tiny tunnel to control supplies headed to the South. Surely there were other routes. I was so lost in a sense of history, I didn't hear footsteps behind me until they were close.

When they stopped I looked back. The spotlights on the sides of the tunnel made it impossible to see more than a silhouette. The person crouched as I looked around, their back to me. It looked as if they were tying their shoe laces.

I started walking a little more briskly. Was I spooked by the bloody history that surrounded the tunnel? Perhaps. Or was it something in the attitude of the mysterious person behind me? Neither of us spoke, but we were alone in the tunnel. I picked up my pace anxious to get to the light at the end of the tunnel.

As I walked faster, so did the person behind me. I shivered and tried to calm myself. Once more I glanced behind me but I could see no more than I had before. Should I stop, confront this phantom, put my mind to rest?

I was being ridiculous.

It was broad daylight outside, but *not* in the tunnel.

Just another one hundred feet, and I'd be back in the sunshine. The footsteps increased to a run. I stood to the side to let the person pass. Instead the person shoved me hard against the stone wall, lost their own balance and recovered with a hand to the wall in front of me as they dashed past. "Get the hell out of here," they growled at me.

I could see nothing but a hunched figure running away and the flash of what appeared to be a Civil War uniform as they disappeared into the light.

Chapter Eighteen

I tried to catch my breath. My attacker was gone. He—or she—had managed to shove me hard into the jagged edge of the stone wall. A sharp pain in my right shoulder shot down my arm.

Gingerly, I moved my shoulder, then my elbow and finally my wrist. I felt along my humerus, my elbow, my ulna, my radius. Everything appeared to be intact and already the pain had lessened.

I wasn't about to see if my attacker was waiting for me at the other end of the tunnel. Turning around I walked quickly back the way I'd come.

In the sunlight I saw I was bleeding, but it looked worse than it was. My shirt was ripped, and my forearm where I braced myself was scraped. I used my sleeve to put pressure on the only abrasion still oozing blood.

I was shaking and took deep breaths to calm myself.

It wasn't the physical injury that unnerved me. It was the attack. Someone saw me enter the tunnel and came after me—not to kill me, thank God, but to scare me off. Or perhaps to injure me enough, so I'd have to leave.

Why would a killer who worked so methodically to alter a cannon, act in such a reckless way? Anyone might have seen him. Was it simply rage at my unexpected presence? I thought about Phil—Josh described him as losing it at his father's party. Ryan had a hair-trigger temper, but why would he consider me any kind of threat? Why was I a threat to *anyone*?

An ominous thought entered my mind. Perhaps the killer wasn't done. Perhaps whoever attacked me was afraid I might interrupt their plans to kill again.

The voice didn't sound like Phil's, but it could have been anyone's—man or woman. It was low, more of a grunt than anything else. I also couldn't tell anything about the attacker's height or build. The person bent over as they ran away. And the uniform, was it Confederate? All I saw was a silhouette of a jacket and a hat.

I tried to hide among the trees to the left of the tunnel entrance. The tunnel led away from the battlefield, and to return the person might have to come back through. My goal was to see him or her but remain hidden. Unfortunately, an officer spotted me first.

"You, miss, what are you doing there?" He approached me. "Are you all right?"

He must have seen my torn and bloody shirt.

"It's nothing. Someone pushed me as I was walking through the tunnel."

"An accident? Why didn't they stay to help you?"

"I guess it was a hit and run, and I don't think it was an accident. The person told me to get the hell out of here or something close to that."

"Can you describe him?"

"I'm not even sure it was a him," I said. "I thought it was someone in uniform but all I could see was his back running away from me."

He looked at my arm. "You need to go to the first aid tent."

"I'm a doctor," I said, "and I'm fine. I need to stay here and see if he or she comes back. Is there any other way to get to the battlefield?

"It would take a while." The officer took off his hat and shaded his face. "It sounds as if you think you'd recognize the person."

I kept my eyes on the tunnel entrance and told the officer about what happened a few miles away in Resaca.

"We all heard about it. I'm a Whitfield County Deputy Sheriff, but that's right next door to Gordon. It's why I'm here. Why we're all here. Look, that arm is still bleeding. You need to get it taken care of."

"Please," I said. "Let me call Mason Garrett. He's a detective with the Atlanta Police Department, and he's here, somewhere."

The officer nodded and I called Mason on my cell. He said he'd be there in five minutes.

Before he arrived, I saw Sally Cutter emerge from the tunnel. She noticed me and came running over. "What happened to you, Ditie? You've got blood all over you."

"I'm fine. Just tripped in the tunnel. What were you doing? I thought you'd be on the field going over drills."

Sally wore a Confederate uniform but no hat. "I'm infantry today, and that doesn't take much preparation. I needed to stretch my legs, so I took a long walk. You walk straight into the countryside through the tunnel."

She could have been the person I saw, but she didn't seem the least bit defensive. Sally wasn't wedded to the truth, but could she be that good a liar?

"Did you see anyone else on your walk?" I asked.

"No, why?"

That remark didn't sound quite as innocent.

When Mason arrived, he examined my arm and looked upset. "I'm taking you to the first aid tent. Now."

We walked a few feet away from Sally, and I told him what had happened. Sally stood next to the Deputy Sheriff, apparently unable to decide if she should go or stay.

I promised to go to the tent if Mason would talk to Sally and stand guard at the tunnel to see who else might appear.

As I walked toward the row of sutlers' tents I went over what happened. Was it possible it had nothing to do with the murder? Someone who was a little too exuberant in his role and took me for a Yankee? I'd heard one of the women dressed in period clothing tell Confederate soldiers to kill some Federals—all in keeping with the day.

No. This wasn't part of the reenactment. This attack was personal—to distract me or get me out of the way—certainly not to kill me and certainly not in fun. I walked to the first aid tent and let a nurse clean me up. She suggested x-rays but backed off when I told her I was a doctor and showed her all the moving parts in my arm were still moving.

I got back to Mason fifteen minutes later.

He stood alone at the entrance to the tunnel. "I questioned Sally and sent the officer on. Sally claims she went through that tunnel half an hour before you did, and she says she went alone. Show me where it happened."

He pulled out a pocket flashlight and held me by my good arm.

I took him to the spot near the end of the tunnel. He shined his light along the surface of the wall and found a small piece of red wool stuck in a rock crevice. He held it up to the light of his flashlight. "Could be from a kepi or a forage cap."

I gave him a blank look.

"The kepi is a lower, stiffer cap with a disc like top. The forage cap is a softer cap, more material, and used for work like foraging in the old days."

He asked me to describe what I'd seen.

"I think it looked stiffer, the way you describe the kepi, but I can't be sure."

When I finished, he said, "Some Georgian Confederate kepis were made of red wool and gold braid—signified artillery officers, lieutenants I think. Of course, Federals wore kepis, too, some of them with red trim."

He studied the small piece of torn wool. "I wonder if it ripped off when the person stumbled against the wall."

"I have no idea. It was on their head when they left the tunnel. How could you possibly know about Georgia Confederate hats, Mason?"

"I'm a Southerner, Ditie."

"You grew up in Atlanta, that's hardly the Deep South. You don't even have an accent."

"My dad's father was from rural Georgia and his mother was from Tennessee. I have relatives who fought on both sides of the war. We know these things even if we don't go around discussing them the way Phil Brockton does."

There was a lot about Mason I still didn't know, but standing in a dark tunnel was not the time or place to learn more. We headed to the light.

It was getting close to the start of the battle.

"Is there another way back to the battlefield?" I asked.

"Sure," Mason said. "It would take longer, but you could swing back along the road. I'll hang onto this piece of material and look for anyone with a torn hat."

"Mason, I'm worried the murderer reacted to my being here because he or she has unfinished business."

"I had the same thought, and I'll alert the officers here. In the meantime I want you out of danger. Someone was obviously unhappy to see you here."

He left me with Lurleen and demanded I stay put. My arm was aching, and I didn't feel like going anywhere. Lurleen jumped in like a mother hen. "You sit, and I'll bring you some iced tea. It was my idea to come here, and now I've put you in danger."

"Lurleen, you had nothing to do with this. Someone doesn't like my looking into things. They didn't try to seriously hurt me—just push me in hopes I'd leave. Have you seen my classmates on the field during the last hour?"

Lurleen squinched up her hazel eyes and thought. "I saw the Confederate Cavalry going through their paces half an hour ago. I think I saw Harper's white stallion—it's a magnificent horse—but the person on it didn't look like Harper. Phil and Danny came by for iced tea at some point."

"So Danny was always with Phil?" I asked.

Lurleen gave me a less-than-happy look. "I'm sorry, sweetie. They weren't always together. Danny was still on break about the time you were attacked. He and I sat behind the tent eating roasted corn."

"That means Phil could have been the one who shoved me."

Did I really think that was possible? Wouldn't I have recognized him even if I didn't see or hear him distinctly?

"What about Ryan, Frank and Andy?" I asked.

"Danny might have seen more than I did. Wait a sec. I did see Ryan, now that you mention it, just before Danny and I took our lunch break. He was looking for Harper. Then he said he needed to talk to you. How could I have forgotten that? I said you were exploring the historic sites and asked if there was a message. He said no. Then he walked off toward the tunnel. Ditie, do you think it was Ryan who pushed you?"

"It could have been any of them." I stood up. "Don't urge me to sit down because I won't take your advice. Do you know where Ryan might be?"

"He's a Federal today. Danny says we all must use that term for Yankees. It's more accurate for the time. Ryan was carrying a gun, so I guess he's infantry," Lurleen said. "Please, Ditie, don't go!"

"No one will do anything to me unless I'm alone somewhere in the dark." I walked off before Lurleen could stop me without making a scene.

I asked directions to the Federal infantry camp from a few men standing near the sutlers' tents. 'Across the field and up a path.' There I found Ryan pacing back and forth in front of a tent. Other men were milling around.

He jumped when I called his name. He asked if I was all right.

"Why wouldn't I be?"

"Your arm. The bandage."

"I'm fine, just scraped it on a rock. Lurleen said you were looking for me."

"It was nothing." Ryan looked upset. "It can keep."

"I'm here now, so what did you want to tell me?"

"More what I wanted to ask. Harper came by minutes ago and tried to reassure me. We're fine really, it's just…"

"What, Ryan? It's just what?'

"Harper said she was with you last night, and I wanted to know—I wanted to know if that was true."

"I'm sorry, Ryan. I haven't spent any time with Harper."

"I knew it! I knew it! And I know who she was with. Ditie, I think Harper's going to leave me."

"You think there's another man?"

"I know there is."

"Who?"

"I thought it was Carl Thompson," Ryan said. "Then when he died I found out who it really was. I think Harper is going to leave me for Phil."

I told Ryan to sit down on a camp stool for a minute. I crouched down beside him and told him to take some deep breaths. Then I asked him to tell me what he knew for sure and what he suspected.

"I was sure it was Carl. He's always been hanging around Harper, even in med school. She kept telling me she didn't want anything to do with him, but I could see her feelings changed when he joined Dr. Brockton's big Buckhead practice. Suddenly, it was all about how smart Carl was, how we'd all underestimated him."

"You can't take that to mean she was having an affair with him."

"Believe me, I know the signs. I've been through this before."

"What do you mean?"

"I've had to set more than one man straight."

"Like Phil at my party?"

"Yes, like Phil. I'm sorry about that, but I can't lose Harper."

I put a hand on Ryan's arm. "You can't control her every move."

He shook off my hand, picked up his rifle, and started cleaning it. Then he put it down and seemed close to tears. "Have you ever loved anyone, Ditie? Really loved them?"

"Yes," I said slowly.

"I don't believe it. If you had, you'd know how I feel. I can't live without her. I don't want to live if she's not a part of my life, and there are all these people who want to take her away from me."

"The problem is between you and Harper," I said. "You need a good therapist, maybe a couple's counselor, to work this out."

For a moment, Ryan seemed to hear what I was saying.

"I'm willing to go. I'm willing to do anything, but Harper won't see anyone. She says everything is fine—it's all my imagination."

"If she won't go, then see someone on your own."

"You mean, like it's all in my head? Harper calls it my paranoia, but it's not paranoia when it's true." He picked up his gun and continued cleaning it. "I won't see someone and let them convince me I'm making the whole thing up."

He glared at me. "You love to fix things, Ditie, but you can't fix this. You shouldn't be here. I'm going to make sure that anyone who shows too much interest in Harper backs off. Like I did with Carl."

"Ryan, do you hear what you're saying?"

"I wanted Carl dead, and now he is. I can't say I'm sorry about that." He stared at me with the look of a tortured animal. "You want to believe I'm a murderer? Go ahead. I don't care what you think."

Ryan stood, grabbed his hat and gun and walked away from me. I tried to imagine him in silhouette. He could have been the person who shoved me.

He left behind a red Confederate hat with a piece of fabric missing. I picked it up intending to take it to Mason, but Sally caught me from behind.

"My hat," she exclaimed. "You found it. I thought I must have left it here when I was talking to Ryan."

Chapter Nineteen

"That's your hat?"

"Yes. Actually, it's Phil's. He let me borrow it."

I showed her the part with the missing patch.

"Oh my gosh, how did that get torn? Phil will have a fit," Sally said. "It's an actual hat from the Civil War. Maybe it was like that when he gave it to me."

"I don't think so," I said. "See, the tear looks fresh."

She examined it and then she inhaled deeply. "I don't have time to worry about it now. I have to get with my group. She grabbed the hat and started to walk away.

"When did you borrow the hat?" I asked.

"I don't remember. Does it matter?"

"When were you talking to Ryan?"

Sally stopped and turned to me. "Why all the questions? Is this still about who killed Carl? Let the police do their work. Stop interfering. Ryan's as bad as you are. He was peppering me with questions about Harper. I told him I hadn't seen much of her lately, but maybe you had. He took off like a rocket, I guess to find you. I've got to go. If I'm not there when the action starts, I'm not in it."

She walked off, hat in hand. I looked at my watch. We were half an hour away from the start of the battle. Maybe I had time to track down Frank and Andy, but I had no idea where they were. I'd find them after the reenactment. I headed back to Lurleen's.

"Boy, am I glad to see you," Lurleen said. "Mason was furious that I let you leave."

She pulled out her cell phone. "Mason, she's here with me, all in one piece."

He showed up moments later. "You're going to sit this one out with me."

I told him about my conversation with Ryan and about finding the hat.

"So it belonged to Phil, but Sally was using it, only she left it with Ryan. Was that before or after she walked through the tunnel?" Mason asked.

"I don't know. She wasn't wearing a hat when we talked to her."

"Ryan seemed wound up?" Mason asked.

"Ryan seemed distraught. He said he was glad Carl was dead. I couldn't tell if he was making a confession or simply relieved to have Carl out of the way."

"Ryan wants you and everyone else to back off," Mason said. "Did I tell you he has a rap sheet? Nearly beat a man to death years ago. He said the guy was threatening Harper. This was during their residency when they weren't even dating. He was lucky not to lose his license."

"A rap sheet. I never heard about that. He could have been the person who pushed me. And we've both seen how he acts when he's mad. He's out of control. You think we need to warn Phil and Danny?"

Mason nodded. "Yes. I'll tell them." Mason ran to the left of the field and was back before the battle started. "I saw Sally standing next to Phil on one side. Danny on the other. They were in a tight formation. I can't see any harm coming to them as long as they stay together."

"But they won't. They'll scatter," I said.

We spoke softly, so no one would overhear our worries, including Lurleen. She was busy offering cookies and iced tea to the spectators."

The action started with the firing of a Federal cannon on one side and return cannon fire from the Confederates. A row of Federals came on the field to be met by a Confederate infantry line. We were too far away to see faces. We saw guns fire and men fall—mostly Union forces. The cavalry from both sides rode onto the field and went hand to hand with make-believe swords before backing off. We could see Harper on her white stallion. Then more infantry, more shots, more dead and wounded. Every now and then medics would run on the field to see who was still alive and carry off a man or two.

The breeze had died, and I could only imagine how the men were suffering from the heat, particularly the Federals in their wool uniforms. The Confederates knew about the South and their uniforms were made of a cotton wool blend, at least some of them—that's what Lurleen took the time to explain to me. She'd heard it from a couple of guys who had partied too much the night before and were sitting out the actual battle.

It was half-way through the battle when we saw Phil's line of infantry emerge. Mason recognized them, and it didn't hurt that Danny waved his cap to us. From a cluster of pine trees, near where I'd seen Ryan, a group of Federals marched onto the field. The Confederates and the Federals faced each other from twenty yards away and fired. Men dropped, and then everyone who was still standing reloaded. There was smoke, noise, and cannons blasting. Bit by bit the Confederates pushed the Federals back.

At first, no one registered there was a problem. Skirmishes were happening across the field with some men on horses, others on foot. The fallen lay on their sides or their backs, some better actors than others. As the reenactment came to a close, two Union reenactors circled back to check on their fallen comrades.

It was then the cry went up. Lurleen and I could hear it from the tent. "A man's been shot!" Three police officers in uniform rushed onto the field. Mason and I ran after them.

I had only one thought. Let it not be Phil. I saw how angry Ryan was as he cleaned his gun. Did he fill it with live ammunition?

"I'm a doctor," I yelled as police tried to keep me away.

"Let her through," Mason shouted, showing his ID. I ran to his side and looked down. At first all I could see was a bloodied chest. A bullet had left a gaping hole near the man's heart. Then I recognized the uniform—a Federal uniform—and finally the face.

Ryan lay dead on the ground, his gun beside him, his eyes mercifully closed. I felt for his carotid, but I knew he was already gone.

Chapter Twenty

I heard Danny and Phil before I saw them. Danny was shouting at Phil to stay down, but Phil was apparently desperate to see what had happened. "Who is it?" I heard him cry. Then he knelt beside me with Danny covering him as best he could.

"Oh, God," Phil said. "I was standing opposite Ryan, shooting at him." He seemed to realize what he was saying and looked around. "I was firing blanks. We all were. Besides, this isn't a wound made by a mini ball—the damage would have been more massive."

Danny peered over Phil's shoulder. "What do you think it was?"

"Don't know," Phil said. He reached over to search the wound, and an officer stopped him from touching anything.

"You know him?" the officer asked.

"He's Dr. Ryan Hudson, a friend…of a lot of us." He looked around. "Where's Harper? She doesn't need to see this."

Danny stood up. "I see her horse. The cavalry has been ordered to stay away, I'm sure. I'll go to her."

"I'll come with you," Sally said.

"No," an officer ordered. It was the same Deputy Sheriff who had spoken to me earlier, but his demeanor had changed entirely. He was not a big man, but he now seemed more commanding. "I'm in charge for now. If you were on the field when this happened you stay on the field."

He ordered another officer to cordon off the area and take names.

"All of you stand over there, keep your mouths shut and your weapons on the ground beside you—understood?"

A second officer led them to a spot at the side of the field, Federals in one cluster, Confederates in another. Men stood or sat and placed their guns beside them. There were thirty or forty men in all, Sally stood next to Phil.

A deadly quiet fell over the field, and all that could be heard was the sound of a few birds calling to each other. A breeze picked up and made it easier to breathe.

I whispered to Mason, "Someone has to tell Harper."

Mason spoke with the officer. "Dr. Brown wasn't on the field. She was with me in a sutler's tent. Could she talk to his wife?"

"I know you both from this morning. She can go. I'll have an officer escort her and bring the wife back here."

The Deputy Sheriff waved me through the line of yellow tape set up to keep some of us in and others out.

The officer said he'd join me in a moment. I walked to where the horses and riders stood. It wasn't hard to find Harper. She was off her horse and sitting on the ground. She jumped up when she saw us approaching.

"What happened?" she asked. "They won't let us through and they won't answer our questions."

"Do you have someone who can take care of your horse?" I asked.

Harper looked alarmed. She turned to a young woman. "Jeannie, can you handle Bullet again?" Jeannie nodded, and all I could think of was the irony of that name.

I led Harper to a place where she could sit down, but she remained standing.

"What is it, Mabel? Just tell me. Has something happened to Ryan? We're hearing all kinds of rumors. Tell me!"

"I'm sorry, Harper. Ryan's been killed."

Harper's face paled and for a moment I thought she might pass out. I helped her to the ground. She put her face in her hands and shuddered. "It's all my fault."

I waited a moment. "What do you mean?"

She looked at me. Her blue eyes were crystal clear. "I drove this madness. I didn't mean to, but I couldn't stand Ryan's hovering any more. I told him I'd go where I wanted and do what I wanted. Ryan thought I was having an affair."

"That's what he told me," I said.

"He told you that? When?"

"This afternoon, just before the reenactment. He said he thought you were involved with Phil."

"Oh God, I knew it. First it was Carl and then Phil. If I ever said hello to a man, Ryan was sure I was about to leave him."

"Were you?"

"I loved Ryan. He never understood how much. I'm gregarious, and he took that to mean I wasn't happy with him."

This time the tears did come. "Was it...was it suicide?" she asked.

I looked at her amazed. "Whatever made you ask that? It was murder."

"I asked because Ryan was so despondent, saying he couldn't live without me. I kept reassuring him, but he wouldn't listen. He said if he did die it would be quick, like on a battlefield."

I wondered if Ryan could have turned the gun on himself. The wound was ghastly enough to be delivered up close. I'd leave that to forensics.

"Frankly, after I spoke to Ryan, I worried he might shoot Phil," I said.

Harper nodded her head slowly. "He did threaten that. I must have spoken to him just after you did. He threatened to harm anyone who paid the least attention to me. I wondered about Carl."

"You wondered if Ryan had killed him?"

Again Harper nodded.

"How would he know about cannons and how to make them malfunction?"

"We all kept our gear in the same locked storage unit—safer than in our homes. That meant the guns, the cannon, even the uniforms. It was a facility with tight security, proper air conditioning."

"Who is all?" I asked.

"Me, Ryan, Sally, and Andy. Even Frank had access. Phil let him choose a weapon and a uniform from his precious supply."

"So you're saying any one of you could have damaged the cannon."

"Anyone who had the time and knowledge."

"Did Ryan have that knowledge?"

"He asked me all about cannons and looked online to see how they worked. I just don't know what he might have done."

The officer joined us at that moment. "Ms. Hudson," he said, "it's time to go."

"Dr. Hudson," she responded. "May I see my husband?"

"I'm not sure you want to see him as he is now."

"I'm a doctor," Harper said. "I need to see him."

"Very well."

We walked back across the field. I stayed near Mason as the officer took Harper five feet from where Ryan lay. "I can't let you come any closer," he said.

Harper looked and nodded. "That's my husband."

Then she broke down. The officer led her back to me and Mason.

She turned to me. "I can't believe it. It really is Ryan. Did Phil take matters into his own hands?"

"What are you talking about?" Mason asked before I could.

"Phil wanted me to divorce Ryan," she said.

"You just told me you would never leave Ryan," I said.

"I meant it, but Phil was sure I'd change my mind. He said Ryan was stifling me. I think Phil hoped to marry me one day."

Mason looked at her. "You do realize you've just given Phil a motive for murder."

Harper looked aghast. "No, no, I didn't mean to do that."

"Were you involved with Carl as your husband suspected?" Mason asked.

"Never," Harper said with disgust. "I don't know where Ryan ever got that idea."

Mason turned to us. "No more conversation," he said. "The Whitfield County investigator is here along with Officer Barden from Gordon County. They'll be asking the questions.

It was Officer Barden who approached us.

"I'm sorry for your loss, but I'll need to talk with you, Dr. Hudson, if you're up to it."

"I am."

The officer led her back across the field to the Clisby Austin House. That must be where they'd set up headquarters. How fitting. It was the old farmhouse Sherman used as his headquarters while he planned his Atlanta campaign.

"They have Phil's gun along with everyone else's," Mason said. "It's an Enfield '53. Sally has the same gun, and she was standing next to Phil. Did she have a grudge against Ryan?"

"I don't know. I have no idea when Sally's telling the truth or making up a story."

"The GBI ballistics team will likely determine where the shot came from. As long as those muskets aren't smooth bore, they can figure out which rifle fired the live shot."

"But Phil said the shot wasn't a mini ball. It was something that was smaller caliber based on the size of the wound."

"I'll check with the Whitfield County investigator. He might already have found the bullet. If it wasn't a mini ball, it's unlikely the GBI will be able to trace the gun."

I watched Mason as he spoke with the Whitfield County investigator who continued labeling evidence in the cordoned area around the body. Another officer worked beside him taking photos. I was too far away to hear the conversation. When it ended, Mason returned with me to Lurleen's tent.

"Barden wants you to stay put for now. He did find the bullet, says it's less than a 50 caliber. He speculates it could have been in the cartridge and not seen by a person loading his rifle."

"That means the bullet might have come from anywhere," I said.

Lurleen was seated next to me, eager to hear every word. "How could the bullet have been hidden in the cartridge?" she asked.

"The cartridge consists of a paper tube, black powder, and a bullet," Mason said. "In a reenactment, there is no bullet. You've watched the soldiers bite open the paper tube, pour the powder into the muzzle and ram down an imaginary bullet."

Lurleen and I both nodded.

"It's possible that a bullet could slide down a musket and not be noticed by the shooter."

"So whoever fired the shot, might not have known he had a live bullet in his gun," Lurleen said.

"Exactly. Or the shooter might have known it would be impossible to trace who fired the shot given the tight formation of the Confederates on the line."

"Can they tell if Ryan was the intended victim?"

"Not for sure," Mason said. "A smaller bullet would have been less accurate but the two lines were only twenty yards apart. It's most likely someone meant to kill Ryan, if it wasn't suicide."

Lurleen stared wide-eyed at Mason. "Do you think it could have been suicide?"

Mason shook his head. "It's doubtful. Those rifles are over five feet. Ryan was tall, but it would have been hard to do. We'll see what the medical examiner thinks."

"If it was suicide, then Harper drove him to it," Lurleen said.

All we could do was wait until the police said we were free to leave. I called Eddie to let her know about the situation and to make sure the children didn't see it on TV. She responded quietly as if I were simply telling her about a busy day. I realized the kids must be nearby.

"Have fun," she said. "I'll be happy to have the kids another night since you and Mason have plans for the evening."

"Thank you. I'll call them later."

I couldn't talk to the kids just then—Lucie would have picked up on my anxiety.

Mason went back on the field while Lurleen and I packed up supplies. From our vantage point we could see most of the battlefield, including the cluster of uniforms and the distant body.

Danny joined us. "Barden has finished interviewing me for now, so I thought I'd see how you two were holding up?"

"We're okay," I said. "We know Inspector Barden found the bullet and it wasn't a mini ball. That means someone could have set Phil up," I said. "He might not have known he was firing live ammunition."

"It's possible."

"Were you next to Phil the whole time?"

"I was."

"Did you see Ryan get shot?" I asked.

"When everyone starts firing, you can't see much of anything beyond smoke," Danny said. "I did see Ryan fall—didn't know it was him—but I remember thinking how realistic it was. Some of the guys have fake blood, and when the smoke cleared for just a second, I thought that's what it was. We were still pursuing the Feds, so we didn't have time to look back over the field."

"You think the shot came from Phil's gun?"

"I can't say. The sound from his gun was loud, startled both of us I think, and then Ryan fell."

"So if Phil was startled, maybe he didn't know his gun was loaded with live ammunition. Maybe he *is* being framed!" Lurleen said.

"Why are you defending Phil?" I asked.

"Phil's smart. Why would he use his own gun to kill Ryan?"

"Maybe he knew the bullet could never be traced or maybe he wanted to promote the idea he was being framed," Danny said. "It's a pretty dangerous way to set up an alibi, but it's possible. Phil hired me as his bodyguard, but he never once seemed worried about what might happen to him yesterday or today."

"Phil has always been cool under pressure," I said. "He would have made a great surgeon."

We sat in the shade of Lurleen's tent, lost in our own thoughts. Lurleen gave us iced tea and then sat beside us looking out at the field, which was still milling with police. The woman who shared the tent had closed up shop and sat talking with several women dressed in vintage costumes. They all fanned themselves, but I think it was more to deal with the anxiety about what happened on the field than the sweltering day.

My mind turned to Phil. Just how cold and calculating was he? He was always reserved, even with me. As I thought about our relationship, he'd never once told me he loved me. I thought he did from his other statements—about how good we were together, how I brought out the best in him, how I was the one who understood him. I was so naive and so willing to believe Phil was the man I wanted him to be.

I stood up abruptly, and Lurleen asked if I was all right.

"I need to take a walk," I said. "My arm's hurting a bit and I need to get a little circulation back in it."

"You want some company, *chérie*?" Lurleen asked.

"No thanks. I won't go far. You stay with Danny. If an officer wants me, I won't be out of sight."

I did need some time alone. Was Harper right? Did Phil want to marry her after all these years? And did it matter if he did? It took me so long to realize he never planned to marry me. Was I still resentful about that?

I sighed loud enough to make people around me glance in my direction.

Phil had none of my father's compassion or concern for others. I was no longer sure Phil had the capacity to love anyone but himself.

How could I have been such a fool and for such a long time, and was I still not seeing Phil clearly? Could he in fact be a murderer, cunning enough to make it seem he was being framed?

Chapter Twenty-One

I looked over the battlefield. Most of the reenactors had left. Andy and Frank approached Lurleen's tent from the near end of the field, and I walked down the hill to meet them.

Andy kept running his hand through his hair. "This is terrible," he said. "Poor Harper."

Frank stood behind him. "What the hell is going on?" he said. His face was mottled— either from the heat or from rage, I couldn't tell which. "First Carl and now Ryan. How do we know we won't be next?"

"Have the police spoken with you both?" I asked.

"They have." Andy said. "We were on artillery, about as far away from the infantry as you can get—on this side of the field. We were near Harper and the cavalry as a matter of fact."

"We didn't know who'd been shot for fifteen minutes at least," Frank said.

"Did you see Harper?" I asked.

"I saw her before the battle started," Frank said, "walking to the stable where the horses were kept. Then later, after we heard that a man was down, she rode over to ask if we knew what had happened? Of course we didn't."

Andy had been staring at my arm the whole time Frank was talking. "How'd you do that?"

"I fell in the tunnel and scraped it against the wall." I looked at both of them to see if either registered something close to guilt.

Andy took my arm gently. "You know you didn't break anything?" he asked, examining it.

"Just abrasions. I must have tripped on something."

Andy looked at me. "On what? The tunnel is asphalt with a narrow row of loose stones along the edges."

"You've been through it?" I asked.

"Sure. I walk through it every time I come."

"What about you, Frank?" I asked.

"What about me?"

"Have you been through the tunnel?"

"I'm not really that interested in history. I'm mostly here as Phil's friend."

"So you haven't been through it?" I asked.

"Sure you have," Andy said. "I told you that you needed to see it—time standing still—and I saw you headed in that direction today. Didn't you walk through it?"

Frank nodded. "Yeah, I did, but as I said it didn't impress me all that much. It was just a hole through a hill."

Andy shook his head. "You're incorrigible. Nothing impresses you."

"Give me a first-class bourbon or an original Van Gogh, and I'm impressed," he said.

I let the matter drop. Frank *had* walked through the tunnel, so why was he so reluctant to say so?

Andy and Frank sat on the tent stools Lurleen offered them and said yes to some iced tea.

She fished it out of a cooler.

"It's good to be off my feet and out of the full sun," Frank said. "What a bloody mess this all is. I wish I'd stayed away. I almost did."

"What were you two doing when Ryan got shot?"

"We were manning a Confederate cannon," Frank said.

"We made sure it was a reproduction, steel reinforced," Andy said. "You can bet I examined it closely."

"There are a lot of people who might be glad to see Carl dead," I said, "but why would anyone want to kill Ryan?"

"Maybe he knew too much," Frank said. "Or maybe Ryan had something to do with Carl's death."

Lurleen pretended to be fussing with putting away supplies. I knew she was listening to every word.

"You're suggesting a second murderer," I said. "Getting even for the death of Carl."

"Or maybe it's simpler than that—someone wants to frame Phil for both murders," Andy said.

"Who would want to do that?" I asked.

Andy flushed and ran his fingers through his hair. "It would be a way to get the spotlight off everyone else."

Frank spoke up. "You do know Sally didn't just disappear second year. She was expelled for cheating."

I nodded.

"Carl blamed Phil for what happened to Sally," Frank said.

"Phil denied he had anything to do with that," I said, "and claimed Carl had invented the whole story."

Frank looked sheepish.

"What is it, Frank?" I asked.

"I guess it doesn't matter now. Phil and I used to talk about how easy it would be to scam the system. We were never going to do it. When Sally was on probation and about to flunk out, I think Phil suggested she talk to an IT friend of ours to see what he could do for her."

"So Phil wasn't as innocent as he claimed to be," I said.

"That's as far as it went. He didn't twist Sally's arm, just made a suggestion."

"And then he gave her name to the authorities," I said. "Not much of a friend."

Frank took a long slow breath. "He's been a good friend to me—told me the truth about Harper when I needed to hear it. But Phil always looks out for himself."

"Sally must hate him," I said.

"I think she did in the beginning," Andy said. "Later she told me that the best thing Phil ever did was get her kicked out of school, so she could pursue her real interest in finance. I didn't know at the time that she didn't have an MBA or a degree in financial planning. I might not have hired her if I'd known."

"You still believe she wasn't involved in embezzling funds from you?"

Andy shrugged. "It's over and done with."

"Maybe it's finished for you," Frank said, "but I don't forget when someone screws me over."

We both stared at him.

"What are you talking about?" I asked. "Did you have a run-in with Carl or Sally?"

"That's none of your business. Why can't you leave all this alone? You have to keep digging up the past. You probably know about all of it anyway, the way this crowd gossips."

"I don't know what you're talking about," I said.

"As far as I'm concerned, this isn't open season on old secrets," Frank said. "I don't know why you turned up here today."

He stood. "I need a walk. Want to come, Andy?"

Andy shook his head and moved over to the stool next to me.

"What was that all about?" I asked.

"I don't know what set Frank off," Andy said. "Maybe it's Harper. She's still a sore topic for him. I think he really loved her. They got engaged at the end of their residencies and planned a big Texas wedding—the kind that gets publicized in the *New York Times* and the *Houston Chronicle*. Then the whole thing blew up. Frank found out that Harper couldn't have children. She'd lied to him about that, so he broke off the engagement. Six months later Harper married Ryan."

"I know about Harper's infertility," I said.

"Yeah," Andy said. "Rough deal, but the problem for Frank was more that Harper hadn't told him the truth. Frank hates to be lied to or taken advantage of. He doesn't get over that—ever."

"How did he find out?"

"Phil told him after he heard about the engagement," Andy said.

"And how did Phil know?"

"I can't answer that one," Andy said. "Sally claimed she was the only one who knew since she took Harper to doctor's appointments and covered for her when she was on call and too sick to come in. Maybe she told Phil."

Andy rubbed his head and asked for more iced tea, which Lurleen happily supplied. She sat down next to him.

"It seemed Harper worked hard to keep her infertility a secret," Lurleen said.

"Yeah," Andy said. "Then when her father died last year, she didn't seem to care who knew."

Lurleen spoke up. "Harper talked a lot about her dad at the party and what a great man he was and how he always got what he wanted in a take-no-prisoners kind of way. What he wanted from Harper was a thoroughbred line of grandchildren. I'll bet she never told him she couldn't give him that."

I turned to Lurleen. "How did you possibly get that out of Harper?"

"She likes to drink, and when she does she gets pretty loose with her words and her actions," Lurleen said. "Maybe she saw me as a kindred soul. She told me how lucky I was to be unmarried, and then she told me about how men had harmed her in the past—giving her sexually transmitted diseases that left her infertile."

Andy looked uncomfortable, but he stayed put.

Lurleen continued her story. "She told me how she'd dealt with the men. I doubt that half of what she said was true, but the other half gave me goosebumps. According to Harper, she made sure all the men had "accidents" when they were too drunk to know what they were doing, so they couldn't harm other women sexually."

"Really?" I said.

"She said it was good for those men to know what it felt like to be impotent."

"I can't believe that," I said. "How would she even know who gave her the diseases?"

"Harper didn't seem to care about that. She said there's always collateral damage in times of war. If a few innocent men were harmed, it couldn't be helped."

"Harper's a big talker," Andy said. "She gets dramatic when she drinks, but I don't think you can believe half of what she says. I've seen her softer side. She was kind to me when I split with Jenna, and she was comforting to Kathy after her miscarriages."

Andy tended to see everyone's softer side I thought. Then I wondered if he'd ever been involved romantically with Harper.

There was a tough edge to Harper—I'd felt it but never been able to put a name to it. I began to wonder if she was capable of murder—now two murders. But she wasn't near either one of the victims at the time. Of course, these murders were carefully planned, maybe from a distance. Still, how could Harper have made sure Carl was the only one killed when the cannon exploded? How could she have gotten Phil to let Carl pull the lanyard and stand alone on the left side of the cannon? How could she have persuaded Phil to fire at Ryan when she was nowhere near Phil at the time? It didn't add up.

Lurleen seemed to be listening in on my thoughts. "I'd put my money on Harper as our murderer, if she weren't so far from the scene of each crime."

Andy shook his head. "I don't want to think one of our friends did this."

"I don't either," I said. "But these two deaths are about vengeance, past or present—that's what I think. They're vicious. The second one means the first was no accident. And that means one of the people we know is a killer whether we like that or not."

Chapter Twenty-Two

Mason stuck his head inside Lurleen's tent. "The Whitfield investigator said we can leave now. He'll be in touch tomorrow to take your statements, unless you saw something he should know about today. I told him about what happened to you in the tunnel and about the torn hat."

Mason helped us carry boxes to my car. Danny remained behind with Phil, and the rest of us drove home.

Hermione greeted us with wild enthusiasm. Her entire body wagged. She didn't like being alone all day. Once she'd greeted us properly, she looked around for Lucie and Jason. I knew she missed them, but the best thing for them and for me was to let them spend another night with Mason's mother.

I couldn't get the image of Ryan out of my mind. First the desperate Ryan and then the picture of him on the field with the gaping wound in his chest.

Mason didn't say anything except to offer me a glass of wine, which I accepted. He sat beside me but didn't urge me to speak. Lurleen busied herself in the kitchen putting my things away.

When Lurleen finally joined us, she broke the silence.

"*Chérie*, tell us what you are thinking." She took my hand. "Whenever I'm quiet for too long, you make me speak and tell you what's on my mind."

I couldn't remember a time when Lurleen had been quiet for too long. That wasn't quite fair. I knew there were times when something triggered an unhappy thought, perhaps from her childhood, but she rarely let those feelings linger.

"I do need to sort through what's going on with my friends—if they even are my friends. Ryan was so sure Harper was having an affair with someone," I said. "First it was Carl he suspected and then Phil."

"Poor guy. So miserable and now he's dead." Lurleen tossed her head. "He had every reason to suspect Harper. Look how she behaved at the party. She could drive a man to—" She caught herself and didn't finish that thought. "If Danny hadn't separated them, Ryan and Phil would have pummeled each other."

"You're right," I said.

"If we wanted a person with a motive to kill Carl and frame Phil, Ryan would have been the one, don't you think, *chérie*?"

"Yes. Are you suggesting Ryan killed Carl and someone else killed Ryan?" I asked.

"I don't know what I'm suggesting exactly—just that Harper could have made Ryan crazy with jealousy."

Lurleen stood. "If we're going to continue a serious conversation I need some food."

She went to the kitchen and returned with a plate of cheese, crackers and fruit. After she passed it around and offered to refill my wine glass, she settled on the chair opposite Mason and me.

"I wouldn't let Phil off quite so easily," Mason said.

Lurleen nodded. "Danny has his eye on him."

"If we're running down the list, let's go through them all," I said. "What about Sally?

She's the one who had the torn hat. She could have been the one who pushed me and ran off. At the funeral service, she told me how fond she was of Carl—how he was a much nicer guy than people realized."

"You are giving her a perfect motive *not* to kill Carl," Mason said.

"But she could have wanted revenge for his killing if she believed Phil or Ryan was responsible."

"And she was standing near Phil," Mason said. "Near enough to fire a live round and not be discovered."

Hermione heard all our talking and wandered in from the family room. She put her head in my lap, and after I stroked her head, she settled at my feet.

"Sally went back and forth about Phil," I said. "On the battlefield after Carl was killed, she said Phil was the most likely murderer. At the funeral she acted as if she might be interested in Phil romantically, now that he was getting a divorce. She asked if I still had feelings for him."

"And you told her what?" Mason asked.

I looked at Mason and shook my head. "I told her the same thing I've told you at least one hundred times. I am not interested in Phil Brockton."

Mason narrowed his eyes and gave me a look I'd never seen before. "For a man you say you have no feelings for, you're certainly at his beck and call."

I could feel my face growing hot, but Lurleen put a hand on my arm and changed the subject.

"I'm not sure what you're thinking, Ditie? Is she a suspect or isn't she?"

I took a few seconds to calm down. Mason and I needed to talk, but not with Lurleen in the room. "I don't know about Sally. She always seems to fly below the radar. She looks so childlike, even now, that I don't think anyone takes her seriously. I can't tell where she fits."

"Let's move on," Lurleen said, "to your friend Andy."

I nodded. "I do like Andy, but he won't tell me the whole story about what Carl did to him. Kathy suggested Carl broke up his marriage."

"I've heard the details," Mason said.

"*Nous sommes tout oreilles,*" Lurleen said.

Mason gave her a blank look.

"We're all ears," she told him.

"Andy is convinced that in addition to stealing money from him, Carl was having an affair with his wife Jenna. They divorced three months later. A couple of powerful motives to kill a man."

"And Andy knew all about cannons." I sighed. "I've always known him to be a gentle soul—I just can't see him as a killer."

"Maybe you don't know what jealousy and betrayal can do to a person," Mason said. "Do you know who Carl worked for before Andy?"

I shook my head.

"Carl had a falling out with a doctor in upstate New York, also about money."

"As in embezzling funds?" I asked.

"Never proven, apparently. Carl left quietly. His boss chose not to prosecute."

"I take it Carl was never censured by the Medical Board in New York."

"He wasn't censured. His former boss kept the whole thing quiet."

"And did he give Carl a reference?" I asked.

"Apparently he did. The boss and Carl kept in touch over the years."

"How do you know this?" I asked.

"Kathy Thompson found a black accounting notebook in Carl's office, in an unlocked desk drawer. In it were initials, dates, payments. Payments were recorded on a monthly basis for a few months to the old boss. Then they stopped for several years and only recently resumed."

"That might well be the blackmail Kathy mentioned," I said. "She told me someone was threatening Carl. She said it might be blackmail and then she denied that later."

"Why does it matter if it was in an unlocked drawer," Lurleen asked.

"If you were paying off a blackmailer, would you keep that evidence in plain sight, where your wife might find it?" Mason asked.

"No, I wouldn't," Lurleen said.

"Does this former boss have a name?" I asked.

I swear Mason smirked. He reached over to the coffee table and picked up another piece of cheese, which he popped into his mouth. He was obviously enjoying himself. When he'd finished eating he finally responded.

"I thought you'd never ask. The initials in the book were F.P. and the boss was Frank Peterson. Dr. Frank Peterson. One of your classmates, I believe."

"You can't be serious," I said.

"I am. Dr. Peterson confirmed the payments. He admitted to the police that Carl had embezzled money from him and agreed to repay him as long as Dr. Peterson kept his mouth shut about what he'd done. Seems Dr. Peterson didn't want the word to get out he'd been taken for a ride, and he certainly wanted his money back." Mason smiled. "Looks like you had a class of mercenary folks in med school, Ditie."

"You look delighted by that fact, Mason! Why would you play a game with me about this? You never play that kind of game. First, you claim I still have feelings for Phil and then you disparage my entire medical school class. What is wrong with you?"

Even Lurleen looked shocked.

Mason slumped into the couch. He rubbed a hand over his face. "I thought it was amusing—that all these doctors weren't quite as high and mighty as they seemed."

"There is nothing about this that's amusing. I know all these people, and now I know they can't be trusted. It's not a joke to me."

"Ditie, I'm sorry. I don't know what to say."

"Then don't say anything!"

Lurleen stood. "This is my cue to leave, *chérie*."

I walked her to the door.

"Don't stay mad too long, *ma chère*. Jealousy makes people do crazy things."

She kissed me on each cheek and left.

Mason stood. "I guess I should go, too."

"Yes, you should. I don't want to discuss this with you right now. But before you leave I need to know if there were other initials in that book?"

"No, but several pages were ripped out," Mason said.

"So maybe Carl was being blackmailed by someone else as well. Someone who knew about his book of accounts and didn't want their names or initials to be found."

"It's possible," Mason said.

I sighed and turned my back on Mason. "Now you can go."

Mason walked to the door. "If I lose you over this I don't know what I'll do."

I didn't respond.

When he left I burst into tears. How could Mason have been so flippant with my feelings? So enraged with my fellow doctors? I was enraged too, but I didn't take satisfaction in discovering how flawed they were. Mason was gloating, and I'd never seen him do that before.

Was this all about jealousy—that raw nasty word? Did Mason actually believe I might leave him for Phil? I remembered what Ryan had said. His words were almost the same as Mason's—that he couldn't bear to lose Harper.

I felt sick and utterly alone—that is until Lurleen called me an hour later.

"I wanted to give you time to finish your argument with Mason. Did you finish it?" she asked.

"For now. He's gone."

"People aren't perfect," Lurleen said, "even Mason. Sometimes people have problems or a history they just can't talk about."

"How can I possibly think of marrying a man who could react like that? I won't live with a man who doesn't trust me or could be so cavalier about my feelings."

"All I'm saying, Ditie, is that you give him a chance to explain himself. You know he's a good man. I don't know what started all this, but I do know he loves you."

"I won't be loved the way Ryan loved Harper. That was desperation, not love."

"Then make him talk to you," Lurleen said.

I took a deep breath.

"You're right, Lurleen. I'm jumping to conclusions. Something's going on with him that I know nothing about."

Chapter Twenty-Three

I called Mason early the next morning before I went to work. Perhaps if I'd been a bit kinder I might have called him the night before.

"I love you, but we have to get through this jealousy thing," I said. "I know your wife died of cancer, and I'm terribly sorry about that. But now I wonder if there might have been other problems in the marriage—maybe related to jealousy or an affair? Perhaps an affair with a doctor? Did you leave that small detail out of our discussions?"

Mason was silent.

"You did, didn't you? No wonder you worried so much about Phil and have such a low opinion of physicians."

"Not all physicians, just the male variety."

"Honestly, Mason, we have work to do before we even think about getting married. You need to talk to me. Obviously, this drove you crazy and you never bothered to tell me about it. You have to let me in."

"I will, Ditie, if you give me another chance."

"You have a hundred more chances with me. I love you. The children love you. But I need to know who you are. I know Eddie couldn't have produced a son incapable of talking to the woman he loves."

"I've never opened up to anyone, Ditie. Not since my brother died."

"That was more than twenty years ago, Mason. You can start with me. I'm a good listener. Jason needs a role model of how to be a man, and he doesn't need another superhero. He needs to know that guys are tender and get bruised sometimes, and that men and women talk to each other and comfort each other. If you plan to be his second dad and my husband, you're going to need to get a move on."

Mason was quiet. "I will, Ditie. I can't believe what I did last night."

"As my wise friend Lurleen said, nobody's perfect and jealousy is a terrible thing."

I drove to work and tried to shove all the pieces of the recent events out of my mind. I turned my phone off and left it that way until I took a break for lunch. Then it was a quick call to Lurleen.

"Mason and I are fine," I told her before she could ask. "Well, not exactly fine, but we will be."

"*Quel soulagement!*" she said.

"Lurleen, it used to be I could understand all your French phrases but not anymore. Am I getting rusty or is your French improving?"

"I said, what a relief, and if you must know Danny is coaching me in everyday useful French phrases. Not that I need it, mind you, but he did major in French at University of Georgia, and I only lived around my French aunt in the summers."

Lurleen claimed her aunt had owned a chateau in Provence. I never pushed the issue and I wasn't about to push it now. Some secrets were harmless.

Of course, that made me think about the secrets that might be deadly.

"You are so quiet, *chérie*."

"I was thinking about the murders. Have you heard from Danny?"

"He's right beside me. Phil told Danny he didn't need a bodyguard anymore. Not with charges of murder or manslaughter hanging over his head—what he needed was a good criminal lawyer. I thought about recommending Tommy, but I wasn't sure you'd like that idea."

"No, Lurleen, I don't. Tommy stays out of this one. I don't mind asking him if he knows someone to recommend, but I'm afraid that might just get his juices flowing. Besides, Phil or his dad will know who to hire."

"Right. I'll keep mum. We'll be at your house when you get home. Will Mason be there?"

"I hope so."

A knock on the door meant I had patients waiting.

"I'll be home around five thirty," I said. "Maybe Danny could scrounge up some dinner? Anything would be fine."

Lurleen put her hand over the phone, and I could hear her murmuring to Danny.

"He asks if coq au vin would suit you?"

"Perfect! Tell him thanks."

The afternoon sped by. I had several follow-up medical screenings to do. In one family from sub-Saharan Africa, I found a rash on a five-year-old's foot. Schistosomiasis was a parasite common to that area. Vic confirmed my suspicions and we sent off the necessary stool and blood samples. I hadn't seen a case before except in text books, which meant that no matter how long I worked in the clinic I'd never manage to see everything there was to see.

I came home tired and a little late, but everyone was there to greet me, including Mason. He held back until I approached him and kissed him hello. Then I kissed Lucie and Jason.

"I've missed you two."

Lucie smiled at me, and Jason paused for two seconds before returning to Danny and his Civil War collection. Danny was letting Jason hold old coins and belt buckles and mini balls. I tried hard not to think of Ryan killed by live ammunition from Phil's gun, but of course that was impossible.

Danny looked at me and seemed to understand what was going on in my head. "We've got to clean up, Jason, and get dinner on the table," he said.

"I'll take him," Lurleen said. "You're not going to give your...other mom a hug?"

Jason looked at Lurleen. He smiled and ran over to give me a huge hug.

"Looks like you could use one too," I said to Lucie, who blushed and let me squeeze her until she begged for mercy.

Dinner was exquisite. Danny would have been a catch if he'd had no idea how to cook, but the fact he could prepare gourmet meals pushed him right over the top. Interestingly, Mason never seemed jealous of him.

After dinner, we watched *Finding Dory* for the hundredth time and then I got the kids to bed. When I came back, Mason made me a Kahlua and cream. I asked him for the news of the day. He gave me a straight answer to a straight question.

"The Whitfield County investigator brought Frank Peterson in for more questioning. Dr. Peterson has changed his story and now denies anything remotely connected to blackmail. He says Carl had agreed to pay back in monthly installments what he had stolen. Frank said the payments stopped years ago and only recently started up again. He said the new payments had nothing to do with blackmail—he was just happy to see the money coming in again."

"Does the investigator believe that?" I asked.

"He's reserving judgment."

"I am too," I said. "Whenever Frank talks about the murders, he comes on so strong, worrying about who might be next."

"That would be a good way to seem innocent," Mason said. "Maybe he doth protest too much?"

"Maybe," I said.

Danny stood up. "Anyone for decaf coffee and some chocolate chip cookies I saw in Ditie's cookie jar? I'll bring out a plateful if that's okay with you, Ditie."

It was all fine with me. I needed to hear more about the investigation but wasn't quite sure what to ask. Maybe over a plateful of cookies we could get into a discussion.

Danny started the ball rolling. "So where is the investigation at this point? I know the Gordon County Sheriff's office is working with Whitfield County, and I guess Officer Barden is more or less in charge of the whole investigation."

"He is," Mason said.

"They have the bullet," Danny said, "but since it isn't a mini ball and a smaller caliber, they can't trace the gun that fired it, right?"

"Right. They do know from the angle of entry and the look of the wound, the shot was fired at close range, not a sniper as some speculated. It could have been any of the Confederate soldiers standing close to Phil."

"They've ruled out suicide?" I asked.

"They have," Mason said. "Wrong angle and the damage would have been more massive."

"Let's assume it was Phil's gun and he didn't know he had live ammunition," I said. "Why would he aim at Ryan specifically?"

"And if he did want to kill him, why would he do it that way?" Danny asked. "He'd be the primary suspect even if they couldn't trace the gun."

"Danny, do you know who had access to the gun, other than Phil?" I asked.

"Phil claims he brought it from home. He left it in a lockbox in a shed on the battlefield while he went over plans with the person in charge of the Confederate forces."

"And who had keys to the box?"

"That's the question, Ditie. Phil had his key, of course, but he doesn't know who else may have had one. Someone could have made a copy—he carried the lockbox with him to every reenactment. I suppose they could have dropped a bullet in his gun, but more likely they would have mixed it in with the black powder in a doctored cartridge. Phil said he had at least one of those in his lockbox as well."

"Harper made it sound as if Phil wanted to marry her and Ryan was standing in the way," Lurleen said. "Phil might have aimed at Ryan to vent his frustration not knowing the ammunition was live."

"That's a lot of conjecture," Mason said. "Maybe it wasn't his gun. Sally was standing beside him."

"We don't seem to have many suspects left," I said. "Frank, Andy, and Harper were nowhere near the scene of the crime. One of them might have had a key to the lockbox, but how could they have made sure Ryan would be the one killed?"

That left us all silent.

"I have work tomorrow," I said. I didn't invite Mason to stay when the others left. We'd be moving slowly for a while. I also wanted a cool bath and twenty minutes to sort through the day.

Ryan had been the most likely suspect, and now Ryan was dead. Could he have killed Carl and could Sally have killed him in revenge? She seemed so devoted to Carl. She also had the hat with the piece of missing red-cotton. Did she attack me in the tunnel in hopes I'd leave and take Mason with me?

I needed to stop thinking and get some sleep, but sleep was elusive. I got up and headed for the kitchen. As I sorted through dinner recipes that might appeal to Jason and Lucie, I had a disturbing thought. What if the murderer still wasn't finished? Frank asked who might be next. What if the killer had a grudge against someone else in our small circle?

Chapter Twenty-Four

Kathy called me on my way to work. She'd been out of town staying with her family. Now she was home and wanted to see me. I also wanted to see her, and we agreed to meet after work. She was running a summer writing program for kids and wouldn't be free until late afternoon.

"I'm surprised you're back at work," I said.

"It keeps me sane. You know how it is—you work with kids. When you have children to worry about, you can't think about anything else. It's when I'm alone that I find it unbearable."

We agreed to meet at my favorite coffee house, Java Monkey in Decatur, as soon as we both finished work. It was a longer drive for Kathy, but she said she didn't mind.

I called Lurleen at lunch and caught her before she took Jason and Lucie swimming. She was fine with my coming home late. "I'll take the kids out to a movie after we swim. We'll have popcorn and hotdogs if that's all right with you."

"Fine with me," I said. It was summer after all. "Danny's not with you?"

"It seems your ex wants Danny to do a little investigating for him despite what he said about not needing him anymore. He wants Danny to find out who might have made a copy of his lockbox key."

"Have they arrested him?" I asked.

"Not yet."

I hung up the phone and finished off my lunch of coq au vin leftovers. Coq au vin is one dish that gets better with age. Then I went to find our triage nurse and see what the schedule held for the afternoon.

"It's light today," Vic said. "If you want to leave early, you can do that."

"Maybe *you* can leave early," I said. "I'm fine. I'm meeting someone at the end of the day."

Vic, always the last to leave, managed to get out early for one day. The nurses and I were able to handle the pace and finish up right on time. I was troubled only by one young boy who didn't look well. His stat labs came back fine, but I urged his mother to bring him back if he wasn't better in a day or two. Sometimes you just get a feeling.

I left the clinic at five thirty and made it to Java Monkey by six. Kathy had settled herself in the back corner of the bar area, sipping a glass of red wine. I joined her.

"I hope you haven't been here long."

"I may stay all evening," Kathy said. "I love the bustle, the funkiness. I feel out of place with no tattoo. Carl had us living in a straightjacket. Everything had to be top dollar and so proper."

"I love this place too. If I ever write a book, this is where I'll come to do it."

Kathy smiled and drank her Pinot Noir.

"I still have trouble imagining you and Carl together," I said. "You seem so down to earth, and I admit I have a soft spot for teachers."

"You made my day," Kathy said. "My father saw teaching as a temporary job until I found a nice doctor to marry. He was very disappointed when I didn't give it up and have a house full of children."

"You never wanted a house full of children?"

"No. It's ironic isn't it. I love teaching kids, but I've never been determined to have my own."

I left her for a moment to order a glass of wine and a piece of the best cherry pie in the world, which came from a local bakery Southern Sweets. It wasn't always available at Java Monkey but when it was I never passed it up. I brought back two forks.

"Oh," she said. "You have a sweet tooth *and* you like children. No wonder I felt an immediate connection to you."

"The feeling is mutual."

We were silent for a moment while we both enjoyed our first bites of pie.

"Sometimes I'm too nosy," I said, "but I am wondering about the children issue—why Carl wanted them and you didn't."

"You're trying to make sense of me. I can hardly do that myself." She took a sip of wine.

"I think Carl believed children would establish him as a full-blooded Southerner, make him a part of the community. That's what he really wanted—to have a home somewhere."

She sighed.

"I've had enough parenting to last me a lifetime. While my father was off giving lectures, writing his books about his idyllic Southern life, I was responsible for my younger brothers and sisters."

She watched me as I split the last of the pie and pushed the plate in her direction. "Nothing my father wrote about our lives was true, and I was expected to keep the secret. Carl and I were damaged goods, so I guess I thought we deserved each other."

"Damaged goods?" I asked.

"When you grow up in a family like mine, you don't get through it unscathed. You hear the arguments and you think you must be part of the problem. Carl didn't judge me—his childhood wasn't any easier than mine. I guess that's what drew us together. It's also what pushed us apart in the end."

The bartender motioned to us from across the wooden bar asking if we wanted another glass of wine. We both shook our heads.

"We married too soon because I was pregnant. Carl kept pushing me for kids, but after the third miscarriage I was done—with babies and probably with Carl."

She stopped talking and I waited. Maybe she wanted to see if I was shocked. When she decided I wasn't she continued.

"You see, I learned the hard way that some people get broken by their past and don't recover from it—that was Carl. I did everything I could not to be like my mother, but Carl became his father. He ran around, had schemes to get money, and always wanted more than he had. I thought I could love him into being a better man, but you can't do that for another person. They have to do it for themselves."

I couldn't keep from nodding as she spoke. "I think I tried to do that with Phil. I saw in him what I wanted to see and not what was really there. When he seemed self-centered or insensitive I thought I could help him grow out of it."

"You have a new boyfriend, right?"

"I do. He's good to me, smart, kind, funny, but for some reason he doesn't seem to understand how much I love him."

"I'll have a talk with him."

I laughed. "That would be great. He doesn't believe it when *I* tell him. Maybe he'll listen to a stranger, or better yet, a friend. Why don't you come to dinner tomorrow, unless you have other plans?"

"No plans beyond grading fourth grade essays about the state of the world." She saw me wince. "Actually, they're remarkably good. I wish our politicians would take their advice." She glanced at her watch.

"We can go any time you want," I said.

She assured me she was in no hurry. "I don't get to talk to many adults."

"I hope this won't spoil our beginning friendship, but I have to ask—were you really pregnant this last time?"

Kathy's fair complexion lit up like a Christmas tree bulb. "I'm ashamed about that. I lied to you. I was late and I thought I might be pregnant. I told Carl I was, and he was ecstatic. Then my period came, and I just couldn't bear to admit I'd lied to you, so I made up the miscarriage story. It's not like me to lie. I don't know why I did it."

"I understand," I said, but I wasn't sure I did.

"I was relieved I wasn't pregnant. I won't say this to anyone but you—I think I'm also relieved Carl is out of my life."

That stopped me.

"He can't hurt me anymore or ask me to clean up his messes."

I looked at her.

"No, Ditie, I didn't want him dead and I'm not a murderer. The photograph was horrible, and I'll never get it out of my mind."

"You still have no idea who might have sent it to you?" I asked.

"I've tried to think who might hate Carl enough to kill him and wish to torture me as well. I haven't come up with any answers." She took a last bite of pie. "Now, I have some questions for you."

"Have at it."

"I heard about what happened to Ryan. It's dreadful. Do police think it's the same murderer?"

I explained the possible scenarios, including the idea that Ryan could have killed Carl out of jealousy, and someone else might have killed Ryan for revenge.

"Why would Ryan have sent me the photograph? I barely know him."

"That's a good question," I said. "Did you think Carl might be having an affair with Harper?"

"Carl clearly thought she was beautiful. He kept telling me I should find out where she bought her clothes, got her hair done. There were a lot of nights he claimed he was working late, and I never knew what he might be up to."

We discussed the other possibilities. There were only six people on the field after the explosion—Phil, Frank, Andy, Sally, Ryan and Harper. Kathy knew them all, some better than others. I asked about Carl's interactions with Frank.

"The episode with Frank Peterson happened before I met Carl. I knew Carl was running from something, but it was a long time before he told me what it was. He said he'd learned his lesson."

Kathy just shook her head.

"The story with Andy is more complicated. I've known Andy most of my life. Andy gave Carl a job as a favor to me. Then Carl did what he'd done to Frank. It was just too easy to syphon off money here and there. I felt horrible and promised to pay back every penny. I've done that."

"Was Andy mad at you?"

"I don't think so, even though I suspect Carl broke up Andy's marriage."

Kathy was silent as she finished her wine.

"I'm sorry, Kathy."

"Don't be. I knew after our first year of marriage what I was dealing with, but I couldn't seem to let go. Lately, Carl and I were barely speaking. The only time he actually talked to me was to say he wanted a divorce and later, when he thought I was pregnant again, that maybe we could work things out."

"You said someone was threatening him, and later you gave the book you found to the police."

"I heard him on the phone, demanding that someone give him more time. When I asked about it, he claimed it was a work issue. But I knew Carl. I knew how he acted when he was afraid. Someone made him feel his life was coming apart."

"Could it have been Frank?" I asked. "His initials were in the accounting book."

"I didn't recognize the initials. I only thought the book was something the police might want to see. They'd searched the house but somehow they'd overlooked it."

"Mason said it was in an unlocked desk drawer."

"Yes, how could the police have missed that?"

"Maybe they didn't. I assume you had visitors after Carl's death."

"Everyone has been by to see me, except Frank Peterson."

"The police said there were pages torn out of the book."

"Yes. It struck me as odd, but the whole thing was odd. Carl didn't keep handwritten notes. It was all on his computer at work."

"And did you recognize it as his handwriting?"

Kathy paused and stared at me. "I never thought about that. It was mainly initials, dates, and amounts of money. Carl did write with a small hand, but these were tiny, meticulous notes. When Carl wrote something out it was more like chicken scratch. I guess it could have been different when he was keeping account of money."

"Or maybe it wasn't Carl's book at all. Maybe it was planted by someone else to look as if it belonged to him."

"You mean like the murderer," Kathy said.

"Who came to visit you after the police searched your apartment?"

"Sally. She seemed devastated and offered to spend the night with me. Ryan and Harper made a visit, and of course, Andy came several times."

"A lot of people might have threatened to tell Dr. Brockton about Carl's misadventures—like Frank or Andy—and then demanded money to keep quiet."

Kathy stood up, and her face took on a hard look I'd never seen before. "Andy would never hurt me in that way! He'd never blackmail Carl. Andy always wanted to protect me, even when we were kids. He'd never do what you're suggesting."

"I'm sorry. I like Andy too, but I had to ask."

I wondered just how far Andy would go to protect Kathy.

Kathy apologized for her outburst.

"I know you're trying to help me find answers, but you must understand that Andy has always looked out for me."

She agreed to come for dinner the next night. This was one invitation that wouldn't upset Mason.

Chapter Twenty-Five

I got home before the kids. Mason called to see if he could come over. He brought some Thai food from a favorite restaurant, and we finally had time to talk over dinner.

"I am sorry, Ditie," he said.

"I'm over what you did, but what needs to change is how we confide in each other. I've been a pretty open book with you, and I don't do that with everybody. It's your turn. I want a partner who will talk to me."

Mason sighed. "You never got to meet my dad, but he was the strong silent type."

"I bet that drove Eddie wild."

Mason laughed. "It did."

"I'm sure your dad was a great guy, but I need someone who can share his feelings. I saw how kind you were the first night we met. You didn't rush me, and I won't rush you either, but we have to start somewhere."

"Where do you want me to start?"

"Why not start with your jealousy, the fantasy you have that I might leave you?"

"You were right about that—it is what my wife did. I thought we had a pretty good marriage, our two boys were great. I was blindsided when she told me she wasn't happy and hadn't been happy for years."

"There was someone else?"

"She finally admitted there was. A doctor friend."

"This was before she got sick?"

"Yes. Just before. When she got sick, the guy disappeared. I don't know if my wife sent him away or if he couldn't handle the situation. After that we had some good years together before she died, but I always wondered what would have happened if she hadn't gotten sick."

"Have I ever given you a reason to doubt me? Most people say I'm loyal to a fault."

"You've *never* given me a reason to doubt you, but you're so self-sufficient. You don't really need me. I'm twelve years older than you. How will you tolerate me when I'm an old man?"

I took his face in my hands and kissed him on each cheek and then on his lips. "I love you now and I'll love you then. I don't need you to support me financially if that's what you mean, and I would find a way to survive if I lost you. None of that means I don't need you. You love my kids, and you make me feel beautiful. A lot of men wouldn't find me beautiful—too much of me they'd say, or as Phil put it—'You could be a beautiful woman if you lost some weight and exercised every day.' You've never once said that to me."

"I've never once thought it."

"I believe you. You don't want to change me, and I don't want to change you. I just want you to rest easier. I'm not going anywhere."

Mason looked at me. "Is that enough talking for now?"

"I guess so."

"Good, because I have other ideas."

"Lurleen said she and the kids would get home around eight."

"That's plenty of time."

* * * *

Lurleen arrived at eight thirty. Mason and I were on the porch swing waiting for them. They ran up the steps, and we made room for them.

"We seed spies," Jason said. "Lots of spies."

I didn't bother to correct his grammar. I raised an eyebrow to Lurleen as she walked up behind him.

"Kid spies," she said. "Nothing too frightening. The movie was about a school for kid spies, and now Jason is sure that's where he wants to go to school."

Lucie looked at me. "It wasn't scary at all, Aunt Di, just funny."

"Good. Thanks, Lurleen. You want some dinner or a drink?"

She shook her head. "Danny's going to pick me up here around nine and we'll go out to eat."

I left her seated next to Mason and went inside to run a bath for Jason. Lucie took a shower upstairs. I was feeling a little guilty that I hadn't been around them more in the last few days, but neither one of them seemed upset about it.

Jason climbed in bed with no fuss. I read a short book and gave him a kiss.

"I love you second Mommy," he said.

"And I love you, my first and only boy."

Lucie wanted to talk. She wanted to know what was going on. I told her some of it, so she wouldn't worry that our family was in danger. I told her Kathy was coming to dinner. Lucie remembered her from the morning they'd spent together.

"Aunt Di, I was wondering..."

"Yes, Lucie?"

"Do you like it when Jason calls you Mommy?"

"I love it, Lucie, but it doesn't mean you have to call me that."

"Would it be okay if I did? Do you think my real mom would mind?"

"Lucie, you and I both know I can never take the place of your mom. I wouldn't want to. But you should know I love you like a mother. I couldn't love you more. So, if you want to call me Mom or Mama or Mama Di, that's all fine with me. And if you want to keep calling me Aunt Di, it doesn't change a thing about how much I love you."

I put my arm around her and she leaned against me as she tried out each name. "I think I'll call you Mama. I never called my first mother that."

"That's perfect." I kissed her, tucked her in, and stayed with her until she fell asleep.

When I came back outside, Danny was seated beside Lurleen on the swing. He jumped up but I waved him back down. I joined Mason on the top step of my porch.

"I've just been filling these two in on what's happening," Danny said. "I assume you want to hear about it from the beginning."

"I do."

"Phil still isn't under arrest, but he can't leave the state for at least another few days. In the meantime, I'm checking out who might have had access to Phil's lockbox key. It seems Phil has had some female visitors in his Whitley suite."

"Like who?" I asked.

"Like Sally. She stayed over more than once."

"So there is something going on between them," I said.

"Nothing serious according to Phil. He claims it's pretty one-sided, but he's not exactly pushing her away."

"You said female visitors plural."

Danny nodded. "Harper stopped by to see how Phil was doing. Phil had me clear out while she was there. And this one is a surprise—Kathy Thompson came by. She wanted to know all about the relationship between Phil and Carl, their past relationship that is. Apparently Carl never told her much about their feud in med school."

"She came by when?" I asked. "I just had a drink with her and she didn't mention it."

"It was sometime yesterday," Danny said.

"Did Phil talk to her?"

"He did. He didn't mention the name of the woman he claimed both he and Carl were seeing in med school, but he did talk about the cheating scandal. He said it was likely to be Carl who was cheating and then blamed it on him. Kathy got a little huffy about that."

I looked at Danny.

"I wonder why Phil is being so circumspect about the woman in question."

"I wondered that too," Danny said. "I told Phil I needed to know everything, but he wouldn't budge. Claimed it was his Southern honor not to sully the reputation of any woman."

"Oh, please," I said. "He'd sully some woman's reputation from ten years ago?" Then I had a different thought. "What if it's not from ten years ago? What if he's still involved with the same woman and what if Carl was too? Kathy said she knew Carl had affairs."

"That would certainly change things," Mason said.

"As far as I know only two women visited Phil in his hotel room who knew him from his med school days," Danny said.

"Harper and Sally," Lurleen said.

I frowned. "I wouldn't mind pinning these murders on Harper, but why would she do it? And how could she have orchestrated those murders from long distance? I can't work that out."

Sally was a more likely possibility—she was such an enigma and seemingly devoted to Carl. If Ryan had killed Carl and sent the photo to Kathy, could Sally have figured that out? Sally had an identical gun to Phil's. Could she have filled one with live ammunition before the fighting started.

I asked Danny about that.

"Hmm. You know, Sally asked Phil to look at her rifle. She thought there was something sticking on the trigger mechanism. Phil checked it out and handed it back to her. She held both guns for a while and handed one back to him when the battle started. She could have filled either one with live ammunition. Phil didn't have time to do more than aim and fire."

"I wonder if she'd realize a smaller bullet couldn't be traced?" I said. "If not, she'd have had time to put the live bullet in Phil's gun."

"And maybe urge him to aim at Ryan," Lurleen said.

"It's time we find out more about Sally," I said. "She comes across as so innocent and a little goofy. She says whatever people want to hear. I also think I need to have another talk with Kathy. She says she doesn't like to lie, but she's lied to me twice."

Chapter Twenty-Six

The next day passed quickly. Phil wasn't arrested. He must have found one very good lawyer. Tommy asked me about it, wondered who it might be and if he could be co-counsel on the case. I told him that was a terrible idea, which only made him more eager to take it on. The fact that Phil *hadn't* been arrested yet seemed to slow Tommy down. He really didn't have time to wait around for that to happen, just so he could appear on local television.

Danny continued to sort through the thorny issue that might prove Phil was being framed—the idea that someone else had a key to the lockbox and had loaded his gun with live ammunition.

I had plenty of time to think about all this as I prepared dinner for Kathy and the family. I poached salmon and prepared three sauces, made wild rice and got summer squash ready for the stove.

Mason had taken the kids swimming, so I could have the kitchen to myself. The doorbell rang at five, too early for Kathy to arrive.

I opened it to find Harper standing in front of me.

"Please can I come in? I'm desperate and I don't know where else to go?"

I opened the door wider and Harper entered. She walked to the sofa and sat down.

"I can't work. I can't do anything. I need to know what the police are doing to find Ryan's murderer."

"You heard it wasn't suicide," I said.

"Yes. I need to know if they've arrested Phil. I need to know if he might come after me."

"Why would you think that?"

"He knows what he said to me. He'll deny it, of course, but I'm sure he thinks I could put him away for life. If he's killed twice why wouldn't he kill me to keep me quiet?'

At that moment, Mason entered the house with two very wet children.

"Oops," he said. "I had no idea you had company."

"It's fine," Harper said. Her whole demeanor changed. "What darling children! What's your name, little one?"

"I'm Lucie and this is Jason."

"You met at the party," I said.

"Of course we did," Harper said. "I just forgot their names. And they might not remember me because I was in a costume."

Lucie and Jason scooted upstairs to change into dry clothes. Mason sat down beside me.

"Do you need any help in the kitchen?" he asked.

"I'm sorry. I must be interrupting your dinner," Harper said.

I didn't reply, and she made no move to go.

"I'm just not sure what to do. If you hear that Phil has been arrested will you call me? I'm afraid of what he might do to me if he's still free?"

Mason stepped in. "What are you talking about?"

"Phil wanted to marry me, and Ryan wouldn't consider divorce. Not that I wanted that. Ryan stood by me when no one else did. I owed him everything."

"You believe Phil killed Ryan and might come after you?" Mason asked.

"I'm scared he might."

Mason stood. "I assume you've talked to the police about this."

"I couldn't. I couldn't tell anyone my suspicions about Phil."

"You've just told us," I said.

"That's different. I'm desperate."

"I advise you to make a complaint to the police and go someplace safe for a few days," Mason said. "Let the police know where you'll be, but don't tell anyone else."

She looked up at him and nodded. "Yes, yes. That's what I'll do."

She got up and left without another word.

Mason waited until we saw her drive off.

"What was that all about?" he asked.

"I have no idea. I'm wondering if it wasn't a grand performance designed to make us believe Phil is a murderer."

Mason nodded. "It was a decent acting job if that's what it was."

Lucie ran downstairs at that moment and looked around the living room.

"Is she gone?" she asked.

"Harper?"

Lucie nodded.

"She's gone."

"Aunt Di, Mama," she said. "Is Dr. Harper your friend?"

"Not particularly, why?"

She came up and whispered in my ear. "She's a phony, Mama."

I held her back at arm's length. "Do you even know what that means?"

Lucie nodded solemnly. "It means someone who pretends to be one thing but is another."

"Go on."

"She pretended she liked Jason and me just now, but at the party she told us to get lost. She said children shouldn't be seen or heard."

I was livid. Mason put a restraining hand on my arm. "She shouldn't have said that, Lucie, and I'm glad you told us."

"Why didn't you tell me before now, Lucie?" I asked.

"I didn't want to get anyone in trouble," she said. "Jason was running around with his bugle, and I thought that might have made her mad."

"You didn't hear any of that, Mason?" I asked.

"Do you think I would have allowed her to stay in your house if I had?"

"You went to get us lemonade, Uncle Mason. We saw Dr. Harper with Dr. Phil, and she didn't like that we were watching." Lucie paused. "They were—you know—kissing."

"I'm glad you told me all this," I said. "Harper won't be welcome in our house again. Are you all cleaned up for dinner? If so, will you check on your brother, and then you can help me in the kitchen or watch a movie with Mason—whatever you like."

"I'll help you, Mama Di."

Mason looked over Lucie's head at me and wrinkled his forehead.

"Lucie's trying out different names for me, aren't you Lucie?"

"I am, Mama Two."

"I like that one," I said. "Is it Mama 'too' or 'two'?" I asked.

Lucie blushed. "You're our second mom."

Lucie ran off to find Jason and brought him back with his musket in one hand and his bugle in the other. Mason extracted them from Jason and said those were for outside. Right now, they'd do something a little more quiet like play with Legos or watch TV. Jason seemed content with that

Kathy arrived a little before seven. She brought a giant bouquet of freesias and snap dragons.

"How could you possibly know those are two of my favorite flowers?"

"A lucky guess. I like them too."

I took them and found a vase while Mason brought out hors d'oeuvres. He called the children in. They remembered Kathy from the day she'd spent with them. Lurleen and Danny arrived a little after seven. Everyone was chatting away when I called them to the dining room. It was too hot to eat outside, and the mosquitoes would have made it more miserable.

"At least it's a cool meal in a cool setting," I said.

People were appropriately enthusiastic about the dinner and the dessert of homemade lemon ice cream and gingerbread.

We kept the conversation light. Thank goodness I had friends who could talk about anything. Kathy was fascinated to hear about what Lucie and Jason were up to, and they were delighted to tell her.

After dinner, I got the kids settled in bed and returned to find Kathy and Mason deep in conversation. It looked serious.

Mason made room for me beside him. "Kathy just asked me about the investigation, and I was telling her what I knew."

"Were they able to do anything with the photograph?" Kathy said.

"No. It was taken on an iPhone and printed on a home computer. Nothing remarkable about it and no fingerprints other than yours and Ditie's."

Kathy nodded. "And the accounting book?"

"They've asked everyone to submit handwriting samples, but the book is basically a series of numbers and initials. Nothing's come back about that yet." Mason hesitated. "I know this may be painful to discuss, Mrs. Thompson, but do you have an idea who might have been threatening your husband?"

"Please, I've just had dinner with all of you. I'm Kathy, of course."

I nudged Mason. "Mason gets a little formal when he falls into work mode."

"I thought you weren't working on this case," Kathy said.

"I'm not, but I'm friends with the people who are. They don't mind getting help from me and I don't mind giving it."

Kathy nodded. "I can tell you the one person who didn't do it."

"Who's that?" Mason said.

"Andy."

"Even though Andy had every reason to hate Carl," Mason said.

"He'd never send that photo to me," Kathy said.

"What about Frank and Sally?" I asked. "Could you see either of them sending you that picture?"

"I don't know Frank well."

"Carl embezzled money from him, and it was Frank's initials in the book," I said. "Maybe the photo was meant to threaten you into paying him what was owed."

"But Frank has never approached me for money," Kathy said.

"He may be biding his time." This came from Mason. "Perhaps he's waiting for the investigation to blow over before he comes to you."

That made sense.

"Do you know of anyone else who might have been blackmailing Carl?" Mason asked. Kathy shook her head. "Carl kept his finances secret from me. I only got involved when I learned what he had done to Andy. Then I made the monthly payments myself, from my trust fund, to pay Andy back."

"What about Sally?" I said.

"What do you mean?"

"Sally was someone I didn't know well in med school," I said. "Apparently she went into investment banking or hedge funds after she dropped out of school. Do you know more about her?"

"Just that Carl always looked out for her. They came as a package in terms of work."

"Was Sally involved in the embezzling?"

"I don't know. Carl never said she was, but then he also claimed *he'd* done nothing wrong."

"Did the three of you spend time together?" I asked.

"Rarely," Kathy said. "I hated all the office talk—I'd grown up with it. When Carl had a dinner with drug reps or something business related, I'd go out with my teacher friends."

"Did you get to know Sally personally, just the two of you?" Mason asked.

"Not really. We never developed a close friendship. She's one of those people who seem almost too sweet to believe."

"I know exactly what you mean," I said. "She greeted me like I was her long-lost best friend."

"Exactly," Kathy said. "That's how she treated me. She really seemed to be into the reenactment thing. I could never imagine why. She wasn't from the South. Maybe she liked all the action. Phil might know more about her than I do."

"Speaking of Phil, I heard you saw him before we met for drinks. I wonder why you didn't tell me."

Kathy's eyes widened. "I guess I forgot. He called me to see how I was doing and invited me over." She stood. "It's late and I should be going." She thanked me for a wonderful evening and that part seemed genuine.

What seemed less sincere was her explanation about seeing Phil and her abrupt departure after I brought him up.

When she left, Mason and I headed to the kitchen.

"We've got it covered," Danny said. "Whoever cooks is not allowed to clean up. Come on, Lurleen, you can help me."

Reluctantly, Lurleen rose from the sofa. She was certain we'd be discussing the case without her.

"I need to find out more about Sally," I said. "She drops out of med school for cheating and then keeps up with all her doctor friends. Maybe I'll have lunch with her," I said. "She mentioned we should get together."

"I'm not enthusiastic about your having lunch with a possible murderer," Mason said. "You're a mother now. Did you hear what Lucie called you?"

"I'll go with her," Lurleen said. She must have been eavesdropping from the dining room. "I've been taking self-defense courses with Wendy, my personal trainer, along with kick boxing. No one messes with me. I keep urging Ditie to come with me, but she's always too busy."

"I have other priorities, Lurleen, and no matter how many push-ups you make me do I will never have your body."

"We only need one Lurleen," Danny said.

"*Ce que je veux dire*," Lurleen continued, "is that I can keep Ditie safe. I will be her bodyguard, and I think lunch with the elusive Sally Cutter is a wonderful idea."

Mason knew when he was defeated. "It must happen in a very public place, and I'd prefer you not accuse her of anything, Ditie."

"I promise not to do that, Mason."

Three primary suspects in addition to Phil remained on our list as potential murderers—Frank, Sally and Harper. Frank could have sent the photograph to scare Kathy about what could happen to her if she didn't pay back what was owed. Sally or Harper might have done it to make Kathy suffer—but why?

Lurleen, Danny, and Mason left. I turned off all the lights, checked on the kids, and walked slowly upstairs.

We were making the assumption that whoever sent Kathy the photograph was also the murderer of two people. Maybe we had that wrong. Maybe the person who sent the photograph was simply doing it out of spite. Or perhaps it *was* Ryan—first a murderer and then a victim.

I'd left Andy off the list of suspects entirely, but perhaps I had a blind spot where Andy was concerned. Andy had probably suffered most at the hands of Carl, financially and personally, but what could he have against Ryan? Unless Ryan had figured out what he'd done. Before I fell asleep,

I realized I hadn't included Kathy as a suspect. She was not at either reenactment, but she'd lied to me twice. Perhaps she wasn't as innocent as I wanted her to be.

I lay in the dark trying to sort through what did and didn't make sense.

Although I didn't like to consider the possibility, perhaps Kathy and Andy were in this together. Two seemingly nice people committing two heinous acts of murder. That was too much for me. It would mean I couldn't trust my own instincts about people. Then I thought of Phil—how little I had understood about the man he was—but I was twenty-one at the time, not thirty-five. Surely I'd learned a thing or two about people in those years.

Chapter Twenty-Seven

I called Sally the next day. She was surprised to hear from me, she said, and delighted. She was sorry she hadn't been the one to make the first move.

We agreed to lunch at the Bistro Niko, Lurleen's favorite French restaurant in Atlanta. I explained that Lurleen wanted some financial advice and suggested the three of us should meet socially. Sally bought it.

"I don't mean to be crass about this," Sally said on the phone, "but Lurleen does understand that I don't give away free advice."

"She's well aware of that, and she has plenty of money," I said.

We met at the restaurant on Thursday for a late lunch. Lurleen insisted on picking me up at the clinic, so she could drive me in her Citroën. "If you are going to a French restaurant, *chérie*, you must arrive in a French car." Obviously she knew rules of etiquette of which I was unaware.

Sally joined us ten minutes late.

"I'm so sorry," she said. "I was checking on Phil and lost track of time."

"Is Phil still considering joining his father's practice?" I asked.

She looked surprised. "I assumed you two talked all the time. He's not considering that at the moment, or to be more accurate his father is not considering it. Not until these murders are resolved. You've seen the papers? The senior Dr. Brockton hates a scandal, and Phil has been named a person of interest."

"What do you think, Sally?"

"About what?"

"About what happened Sunday," I said.

Our waiter came over and brought our menus and water. When he left, she responded.

"You know Phil," she said to me. "Can you see him killing anyone?"

"In med school, I would have said that was ridiculous. Now, I don't know for sure."

Sally took a sip of water. Her pixie face looked less childlike and more intense. "I guess I don't know for sure either. I'm choosing to believe that someone set him up."

"How did someone get him to fire a bullet at Ryan," I asked, "if it was his gun?"

"What do you mean if it was his gun? Of course, it was his gun."

"The police can't say who fired the live shot," I said.

"What are you implying, Ditie?"

"Nothing. I'm simply stating a fact."

"It wasn't *my* gun, I can tell you that. It was Phil's, and he either knew he had live ammunition or someone planted it in his gun."

I heard Mason's admonition in my head—don't accuse her of anything—and I remained silent.

Sally put a hand over her red cupid lips. "I guess I haven't helped Phil's case much, have I?"

"Phil and Ryan acted as if they hated each other. We saw that at Ditie's party," Lurleen said.

"Oh yeah," Sally said. "Ryan got jealous all the time, and Harper is, well, Harper is just Harper."

"You don't think there's anything going on between Phil and Harper?" I said.

For a moment Sally's dark eyes flashed. "Do you?"

I shrugged and Lurleen took over. "Much as I enjoy this talk of murder and intrigue, I'm really here for some financial advice. I've had such bad luck with financial planners," she began.

"You'll be happy to know I'm not a regular financial planner. I'm sure Ditie told you I was on Wall Street for a few years and left when I'd soaked up all the information I could," Sally said.

"She did mention that, but I always do my own homework before I make any major decisions. Do you mind if I ask you questions?"

"Not at all."

Our waiter interrupted us to take our orders. "The usual, *mesdames*?"

I nodded. The usual for me was the croque monsieur with extra cheese. Lurleen got the salade niçoise.

"And for you, *mademoiselle*?"

"Anyone who still calls me mademoiselle can bring me anything he wants. What do you recommend?"

"The salade niçoise. is a house specialty. The bouillabaisse is also excellent. May I ask what you are in the mood for?"

"I'll start with the house Chardonnay and then the bouillabaisse."

She nodded at Lurleen. "What are your questions, Lurleen, if I may call you that?"

"Of course. I wondered about your education."

Sally looked at me. "I suppose you told her I dropped out of school." She did not sound pleased.

"I told her what little I knew," I said. "I'd love to hear the whole story about why you left school and what you did next."

For just a moment Sally lost her sweet demeanor. "You make me sound like I couldn't cut it."

"Not at all," Lurleen said. "I have been many things in my life, and I admire a woman who makes changes when those changes are necessary. I'm curious to know why you made yours."

Sally drank some wine and recomposed her features. "School and I never agreed with each other. I believe in practical experience. I think people misunderstood my leaving school. They thought I couldn't take the pressure, but it wasn't that at all."

The waiter arrived with our food, and for a few moments we simply enjoyed our meals.

Sally looked at me. "It was so easy for you, Ditie."

"What do you mean? It was anything but easy," I said.

"You just studied all the time. And then Phil waltzed into your life. You made room for him, but you never seemed to care about anything but school work and Phil. I wasn't made like that."

"I didn't really care about the social stuff if that's what you mean. But I certainly worried about whether or not I could actually become a doctor, whether I could learn everything they were throwing at us, whether I could make life and death decisions."

"You never showed that side of you. I wasn't like you. I needed to have a good time. I couldn't hole myself away as if I were in a monastery. So I quit." Sally looked over at Lurleen. "I had to decide what I really wanted to do. I took a year off and realized medicine would never be my calling."

I wondered if Sally needed a break from her untrue confessions. "How's the bouillabaisse?" I asked.

"It's all right." She called the waiter over for a second glass of wine.

Most people raved about the bouillabaisse, but not Sally. She was feeding us a lot of lies, and maybe that made her lose her appetite.

Lurleen gave me a break, so I could eat my croque monsieur before it got cold.

"I like someone who thinks for herself," Lurleen said. "Tell me what happened next."

Sally gave her a startled look. "What do you mean?"

"What was your calling?"

"I worked on Wall Street for a while," she said, "but I got tired of all the testosterone. I decided to go into business for myself. You haven't been spreading any rumors about me, have you Ditie?"

I nearly choked on my cheese sandwich. "Rumors? I don't know any rumors about you."

"I was only kidding," Sally said. "You know there was that big rumor that Phil organized a cheating ring in school, that he got hold of the tests ahead of time."

"Phil claimed that Carl started that rumor," I said, "because he and Carl were involved with the same girl and Carl was furious about it." I looked at Sally. "You were in Phil's group. Did you know who the girl was?"

This time it was Sally's turn to have trouble swallowing her food. "You're kidding me, right? You honestly didn't know who it was?"

"No."

"It was Harper, who else?"

"Harper?" I stared at her.

Phil, Andy, Harper, and I were in a study group together. There was plenty of time for mischief in that group."

Lurleen sat quietly during this exchange, sipping her wine, eating her salad. She smiled sweetly at Sally.

"I guess that's ancient history by now," she said. "Are you married, Sally? I hope that's not too personal a question. I just wondered if you could understand a person like me who chooses to be single."

"I'm not married, and believe me, I can understand a woman like you. Why give up our freedom when we can have it all?"

"*Exactement*," Lurleen said and smiled broadly at me. "Now, Ditie here, was all ready to tie the knot with Phil when he stepped away from the table. All for the best I'd say."

I shot her a look before I understood where she was headed.

I took up the thread. "Sally, the last time we spoke, you seemed really pleased that Phil was getting a divorce. You asked if I still had an interest in him, and I said no. I assumed that meant you did."

For just a second, Sally seemed to be caught off guard, and her face fell. She twisted pain into a smile. "I was only teasing you. To be honest

Phil asked me to find out if he might have a chance with you. I told him what you said."

"Are you planning on working for the senior Dr. Brockton?" I asked.

"Where did you hear that?" Sally asked.

"From Josh Nettles. He's an internist who was at a meeting at Dr. Brockton's house a few weeks ago."

"I remember him. Things got heated at the party between Carl and Phil, and I decided that wasn't the right work environment for me."

"Josh decided the same thing."

"I want to be my own boss. Work with individual clients on their portfolios. Lurleen, if you'd like to follow up with me, here's my card. I think we could have a great working relationship."

"I think so too," Lurleen said with her best Southern charm. "You're a sweetheart, if that's not inappropriate to say. And I'm really glad you found your calling in the world of finance."

"So am I."

"I want someone who understands me and will be looking out for my best interests."

"Great. Then I'm your gal."

Sally stood up and said good bye to both of us. "I'm sorry to rush off. I have another meeting I'm already late for."

I stopped her as she started to leave. "I do have one more question. You and Carl were very close. Did you know he had an accounting book apparently filled with payments he was making to people?"

Sally blanched. "Why would I know about that and what does that have to do with me?"

"It's just that some pages were torn out of it," I said. "I thought you might know who Carl was paying off privately."

This time her face reddened. "What are you up to, Ditie? Is this really why you invited me to lunch? To see what I knew about Carl's life and who might have killed him? I know nothing about any little black book."

She left us with no goodbye and no backward glance.

Lurleen gave her five minutes to leave the building. "What was that all about?"

"I just wondered what Sally might know about those missing pages. She obviously did know about the book. I never mentioned it was little or black."

Lurleen nodded. "Here's another one of your friends I don't like much. She didn't even offer to pay her share—and for her it was a business lunch."

"I have to say, Lurleen, we got our money's worth. Sally is not my friend by the way or your gal."

"Believe me, *chérie*, I knew that after the first five minutes."

"I'm not sure she made one honest statement to us."

"You think she's our murderer?"

"I think it's possible. She obviously knows more about Carl's book than she cares to say, and I'm wondering if the girl Phil and Carl were both dating in med school was Sally not Harper. I'm going to have a serious talk with Phil."

Chapter Twenty-Eight

Lurleen dropped me back at the clinic and then headed for a spa afternoon. Mason had just finished up a big case and was taking a vacation day to watch the kids.

I got home after a busy afternoon in time to see him playing hide and seek in my backyard. It was pretty hysterical—Mason hiding behind my Crepe Myrtle, with a trunk that was half his width as Lucie pretended she didn't see him, and Jason ran around with his bugle. Apparently, when anyone was spotted, Jason announced the discovery with his one-note bugle call.

I brought out a pitcher of lemonade and five glasses. Lurleen and I sat on the deck until they finally noticed we were there. Mason raised his hands in surrender.

"Drinks!" he shouted. He ran up the steps and planted a kiss on me, whispering in my ear, "How'd it go?"

"Useful," I said.

"Do we have a murderer yet?" he whispered again as he poured himself some lemonade.

"She didn't come right out and confess, but I suspect she was the girl Phil and Carl were both seeing in med school. She claimed it was Harper, and she seemed very concerned with what Phil and Harper might be up to."

"That was a decade ago. What does it matter who Phil was seeing then?"

"I'll tell you more after the kids go to bed."

Jason scrambled up the steps. "I catched him every time, Mommy, every time! Didn't I Uncle Mason?"

"You did, my boy. Thank goodness you gave me fair warning with your bugle."

I gave Jason a hug and then handed him a glass of lemonade.

Lucie came up more slowly.

"Are you all right, Luce?"

"Yes," she said. "Mason showed us a bird's nest in your big tree and I wanted to see if there were any babies in it."

"Were there?"

"I couldn't tell."

I led her over to the rail that looked down on that part of the yard. "Where's the nest?"

"Just there." She pointed to a middle branch of my cryptomeria. It was a fir tree that had grown a couple of feet every year since I planted it and now loomed over my pergola and wooden swing.

"Mason, can you bring out the binoculars?" I asked.

"At your service." He returned two minutes later with the binoculars in hand. "Let me take a look first." He focused on the tree. "It's a brown thrasher, Lucie, our state bird. Look right there."

He steadied the binoculars for her. "I see the nest, Uncle Mason." Then she squealed. "I see the babies!"

We all took turns and did our own count. Even Jason managed to see the babies or he claimed he did. One mother bird and two babies. Amazing.

It was too hot to stay outside any longer.

"Why don't you each take a bath, and you won't have to do that after dinner?"

Lucie trotted upstairs, and Jason went to the bathroom the two children shared.

Lurleen jumped up. "Let me get things started for you, Jason." He didn't protest, much to my surprise. Mason must have worn him out.

"I love you," I said to Mason.

"What's that all about, not that I'm complaining?"

"You are so good with the kids."

"I have had practice you know with my own two."

I know, and they've turned out to be wonderful young men."

"You've only met them twice," Mason said.

"I'm a very good judge of character." I saw this as a rare moment for the two of us alone. "Can I ask you a little more about your marriage? I promise I won't bombard you with questions. It's just that I thought you had this idyllic relationship before your wife died, and now I know that wasn't true."

"It wasn't true, Ditie. I told you about the one affair that ended when she got the diagnosis of breast cancer. I suspect there were others. I was so consumed with work, I just didn't see what was going on at home. When she got sick, then everything changed—my priorities and hers."

I stood up and put my arms over his shoulders. I rubbed his bald head. "I'm sorry it was rough."

That was about all the sharing Mason could take for the moment. "Tell me about the lunch," he said.

When I finished he shook his head. "I have to say, Ditie, you aren't making medical students sound like a terrific group of people."

"I know, but we're talking about a very small group—Phil's group to be specific. My other friends were great. I could spend a day on them, but that wouldn't help us solve this murder. I have to talk to Phil again."

"I want to be present when you do—not because I'm jealous of him—but if he knows more than he's saying, I want to be there."

"I agree. Will the investigators tell me to stay away?"

"Not if I'm with you. I'll talk to them about it. See what you can set up?"

I called Phil, and he answered on the first ring.

I asked how he was.

"I haven't been arrested if that's what you mean. They say I can go back to New York in a few days."

"Could we meet before then? I have some questions."

"Like what? Am I guilty of murder?"

"No, Phil. I'd just like to talk to you before you go."

"Now's not a good time." He sounded nervous.

"Someone's there with you, is that it?"

Phil was silent.

"Call as soon as you're free," I said. "We need to talk."

"All right."

I hung up the phone and suddenly felt panicked. I seemed to be having one of Lurleen's intuitive moments. Mason saw how agitated I'd become.

"What is it, Ditie?"

"I don't know. Probably nothing. Phil's not alone, and he sounded—I don't know—scared maybe? I just got to thinking—if he isn't the murderer and if he is still a target, then maybe he's in danger. He sounded as if he couldn't speak freely. I think I need to call Danny."

Lurleen walked into the kitchen with a well-scrubbed little boy. "Did I hear Danny's name mentioned? Is he joining us?"

Mason nodded at me. "I'll fill her in."

Lurleen followed him into the living room, and I heard them speaking quietly for a few seconds.

"How's my boy?" I said to Jason. In the last few weeks, he no longer ran around with his cape and superheroes. I kind of missed those days.

"Can I read to you?"

"What do you mean, Jason?"

"I can read now, Mommy."

"You'll have to show me." Together we walked into the family room. Mason and Lurleen were seated outside on the front porch.

We found a book Jason and I both loved—*Where the Wild Things Are*. I turned the pages and Jason read to me. Mostly, I suspected he'd memorized it the way I had. When he forgot we said the words together. Lucie joined us.

She saw that I thought Jason was pretending to read. "No, Aunt Di, Jason really can read. Show her!"

Lucie pointed to a word, and Jason pronounced it clearly.

"When did this happen?" I asked.

"It was supposed to be a surprise," Lucie said. "Lurleen and Jason and I worked this summer to get Jason ready for kindergarten."

"You don't have to be reading in kindergarten," I said.

"It can't hurt," Lurleen said as she joined us. "And besides Jason pretty much did it on his own, didn't he Lucie?"

"He did."

"You are all full of surprises!" I said.

Jason grinned.

"Lucie, you two want to read some more, while Lurleen and I fix dinner?" Lucie nodded.

Once we were out of earshot, I asked Lurleen about Danny.

"Phil told him to take a break, which meant someone was coming over. He's going to check on him now."

"Good. I may be overreacting, but I'll feel a lot better knowing Danny's there."

"If it is just a one night stand you're interrupting, Phil *will* be annoyed," Lurleen said and smiled.

"I don't care if Phil's annoyed as long as he stays alive."

Chapter Twenty-Nine

I tried to keep myself occupied in the kitchen. It was too hot to eat a heavy meal, so Mason agreed to grill hot dogs and hamburgers. Lurleen and I worked on a fruit salad and shucked corn she'd bought from the Dekalb Farmer's Market.

I waited for the phone to ring saying Phil was safe and I'd sent Danny on a wild goose chase. Lurleen could see how anxious I was.

"Danny's in five o'clock rush hour," she said. "You know how Buckhead is at that hour. He won't even be close."

"If that's supposed to make me feel better, it isn't doing the trick. Maybe I'll call Tommy. He's lives five minutes away from the Whitley."

Before Lurleen could stop me, I had Tommy on his cell.

"You're going to think I'm crazy, but are you at home?"

"I am," Tommy said. "Josh and I are deciding what to do this evening."

"I have an idea for you. Would you mind going to the Whitley for a drink and calling up Phil Brockton while you're there?"

"What's going on, Ditie?"

I explained my irrational worries to him as best I could. He responded that he'd never seen me in this state before. He was clearly skeptical, but he and Josh agreed to head to the Whitley anyway.

Now I had three people involved with what was probably a completely unfounded worry, and I had nothing to do but wait. Danny called to say he was still a couple of miles away from the hotel. He'd tried to reach Phil and gotten no answer. He'd keep trying.

Tommy called me ten minutes later.

"It's okay now, Ditie," he said. "Josh is taking care of Phil."

"What do you mean taking care of Phil?"

"Just listen and don't interrupt," Tommy said.

I sat down on a stool at the island. I held the phone so Lurleen could hear Tommy, but I didn't put him on speaker phone for fear the kids would come in. I listened to the whole story before I said a word.

Tommy and Josh got there before Danny. They'd called Phil's room, and when he didn't respond, they went upstairs to find him. They knocked on his door, saw it was partially open and went inside. Phil was in the bathroom holding a wash cloth to the back of his head.

"He nearly had a heart attack when he saw Josh in the mirror," Tommy said. "He obviously didn't recognize him. 'How'd you get in here?' he kept asking. 'Who the hell are you? Take whatever you want.' He must have thought Josh was his attacker. He settled down when he saw me, and I explained why we were there. I talked to him while Josh tended to his head."

Josh got on the line at that point. "It's a superficial wound, Ditie. I think someone whacked him from behind and it stunned him. A sharp object, like the edge of a book. We found one near where he fell."

I heard Tommy say something to Josh and then he took the phone back. "I'm in the living room. It's a lot easier to talk here while Josh finishes patching up Phil."

"Thank you, Tommy. Tell Josh he's a life saver."

Mason came inside to say the hamburgers were ready, and the kids bounced into the kitchen behind him.

"Hang on, Tommy," I said. I ushered the kids back outside to set the table on the deck. It would buy me five more minutes to talk to Tommy.

"Tommy, are you there? I'm putting you on speaker, so Mason can hear what's going on."

"Sure. It seems that Phil was entertaining Harper Hudson when she got an urgent call from someone. It was an intimate moment according to Phil, but she pulled herself together and ran out the door five minutes later. Phil noticed she'd left her belt and caught her at the elevator. When he got back, he went into the bedroom, and it was then someone threw a book at him."

"Hit him with what?" Mason asked.

"A medical school yearbook, if you can believe that. Phil said he brought it for the folks who were coming to the reenactment. "

"Has Phil called the police or the county sheriff?" Mason asked.

"He's reluctant to do that," Tommy said. "He's concerned about how it might look—his spending time with Harper when her husband was just killed."

"He's right about that," Mason said. "Did he see who attacked him?"

"He didn't see anything. He fell forward and by the time he got up, the person was gone."

"I'm coming over," Mason said, "after I call Barden."

"Barden?" Tommy asked.

"Investigator Barden with Gordon County. He's been on the case since the cannon explosion. He needs to know about this."

Mason handed me the phone.

"I'm coming too," I said.

We hung up, and Mason looked at me. "I don't suppose there's any point in asking you to stay put."

"No point at all."

We both went out on the deck. Mason sat with the kids while I told Lurleen where we were headed.

"But I want to go too," she said.

"Not this time. The kids."

Lurleen sighed dramatically. "All right. I'll feed the kids and take them for ice cream after dinner."

I didn't say much to the kids except that their uncle Tommy asked us to come over. Lucie looked as if she didn't quite believe me, but she didn't ask any questions.

Mason called Barden. He said he'd meet us there. Apparently, Atlanta police were already on the scene.

Traffic had calmed down by the time we left the house. We got to the Whitley a little before seven and found Tommy waiting for us in the lobby. "Danny, Josh, and Phil are upstairs."

He took us to Phil's suite. We knocked and an Atlanta police officer let us in. "We have a team in the bedroom, so we'll talk out here. Dr. Brockton says he interrupted a burglary. Nothing was taken, including his valuable Civil War guns—he keeps those in a lockbox in the closet."

Phil joined us in the living room. "The guys probably didn't know what they were looking for, just a snatch and run through an open door."

"Phil, are you saying this is not related to the murders?" I asked.

"I'm alive, aren't I?" Phil said.

."He could be right," the officer said.

"Or he could be very wrong," I said. "You have two deaths. Do you really think this assault is unrelated?"

Inspector Barden joined us at this point. He'd gotten the quick version of events from the officer in charge. "Throwing a book at someone isn't a way to commit murder," he said.

"You're right," I said, "but the simplest explanation is that all of this is part of the same story, not some random coincidence. That's the way we'd approach it in medicine—look for one diagnosis that fits all the symptoms."

"Sometimes the simplest story isn't the right one, Ditie." This was from Mason. "What does a relationship between Phil and Harper have to do with Carl's death or Ryan's death for that matter? The only people who might care about it are dead."

"Maybe it's a woman who cares, like Sally Cutter. I suspect she was the woman involved with both Phil and Carl during med school. I think she's still interested in Phil. And there's more."

That got everyone's attention.

"When I asked Sally if she knew about Carl's book of payments, it was clear she did. She denied it, of course, but I wonder if she also knew about the missing pages."

"What does that mean?" Mason asked.

"I'm not sure, but I intend to find out."

"I better be at your side when you do," Mason said.

"And I better not hear that you are interfering with my investigation," Inspector Barden said.

Chapter Thirty

Mason and I got home a little before nine. The kids were tucked in bed but still awake.

Jason wanted to talk.

"I got *two* scoops of ice cream. Lurleen said promise not to tell, and I said I wouldn't."

It was hard not to laugh. Someday, Jason would be a lot better at keeping secrets.

"What flavor?" I asked.

"You know, Mommy, vanilla with sprinkles!"

"Silly me. How could I forget!"

I gave him a kiss and a hug and found Lucie curled up in bed with her book *Harriet the Spy.*

"I'm going to be a detective when I grow up," she said, "like you and Uncle Mason."

"I'm a doctor, Lucie, what do you mean?"

"I mean your real job. You want to find out who is trying to make Dr. Brockton look like the murderer, but you don't think he is the murderer."

"Good grief, Lucie, where are you hearing all this?"

"I'm not listening at doorknobs," she said, and then she blushed. "Sometimes you talk kind of loud, Aunt Di, and sometimes Lurleen tells me what's going on. She says a good spy should always know what's going on."

"Do you know what's going on?" I asked.

"I know someone got hurt when a cannon exploded and some people think Dr. Brockton did it, but I don't."

"Why not, Lucie?" I asked.

"Because he was your boyfriend once, and I don't think you would ever have a boyfriend who hurt people."

"I hope you're right." I looked at her. "Since you are very good at listening, but not at doorknobs, do you have an idea who might have made the cannon explode?"

"No, I don't know that. But I'm keeping a list of people like Harriet did. Do you want to see?"

"You bet I do."

Lucie pulled a spiral notebook from under her pillow and showed me what she had so far.

Page One: People at the party

Page Two: People I like

Page Three: People I don't like

I read through the pages. On the top of page three was Harper Hudson. Lucie wrote what she'd already told me. "Phony. Doesn't like kids or dogs. Doesn't like Dr. Ryan. Likes men and doesn't like women."

"That is quite a description," I said to her. "How do you know she doesn't like her husband."

"I didn't mean to listen, Aunt Di, honestly, but they were in my bedroom and I was just about to go in there when I heard them. The man Dr. Hudson said, "This has got to stop! You are making a fool out of me, right here in front of my friends." And the woman Dr. Hudson said, "It's your own fault. You hate everyone I like—you hated Carl. I wonder if you killed him!"

"That's quite an argument you heard, Lucie."

Lucie nodded solemnly.

I looked over her lists. "You have Frank Peterson on your 'do not like' list. Why?"

"I watched him walk around your house, Aunt Di, and he said mean things, He said, 'Those pictures are done by amateurs. What does Mabel Brown do with her money? She sure doesn't spend it on art or nice furniture.' I love your house and your furniture and your paintings."

"Thanks, Lucie, I do too. You have Frank Peterson pegged about right. All he seems to care about is money. Who was he talking to when he said those things?"

"He was talking to Sally Cutter."

I looked at her list. "You wrote her name with a question mark. What does that mean?"

"It means sometimes she was nice and sometimes she wasn't. She agreed with Dr. Frank, but then later she agreed with Dr. Andy when he said it was a beautiful house and then she agreed with Dr. Brockton when he said he was having a hard time. She seemed to agree with everyone, so I didn't know about her."

"You are amazing, Lucie. May I keep this for tonight?"

Lucie nodded. I tucked her in bed and put *Harriet the Spy* on her nightstand.

She motioned me down close to her. "Do you mind if I keep calling you Aunt Di?" she asked.

"I don't mind a bit," I said.

"It's just I don't want Mommy to think I've forgotten her."

"I understand, Lucie." I stroked her face. "We never forget our mothers."

I turned off the light and closed the door to her bedroom. For a moment I thought about my own mother, and for the first time I wondered if I'd judged her too harshly. Her life hadn't been easy. Her mother had been a no-nonsense woman who lost her husband at an early age. How could my mother have been soft and survived?

Lucie was a miracle of insight—about the suspects, about mothers and daughters. I wondered what she would become when she grew up and the thought of watching my daughter grow up made me cry.

Lurleen found me in the hallway, rubbing my eyes.

"It's all good," I said, before she could say anything. "It's just that Lucie is the most amazing little girl. Look what she did."

Lurleen took the notebook and glanced through it. "Where did she get this idea?" she asked.

"She's been reading *Harriet the Spy*," I said.

'Didn't Harriet get in trouble with her notebook about her friends?" Lurleen asked.

"How do you know that?"

"I was the one who gave her the book."

We took Lucie's notebook out to Mason. He looked it over and then looked at me.

"You agree with this assessment?" Mason asked.

"Every word, and I didn't coach her. These are all Lucie's thoughts. Did you notice she was writing in a notebook all evening?"

"She kept it tucked away," Mason said. "Occasionally, she'd pull it out and write something."

We sat on the sofa together and read each page. Lucie had a fourth page—"What Happened at the Party." She kept an account of every hour and listed who was where. On the list were a few names I'd never heard of. I skimmed over those.

There was one addition to the list I didn't expect to find, one person at the party I thought had come and gone in a flash. Kathy. At 8:00 pm Lucie described someone she couldn't name—"a thin woman with brown hair and eyes, wearing white shorts and a purple top." That was a description of Kathy. Lucie saw her talking to Dr. Andy at the side of my house just inside the wooden gate that led to my backyard. It was the one place two people might have spoken in private. It couldn't be seen from inside the house, and Lucie must have been crouched somewhere, perhaps behind the wooden break for the garbage cans, to hear and see what she did. I read the passage aloud, so both Mason and Lurleen could hear.

"Dr. Andy gave her a big brown envelope. The woman gave Dr. Andy some money. Then the woman left."

Chapter Thirty-One

I looked up from Lucie's notebook. Mason and Lurleen were as stunned as I was.

"I need a moment," I said. "Kathy came to the party around six or six thirty I'd say. She left within ten minutes. Andy followed us out to the car. She came back around eleven, after everyone had left, and she was hysterical. Was she making that up?" I looked at both of them. "She fainted. Was that for my benefit?"

I didn't wait for a reply. "At eight, according to Lucie, she made a secret visit to the house, this time to see Andy. That had to be an arranged visit obviously. He hands her an envelope, maybe an envelope with a picture in it, and she pays him some money."

Mason suggested we talk in the kitchen over a cup of coffee. I checked to be sure the children's bedroom doors were closed.

I made decaf and brought out some brownies, left in the freezer for emergencies like this, for times when we needed to think.

"Remember," Lurleen said, "I was the one who told you Andy Morrison was the murderer and you scoffed at me, Ditie."

"Yes, and if that meeting was about the murder, then that means Kathy is involved as well. I just can't believe it."

"Perhaps you could believe it if you took your personal emotion out of it," Lurleen said.

Mason and I both stared at her.

"What?" she said. "You think I can't be logical? I worked at Sandler's Sodas as an accountant for years. You can't get more logical than that. And you know the saying—follow the money."

"The money poses a good question, Lurleen," Mason said. "Why would Kathy give Andy Morrison money in exchange for an envelope?"

Lurleen said aloud what we were all thinking. "The obvious reason is that she was paying Andy to murder her husband, and he was providing the proof that he'd done so." Lurleen pointed a long slender finger in my direction. "And then perhaps when she finally looked at the picture, she couldn't bear what she'd done. Maybe that's why she showed up on your doorstep late at night."

"I'm sorry," I said. "I can't wrap my head around that and there's a flaw in the logic. She didn't need to see a picture of Carl dead. She knew he was dead. Why would either one of them risk being seen with that photograph? It doesn't make sense."

The three of us were silent, drinking coffee and eating brownies.

"You're right," Mason said, "unless she was determined to make herself look like the victim and not the perpetrator by bringing the photo to you. But even that doesn't work well. Her best bet, if she were involved, would be to lie low and hope Carl's death would be declared an accident."

"So, if Andy wasn't giving her that gruesome picture, what was he giving her?" I asked. "It was done in secret or was it? Maybe Lucie saw it that way. Maybe they just met up at the most convenient spot?"

Lucie trotted into the kitchen at that moment and saw the three of us poring over her notebook.

"Was I talking too loud, Lucie?" I asked.

"No, I couldn't sleep and I wanted to get some water."

I gave her some.

"Why are you looking at my notebook? Did I do something wrong?"

"No, Lucie," Mason said. "We're looking at it because you kept such good notes. Do you mind telling us about seeing Dr. Morrison and the thin woman with brown hair? Did they act like their meeting was a secret?"

Lucie thought about it. "Kind of. Dr. Andy stood at the back gate and looked at his watch. That made me look at my watch. That's how I knew it was exactly eight o'clock. The thin woman opened the gate like she was trying to be quiet." Lucie's eyes suddenly grew large. "The thin woman was Kathy Thompson—that's who she was. I didn't recognize her then, but I do now. She looked around like she didn't want anyone to see her. Dr. Andy pulled the envelope from his pocket and gave it to her. It was folded over and she unfolded it."

"Did she look inside?"

"She did, Aunt Di. I forgot that part. She looked inside and said, 'It's all here.' and Dr. Andy said, 'Of course it is,' and then she gave him some money."

"Were you close enough to see how much money she gave him?" Mason asked.

"No, but I think it was a lot of money. He put it in his pocket and kissed her on the cheek. And then she left."

"Thanks, Lucie," I said. "You are going to be a great detective one day or maybe a reporter. Do you want a brownie before you go back to bed?"

"No thank you, Aunt Di."

I took her hand, walked her back to her bedroom, and tucked her in bed. When I came back Lurleen and Mason were whispering to one another.

"What did I miss?" I asked.

"Nothing much," Mason said. "Lucie said Andy kissed her on the cheek. That's an odd occurrence for a secret business deal."

"I could ask Kathy," I volunteered. "It's a place to start. I just can't believe she was involved with the death of her own husband. And certainly not with Ryan's murder.

"I don't want you to see Kathy on your own," Mason said, "and I'm going to give this information to the investigator."

"I'll be careful, Mason. If we do meet, I'll make sure it's in a public place. Before we call it a night, shall we see if there's anything else we missed?"

Together we read the rest of Lucie's account of the evening.

She seemed to be everywhere at once. She saw Harper make a move on at least two other men besides Phil. She saw Ryan drink at least five beers. Sally Cutter was often next to one of our male classmates. What wasn't obvious was where Phil was for the middle chunk of the evening. He was there early. An hour and a half later he was cornered by Harper near the pond at the far end of my backyard. Then there was the fight that didn't quite happen and then he got everyone out the door around eight thirty. But from six to seven or so there was no mention of Phil. I checked back to the notes on Sally. She was also not mentioned during that period of time.

"Sally seemed very happy to hear Phil was getting a divorce," I said. "I wonder if she and Phil were somewhere together during that hour lag time."

"Meaning what I think you mean?" Lurleen asked.

"Yes. Did they leave the party, I wonder. Would we have noticed?"

"I was occupied with the kids," Mason said. "Danny should know—he was the bodyguard."

Lurleen took out her cell, but Danny burst into the kitchen before she could call him.

"Ah, Ditie's brownies—I'm starving. What a night!" He ate the last four brownies and poured himself a large glass of milk. "Not much to tell. Whoever went after Phil didn't take anything and didn't do much damage. It was a pretty amateur assault. Looked like someone threw a book at his head and it landed. Nothing more than that."

"The book was a med school yearbook," I said.

"Yeah. That's odd, I'll give you that. Maybe it was the only heavy object around."

"Dan, we have a question for you," Mason said. "Did you stick with Phil all night at the party?"

"As a matter of fact, I didn't. He told me to take a break around six. Said he'd call me when he wanted me back on duty. I said that wasn't a good idea, but he ignored me."

"Did he go somewhere?" I asked.

"Yeah. He said he needed to get away for a bit. I offered to go with him, and he said that wasn't necessary."

"Was anyone with him?"

"I didn't see anyone when he walked out the door, but he told me not to follow him to his car. Can someone fill me in here?"

I described what was beginning to coalesce in my mind. Sally Cutter left school at the end of second year after the cheating scandal when Carl and Phil were reportedly seeing the same woman. Sally said it was Harper, but what if Sally were the woman as I suspected? What if she'd gone off with Phil during the party—perhaps rekindling what had started in med school? What if she'd gotten wind of Harper's interest in Phil and was spying on them? A woman scorned.

The others nodded.

"How does Carl fit in?" Mason asked.

"Do you think Sally could have been involved with both of them again?" I said. "She spoke so highly of Carl, as if he were misunderstood, and they'd stayed close over the years."

Mason was rubbing his bald head. "You're describing two women—Sally and Harper—with a propensity to carry on with more than one man. Why would that make either one of them angry enough to kill Carl?"

"It's a good question," I said. "I've always thought of Harper as someone who liked to be adored by every man she saw. She always had Ryan to fall back on. Sally didn't seem to have anyone. Maybe she wanted to get married. She talked that way in med school, wondering if marrying a doctor wouldn't be easier than becoming one."

I remembered something else.

"There was always a rivalry between Sally and Harper, like the game some guys play in college when they rate the women they can get to sleep with them. I think Sally felt like she couldn't quite keep up with Harper."

"That might explain Sally's throwing a book at Phil in his hotel," Mason said, "if it *was* Sally, but how would it explain Carl's murder?"

I poured myself another cup of coffee and thought out loud.

"Kathy said she and Carl were on the verge of divorce. Perhaps there was another woman at that point, and that woman was Sally. Then, when it appears Kathy is pregnant, Carl wants to keep the marriage intact. Sally would be so close to getting what she wanted only to find it snatched away from her."

"You think she could have been angry enough at Carl to kill him? Lurleen asked.

"She knew about reenactments," I said. "She'd be smart enough to know how to set up that cannon to explode. And maybe she'd be angry enough at Kathy to show her that horrible picture."

Lurleen nodded. "That still doesn't explain why Ryan was killed or the mystery encounter between Andy and Kathy."

"No, it doesn't," I said.

We'd done all we could do for one night. Lurleen and Danny went home. Mason made noises about leaving and I asked if he wanted to stay for a while. He did. It seemed we were over the hard time of his jealousy. Maybe it helped him to realize Phil was happy to sleep with Harper *and* Sally, even if it didn't make either one of them particularly happy.

Chapter Thirty-Two

Friday was normally my day off, but I'd missed a lot of work and wanted to make up the time. I called Kathy at the end of the day to see if we might meet for a drink.

"You have news about Carl's murder?" she asked.

"More questions than news."

I felt like a hypocrite. Kathy thought I was working on her behalf, and at that moment I wasn't. We agreed to meet at a coffee and wine bar midway between us.

She was there, sipping a glass of wine when I arrived. She looked expectantly at me.

"Do you want to get something to drink first?" she asked.

"Good idea."

It would give me a few minutes to determine how to ask her what I wanted to know. I started with an easy question when I returned. "How are you?"

"I'm not bad," she said. "My family left yesterday, and I'm glad to have the apartment to myself. I won't stay in it forever. It doesn't suit me." She smiled at me. "You said you had questions not answers, and you look a little nervous. What is it?"

"There's no easy way to ask this," I said. Then I recounted what Lucie had seen.

Kathy took a moment, perhaps stunned that someone had seen Andy and her together. "I did come back to the party," she said. "Andy called me after I left and said he had some information for me and could I stop back by?"

"It wasn't a secret meeting?" I asked.

Kathy hesitated and then laughed. "Of course not," she said. "Lucie is what, nine?"

"Almost," I said.

"I teach kids that age. They are all about secrets and mysteries—the girls are anyway. There was nothing secret about the meeting. I asked Andy to get me some information about real estate in South Carolina. I'm thinking of moving closer to home. He brought me pictures of available houses in my old neighborhood."

"You gave him money."

"I did. He'd handled some expenses for me right after Carl was killed, and I wanted to pay him back."

"I see."

Unfortunately, I didn't like what I saw. Lucie wasn't making up the fact that the meeting was supposed to be secret, and Kathy wasn't telling me the truth.

"Did you like what you saw?" I asked.

"What I saw?"

"The real estate options," I said.

"I did as a matter of fact. I wouldn't mind living closer to Andy." She paused. "We've both been through rough times because of Carl."

"Were you shocked when Andy and his wife broke up?"

"Not shocked exactly. There were a lot of arguments even before Carl started working for Andy. You know Andy, he's so even keeled and polite—he'd never say anything bad about his wife, but she could be pretty hard to take at times. She always wanted the best of everything when all Andy wanted was a simple life."

"You could be talking about the differences between you and Carl," I said.

"You're right, I could be."

"Did you have any more thoughts about Carl's book of accounts? You weren't sure it was his handwriting."

Kathy shook her head. "No new thoughts."

"The only payments in the book were to Frank Peterson," I said. "I wish we knew about the missing pages."

"I've told you, Ditie, I didn't know who was threatening Carl or anything more about the book. You act like you don't believe me."

I let that comment pass. "Do you think Sally would know who was threatening Carl?"

Kathy shrugged. "I don't know. They had a falling out before he died. When he mentioned her, it was to make some crack about how she was living high on the hog while he was struggling."

That felt like enough interrogation for one evening. We talked about other things, and when I finally said I needed to go, I swear Kathy looked relieved.

"I'm glad you spoke to me about what Lucie thought she saw. I'd hate there to be any misunderstanding about Andy and me."

"Misunderstanding?" I asked.

"That we were up to something when all we are is good friends."

We left together. I got home around seven to two starving children and one hungry boyfriend.

"I took the liberty of ordering Chinese," Mason said. "You want to walk me to the car, and I'll pick it up."

When we were away from the kids he asked if I'd learned anything. I told him what Kathy had said.

"So she wasn't ready to tell you the truth."

"She said she didn't want anyone to get the wrong idea about her and Andy. I wonder if the wrong idea might be the right one."

"That she and Andy are involved with one another romantically?" Mason said.

"That's what I'm wondering. It doesn't explain the private meeting. All I know about that so far is that Lucie thought it was secret, and I bet she got that right."

"Me too," Mason said. "All these encounters are starting to sound like Peyton Place."

I had to laugh. Mason and I loved many of the same things including old movies.

"I agree, and a lot of it started in med school. I had no idea. I just studied and saw Phil when he was available. That was *my* med school experience."

"Good," Mason said.

I left him and went to find the kids waiting for me inside.

"Are you hungry?" I asked.

"Uncle Mason gave us a snack," Lucie said. "Apples and peanut butter."

"Perfect. I'm sorry I was late."

"Were you solving the case?" Lucie asked.

I just smiled at her. "Tell me about your day, you two."

Jason went first. "Lurleen showed us how to catch butterflies."

"We didn't catch any," Lucie said, "but she made us butterfly nets. She said it was better that we didn't catch any."

"I'm with her," I said.

"Then she got a call from Uncle Danny, and she looked kind of upset and Uncle Mason came over and Lurleen left like a bat out of hell."

"What? Where'd you get that from?" I asked.

"Lucie said a bad word," Jason said.

Lucie blushed. "It's what Lurleen said—'I don't mean to leave like a bat out of hell, but Danny needs me.'"

"Do you know if anything was wrong, Lucie?"

Lucie shook her head. "Uncle Mason said everything was fine."

"I'll give her a call," I said.

I left the kids in the family room, Lucie with her book and Jason on the tiled floor playing with his Legos.

Lurleen answered on the third ring. "Ditie, I was about to call you. I'm with Danny, but he hasn't seen Phil all afternoon. They were supposed to meet for lunch but Phil never showed up. He hasn't been in touch with you, has he?"

Chapter Thirty-Three

"Why would Phil disappear and not tell anyone?" I asked. "I assume you're in his hotel room?"

"We are."

"This sounds like what he did at the party—just take off and then reappear when he felt like it," I said. "Have you called anyone else to see where he is?"

"Danny thought that might come better from you."

"I doubt that I have all their numbers. I do have Andy's card and Sally's as well. Maybe they'll know how I can reach everyone else."

I went back to check on the kids and they were sitting side by side in the family room as Lucie helped Jason read a book. I sat in the living room to make my calls. I started with Andy. He stammered into the phone.

"What is it, Ditie? Is everything all right?"

I told him I was trying to find Phil.

"It's about Phil!" He sounded relieved. "I haven't seen him since Sunday."

He gave me numbers for Harper and Frank.

"I just saw Kathy," I said before I hung up.

"I know. She called me. She told me what Lucie thought she saw."

"I have to be honest with you, Andy. If Lucie thought it looked like a secret meeting, I don't think she made that up. What's going on?"

Andy was quiet for a second. "It's not for me to say."

"What?"

"Ditie, I can't talk about it unless Kathy says it's okay. It's got nothing to do with Carl's death, that much I can tell you."

I hadn't really asked that. I had a friend who was a psychiatrist, and she loved to talk about "spontaneous denial." That's when someone denies something you never asked about. When they did that they were often lying.

"Is that all, Ditie? I need to get back to my kids. It's my night with them."

"So you and Jenna *are* divorced? You didn't tell me."

"It seemed kind of personal for a party. I'm not keeping it a secret or anything."

"Did Carl make a play for Jenna?"

"A lot more than a play. Jenna was my office manager. She and Carl were involved for most of the time he was there. Look, I gotta go."

I called Harper, but she didn't answer.

Frank picked up on the second ring.

"Are you still in town?" I asked.

"The police won't let us go anywhere for another few days. It's outrageous. They say they're waiting on some forensic evidence. What the hell does that mean? I only get paid when I work, and now I haven't been working for two weeks."

"Have you seen Phil today?" I asked.

"Nope, and I hope I don't see him again for a good long time."

"I heard about what Carl did to you. He was paying you back?"

"Who told you that? Carl made a few payments of about $10,000 each. Then he stopped. When I said I'd bring him up on charges, he said I would be the one to suffer—he'd ruin my reputation—make me look like a fool."

"You must have been furious when he turned up for the reenactment," I said.

"When I heard he was working for Phil's father, I thought finally that creep could pay me back. I told him I expected regular payments—that was the only way I'd keep my mouth shut about his previous indiscretions."

"And he agreed?"

"More or less. Look, Ditie, I don't feel like spilling my guts to you or anyone else. I just want to get the hell out of here."

"It sounds as if the only person you might have been happy to see was Phil."

"Phil put me straight about Harper, and I owed him for that. When he came up with this reenactment idea I actually thought it might be worth the trip. Boy, was I wrong. Same old intrigue."

"Same old intrigue? What are you talking about?" I asked.

"You know how every medical school class has its own personality? Well, yours was known for all the complicated liaisons."

"I never knew that," I said.

"Then you were the only one who didn't. And it was your boyfriend who was in the middle of it."

"What are you talking about? "

"Phil collected his followers and reaped the rewards. Carl couldn't stand it when he wasn't invited into Phil's inner circle. That started the rivalry. Then Carl did everything he could to bring Phil down."

"Like implicating him in the cheating scandal?"

"Yeah. Then of course there was Sally. Phil strung her along just to get back at Carl, that's what he told me."

"So Phil and Carl *were* both dating Sally?" I asked.

"You got it! Carl really hated Phil. He thought he was going to marry Sally, although I don't think Sally thought that. I wouldn't be surprised if Sally was screwing the poor guy who got the tests for her."

It really was Peyton Place. I kept that thought to myself.

"Anyway, Carl made it his life's work to destroy Phil. You can imagine how Phil felt when he learned Carl was working for his father."

"I can."

"I got to go, Ditie."

"Do you know where Phil is? That's really why I called."

"Maybe he's hiding somewhere from the police."

My next call went to Sally. I was surprised she picked up. My theory was that she and Phil were somewhere together.

"Phil is missing in action," I said. "Any idea where he might be?"

"Did you call Harper?" Sally asked.

"I did. No answer."

"That's your answer don't you think?"

"Were you the one who slammed a book onto his head?"

"Where do you get off?"

I'd never heard Sally really angry before. I thought she might hang up on me but she didn't, so I kept talking.

"I know you've been seeing Phil at the hotel. And I know Harper's been doing the same."

I could hear Sally take a deep breath before she answered. "There's no crime in that. At least not for me. I don't have a husband who was recently murdered."

"Do you think Harper and Phil might have been involved in both murders?"

"I wouldn't put anything past those two," she said. "They're both determined to get what they want, and they don't care who gets hurt along the way."

"Harper says Phil wanted to marry her. Do you know about that?"

"Part of Harper's vivid imagination if you ask me. I'm done with both of them. They're not worth my time, and as soon as I can get out of here, I'm gone."

"Sally, I know you were devastated by Carl's death, but Kathy made it sound as if you two had a falling out right before he died," I said.

This time she did hang up on me.

I called Danny to tell him I'd done all I could to help find Phil. Best bet was that he was off with Harper. Strangely, I didn't have the same sense of panic about his safety that I'd had so recently. Maybe I no longer saw him as a potential victim.

I heard Mason enter the house announcing dinner was about to be served. I found him and the kids at the kitchen island waiting for me to show up.

"Did you get me Mongolian Beef?" I asked.

"Of course."

"And egg rolls?"

"I'd never forget those," Mason said and gave me a kiss.

Jason made a face and Lucie giggled. Mason passed out chopsticks and for half an hour we enjoyed ourselves right down to the fortune cookies.

After dinner, I got the kids in bed, and then Mason and I talked.

"Still no word on Phil?" Mason said.

"Nope."

"Your ex-boyfriend seems to disappear a lot."

I told him about my conversation with Sally.

"Sounds as if you ruffled a few feathers," Mason said.

"My mother and brother would say that's what I spent my life doing. You know for some reason I'm not really worried about Phil, like I was the other day," I said. "What does that mean?"

"Maybe you believe he actually is capable of murder. Of course, it would be foolish for him to run from the police. He'd know that, but perhaps he needed time to sort things out."

Mason led me out back where we could sit on the deck and not worry about the kids overhearing us.

"Does Barden know any more?" I asked.

"About as much as we do," Mason said. "The sheriff from Gordon County is waiting for forensic evidence regarding the cannon to determine whether or not the explosion could have been an accident."

"I thought they'd already decided that."

"Phil Brockton's father called in his own private investigator, an expert on munitions, and that guy is presenting all kinds of different scenarios," Mason said.

"He can't come up with anything to explain the live ammunition that killed Ryan."

"No."

"So why haven't they arrested Phil?" I asked.

"All the evidence is circumstantial. No smoking gun, so to speak. Phil would have been smart enough to know the bullet couldn't be traced to his gun."

"Any word on the mysterious accounting book?" I asked.

"Not yet. I wish we could turn up those missing pages, but you can bet they've been destroyed."

"No information on the handwriting analysis?" I asked.

"One curious fact. When handwriting experts compared Carl's handwriting to the ledger, they did discover a difference. Carl never crossed his sevens."

"You mean the way an accountant might do?" I asked.

"How would you know that?"

"Lurleen explained it to me, so the number couldn't be confused with a one."

"It's lucky Lurleen's not a suspect," Mason said.

"Right, and the only other person likely to write like an accountant is—"

"Sally Cutter," Mason finished for me. "People claim she's not all that smart, not clever enough to embezzle money."

"I think she's a whole lot smarter than people give her credit for," I said, "and I have wondered how she had the money to dress in designer clothes and stay in a hotel like the Whitley. I assumed she got her money from her father, but maybe she got it somewhere else."

I looked at Mason.

"Did the book make it clear that the money was going out and not coming in?"

"I don't think it did, but the payments coincided with money leaving Carl's account."

"Any chance Lurleen and I might see the book?" I asked.

"Highly unlikely," Mason said. "The police do know what they're doing, Ditie."

I suddenly remembered something. Sally had written her cell number on the card she gave me at the funeral service. I'd just used it to call her, but I hadn't paid any attention to the way she wrote her numbers. I fished it out. "There you go. Every seven is crossed. Sally's our girl."

"She might be our girl, but there may be a lot of people who cross their sevens. I'll tell the police to check this out."

My cell phone rang. It was Dan. I listened and after he hung up I relayed the information to Mason.

"Phil finally called Dan. He told him he was going stir crazy, so he took off to be by himself for a while. He said he'd be back in an hour or two."

Mason looked angry. "He didn't bother to tell Danny where he was going?"

"Apparently not. He apologized to Danny and then said some things were private."

"You believe all that?" Mason asked.

"I don't believe he was alone. I'll bet he was with Harper."

I went inside to check on the kids. Jason was asleep but Lucie was writing in her notebook. She put it aside when I walked in.

"You've been doing some more thinking about the case, Lucie?"

She blushed. "Are you teasing me, Aunt Di?"

"Not at all. You have a remarkable eye for detail, and detail may be what we need right now."

"I was making a list of people who might want to hurt Dr. Thompson," Lucie said.

"May I see it?"

Together we went over the list. Lucie described Carl Thompson as someone who was not a nice person. When I asked her what she meant, she said she'd heard people at the party talk about him. That he stole money. That he was mean to people. They said he was mean to his wife. They said he took whatever he could get, and if it belonged to someone else that didn't matter."

"Who said these things, Lucie?"

"Dr. Frank and Dr. Andy and Dr. Ryan."

"They were together?"

"Yes. They were all together in a group and then when the woman named Sally came over, they stopped talking."

I nodded, kissed her and turned out the light.

I found Mason on the deck where I'd left him. The mosquitoes didn't love Mason, but they certainly loved me. It was just growing dark, and after a minute I claimed defeat.

"I'm being eaten alive."

"We can't have that." Mason took my hand and headed for the living room. "You were gone a while."

"Lucie's doing more detecting. She confirms what we already know. We have a lot of suspects who might have wanted Carl dead."

My cell rang.

"Hi Mabel, it's me Harper. I hope it's not too late to call. I got your message that you were looking for Phil. I don't know where he is. Have you found him?"

"Yes, he's fine."

There was a brief silence.

"I don't know if this is possible, but I wondered if I might come over for a few minutes tonight. I was a little hysterical when I saw you last, and I want to straighten that out."

"Okay. Mason Garrett is here. I hope that's not a problem."

"Not at all. I'd be happy to talk with both of you. I want us all to be on the same page."

I made a fresh pot of decaf coffee, defrosted some macaroons, and then we waited. I'd said she'd never be welcome in my house again, and I meant it. But this wasn't a social visit, and I needed to hear what she had to say.

Chapter Thirty-Four

Harper arrived thirty minutes later, looking calm but somber.

I ushered her into the living room and made sure the kids' doors were closed.

"We'll have to speak quietly, so we don't wake the kids," I said.

"No problem," Harper said. "I don't know if Lucie mentioned anything about my behavior at the party, but I wanted to apologize for it anyway. I don't think I was very nice to her."

I didn't respond.

"Actually I wasn't very nice to anyone at the party. I'd had too much to drink. I think we all did. Anyway, when I shooed Lucie away, it was really because I find it hard to be around children."

She paused, and again Mason and I remained silent.

"I've never really gotten over the fact that I can't have my own."

Mason looked at her, eyebrows raised.

"It's not a secret." She turned to Mason. "I got sick, and it left me infertile."

She didn't add that her infertility was caused by multiple sexual contacts and sexually transmitted diseases.

"So, you see it's hard for me to be around children. I was a young woman when it all happened. Ryan was incredibly loyal to me even though he wanted a family. At some point he said we would adopt. Now, he's gone, and I'm totally alone."

"How are you coping?" I asked.

"It's hard. Harder than I imagined. I lost my father last year, but in many ways this is more painful."

She ran a hand through her sleek blond hair.

"Ryan was so upset before he died. I don't think he understood how much I loved him."

I was having a hard time with this conversation. I stuffed a macaroon in my mouth to avoid saying something I might regret.

"I know you don't like me much, Mabel. Sometimes I don't like myself either. I think I've always felt I had to prove I was attractive to men since I couldn't give them what most men wanted—children."

I couldn't stop myself. "If you were so devoted to Ryan, why were you in Phil's hotel room before he was attacked?"

"Attacked. What are you talking about?"

"After you left someone threw a book at Phil and sliced open the back of his head."

"But I just saw him. He's fine."

"That means you were with Phil this afternoon, and you lied to Ditie," Mason said.

"How would it look for a widow of a few days to be with a man accused of murdering her husband?"

"Not good," I said.

"Maybe you've never lost anyone important to you, Mabel, so you wouldn't understand. I needed comfort, and Phil provided it." She paused briefly. "Do the police think Phil killed Carl and Ryan?"

"Do you?" Mason asked.

"He tells me he didn't kill anyone, and when I'm with him I believe him. When I'm away from him, I'm less sure."

She looked at us as if she expected us to say something. We didn't.

"I won't keep you any longer." She stood. "If you have the time, Mabel, I might want to come back and talk to you about what it's like to raise children who are not your own."

"They are my own. I didn't give birth to them if that's what you mean, but I couldn't love them any more if I had."

Harper nodded. "You know what I mean. I'm so lonely—I'm thinking I might want to adopt. It's what Ryan always wanted, and I was never quite ready. Now I think I am."

I was speechless. The idea of Harper as a mother made my blood run cold.

When Harper left, I turned to Mason.

"Why is it that every time I talk with Harper, I feel like she's onstage delivering a performance?"

"Because she is?" Mason said.

"I wonder if she came tonight to check on the investigation, to see what the police know," I said.

Mason nodded and helped me collect coffee cups and carry them to the kitchen.

"And what's all this crazy talk about adoption? Harper hates children," I said.

Again he nodded.

"I wish we could pin the murders on her," I said, "but she wasn't near either man when he was killed."

"No, she wasn't," Mason said. "Regardless, I don't want you meeting with her alone."

"Agreed."

Mason put the dishes in the dishwasher, gave me a kiss and went home.

While I wanted Harper to be the murderer, there were other contenders, closer to the scene of the crimes, like Sally for one.

There was something about the photo sent to Kathy that sounded so vengeful. I wasn't sure if I was being unfair to women, but it sounded more like what a woman would do than a man. A man could have killed Carl for a dozen reasons, but would he show the photo to Kathy out of spite? Frank could have simply been in touch with Kathy and demanded the money that was stilled owed to him. If it was a woman, then we had only two candidates—Sally and Harper. Of course, if I left my emotion out of it as Lurleen suggested, I had to include Kathy. She could have orchestrated all of it through Andy and pretended to be devastated by the photo. That still seemed so farfetched.

* * * *

I woke up the next morning determined to talk to Phil. He was at the center of this, and if he wasn't the guilty party he might have ideas about who was.

I went to work that morning and focused all my energies on the children in front of me. At lunchtime I made a call to Phil, and he actually picked up.

"We need to talk."

"Why do you sound so intense?" he said. "I'm the one in trouble."

"Why do you sound so casual, as if someone is threatening you with a parking ticket? You're under investigation for murder."

"I know that, Ditie, but it doesn't do me any good to dwell on it. My father's hired two of the best lawyers in Atlanta, and he's got his investigators swarming all over the case. I can't do anything but wait."

I'd forgotten how good Phil was at compartmentalizing. If something didn't need his immediate attention, he set it aside. He wasn't one to waste his time worrying about a problem he couldn't solve.

"Phil, I need to see you face to face."

"I'm pretty busy," Phil said.

"Doing what?"

"My dad and I have to make plans. We have to deal with patient overload now that Carl is gone. We have to let them know what happened if they don't already."

"Are you going to work with your father after all?"

"I might."

"Phil, I'm asking for half an hour. No, I'm not asking. I'm demanding half an hour of your time."

"We can't do it over the phone?"

"No, we can't."

"All right, but it'll have to be tonight."

"That's fine. Then Mason can come."

"I don't want your boyfriend there," Phil said.

"You can't always have what you want, Phil. Not this time."

"You sound like every other pushy woman I know," he said, and it didn't sound like a joke.

"Really? Like whom?"

"Never mind. Let's meet at ten tonight in the lobby here at the hotel."

Phil was doing everything he could to make things difficult for me. It would take an hour to get to Buckhead on a Saturday night, but Phil could have told me to meet him on the moon, and I would have gone. I hoped Mason would be as obliging.

He was my next call. He agreed. Then I called Lurleen. She said she could stay over with the kids.

"I have some news for you," Lurleen said. "Phil fired Danny today. He said he didn't need protection anymore. No explanation. Just thanks but no thanks. He paid him in cash with a bonus."

Chapter Thirty-Five

I stayed at the clinic Saturday afternoon, so Vic could have a weekend off. Fortunately, two seasoned nurses were working with me. We had one six-year-old boy with a bad asthma attack who was immediately sent to the ER. I didn't get out until six, but since Lurleen was staying over with the kids, it didn't matter how late I finished up.

I came home to find Danny in the kitchen and Lurleen in the family room reading with Jason and Lucie. "You've got to listen to Jason," Lurleen told me. "Pick up any book and he'll read it to you."

I picked up *Where the Wild Things Are.*

"Not that one, Aunt Di," Lucie said. "Jason reads that one all the time."

"You pick one out, Jason," I said.

Jason grabbed one about a dragon. He read each page flawlessly.

Lurleen handed him two more, and he read them without a single mistake. I watched him read. He seemed to be looking more at the pictures than the words. I began to wonder if Jason had memorized the stories. Maybe he had the same kind of memory Lucie had. She could repeat conversations verbatim.

Danny called us to dinner.

"Mason has to work late tonight. He said he'd pick you up around nine," Danny said.

The kids looked at me. "I have to go out tonight to talk with someone, so Lurleen is staying over."

Lucie whispered to me, "Is it about the case?"

"Yes," I whispered back.

Jason heard us. "Mommy said no secrets at the table. Mommy Two, you shouldn't have secrets either."

"No secrets, Jason. I'm visiting a friend."

We settled into a very fine dinner of chicken piccata, wild rice and broccoli au gratin.

This night I had plenty of time to spend with the kids. I tucked Jason in bed and found a book I didn't think he'd read before.

I pointed to a page in the book. "Can you read me a little of this, Jason?" I asked.

"You read it to me first."

"You try and then I will."

Jason looked at the page and then looked up at me. I thought he might cry.

"It's okay, Jason. In fact it's pretty amazing. I think you hear the words of the story and then you remember them. Nothing's wrong with that."

Jason didn't seem convinced.

"It takes a very, very smart boy to memorize a story."

"Memberize," Jason said.

"Memorize. That just means you remember what you hear and then you can repeat it."

"But I want to read! Like Lucie."

"You will, Jason. Look at this word. Can you tell me the letters?"

Jason looked at the word. "T .E. H."

"T. H. E. The," I said.

I did a couple more words. Like a lot of kids his age he reversed the letters. It might mean nothing, or it might mean something. "That's enough for one night. We'll practice this whenever you want. You don't have to read before you go to kindergarten."

"Lucie said I did," Jason said.

"You should know your colors and you do. You should know how to hold a pencil and you should know your numbers and how to listen. You know all those things, Jason. You're ready for school. You remember how smart your pre-K teachers said you were."

Jason nodded and looked relieved. "They said I was very, very smart. But I can't really read. I was just tending for Lucie."

It took me a moment to realize what Jason was saying. "Pretending," I said. "You don't have to pretend about that. When you're ready to read, you will. And if you have trouble with that, we'll help you. That's what school is all about, to help you with your numbers and your letters. You'll have a great time."

I kissed Jason good night. "Can I explain this to Lucie?"

"Okay," Jason said, "but don't tell Lurleen."

"Why not?"

"She'll be mad at me."

"Lurleen won't care. Why would you think she'd be mad at you?"

"She says I'm a big boy to read so well. I don't want her to think I'm not a big boy."

"Jason, we all have trouble doing things once in a while. Even Lurleen. Lurleen can't cook, and I can't sing on key. It doesn't matter."

I'm not sure Jason believed me, but he did seem less upset.

When I talked with Lucie, she wasn't surprised.

"When I ask him to spell a word, he gets the letters mixed up," she said.

"I know. Sometimes kids do that."

I didn't add that it could be an early sign of dyslexia, and that Jason might have more trouble reading than other kids. We'd cross that bridge later if we needed to. I tucked Lucie in bed a little before nine and found Mason waiting for me in the living room.

We left Danny and Lurleen watching a favorite old movie of theirs, *Love Actually.*

"We'll be back as soon as possible," I said.

"Take as long as you want," Danny said. "Lurleen and I haven't had much time together."

Mason and I reached the Whitley a little before ten.

"Phil knows I'm coming?" Mason asked.

"Yes, and you can imagine he wasn't happy about it. He wasn't happy about seeing me at all."

We waited until 10:10, and when Phil didn't show in the lobby we called him.

"I was just about to text you, Ditie. Now is not a good time."

"Phil, we drove an hour to get here. We are not leaving without talking to you."

"Okay, okay. I'll be down. Have a drink in the lounge. I'll get there as soon as I can."

I hung up and repeated the message to Mason. "He wants us to wait in the lounge and have a drink."

"Then I think we'll stay right here in the lobby. See if we know anyone who's leaving," Mason said.

"I'm with you. You think it will be Sally or Harper?" I asked.

As it turned out, it was neither of them. Frank Peterson walked off an elevator and out the front doors. He never looked in our direction.

Phil arrived five minutes later.

The three of us took a seat in the lounge. At this time of night, we were virtually the only people in the heavily paneled room. Even the piano player had stopped for the evening.

Phil ordered a martini. Mason and I ordered decaf coffee.

"What was Frank doing here?" I asked.

"What are you talking about? Frank wasn't here, and if he was, what business is it of yours? Are you spying on me now?"

"You asked for my help and I gave it. How did I suddenly become the enemy?"

That seemed to bring him up short.

He looked at me and shook his head. "I'm sorry. It's been a hell of a couple of weeks," he said. "I don't know who I can trust. I started to think you and Mason were here to get me to confess to something I didn't do. I didn't kill Carl or Ryan."

"They haven't arrested you," I said.

"That's only because they don't have enough evidence to make the charges stick."

Mason spoke up. "Have you told them everything you know?"

"My lawyers said I should keep my mouth shut."

"Can you talk to us?" I asked.

"They said I was a fool if I talked to anyone."

"Phil, we've been through a lot. I've been angrier at you than any other person I know. But I'm over all of it. Mason is as honest as I am. Talk to us."

Phil sipped his martini and said nothing for thirty seconds. "You've never betrayed me, Ditie. I know you wouldn't say the same thing about me, and I'm sorry about that."

Two apologies in one evening from Phil? I looked at Mason. He kept his face blank.

"I accept your apology," I said. "Now what do you know about this mess that you haven't told the police."

"More than I'd like to know.

"We're listening," I said.

Chapter Thirty-Six

Phil looked at me and then at Mason. "I wish your boyfriend wasn't here."

"He's here and he's staying," I said.

Phil sighed. "I have to start at the beginning. I was so young in med school and so cocky."

"Like half the class," I said. "The other half was just scared to death. That would be my half—afraid we would never know enough."

"You never seemed that way, Ditie. You always had such a cool head and you weren't caught up in status. It was a relief to be with you."

I let that pass.

"You know why I had the group of friends I had?"

"No."

"I gathered them around me for one purpose. They each had some flaw that I could use to my advantage. They all wanted to get ahead, and I knew the ropes. I knew the right people. I had an in with administration. I had my dad who knew everyone in town. It was my fiefdom, Ditie."

I looked at Phil. "How could I have missed that?"

"You didn't really hang out with any of them. You didn't join the study group I formed. You always said you needed to study alone."

That was true. I'd do my studying away from school, at the laundromat or a coffee shop. That was how I met Lurleen, and it was Lurleen who helped me keep some perspective in med school.

"Why would you want a fiefdom?" I asked.

"Ditie, you don't seem to realize how intoxicating power can be. I learned that in boarding school. You fight your way to the top and then you reap the rewards."

I thought about my brother, sent off to boarding school as a young teenager. Is that what he'd learned there?

"But you started at the top, Phil. You came from a long line of Southern docs. You were smart. What more did you need?"

"Once you know you have power, you want to keep it, and you want more. I'm not proud of what I did, but I was twenty-three. I thought I had a right to take anything I wanted."

I sipped my coffee and tried hard not to react to what I was hearing.

"I collected them bit by bit," he said. "The ones who were smart but not very sophisticated—like Andy and Ryan. I gathered the most attractive women I could find."

"Harper and Sally," I said.

"Yes. I offered them a safe haven, like what you offered me, and then I figured out how they could be of service to me. I figured out what each of them was afraid of and I used that fear to my advantage."

I was starting to feel sick.

"What was my flaw, Phil? How did you use me?"

"Your flaw was that you were young and idealistic. You saw the best in me, and I needed that."

"And the others?"

"Ryan was easy to rouse. If I needed someone to fight a battle for me, Ryan was my man. In return, I helped him deal with Harper. She was a handful, but Ryan could never see beyond her beauty. She cast a spell on him, I swear she did. Harper could be very convincing when she wanted to be. When I learned she could never have children, I convinced Ryan to wait his turn—be a loyal friend to her. Ryan wanted Harper more than he wanted kids, so he managed to bide his time. When Frank broke off his engagement to Harper, Ryan was there, ready to marry her on the rebound."

"Andy?" I asked. "What could you possibly offer him?"

"Andy was Mister Affable. He liked me, and he was good for my image. When people started saying I was an asshole, Andy was my defender."

"Sally?"

"Sally was a chameleon. Whatever you needed her to be, she'd be."

"What did she get out of it?"

"A chance to belong to my group of course—to mix with the movers and shakers."

"And Carl?" I asked.

"Carl wanted to belong to my group, and he had nothing to offer me. Nothing. I didn't have time for him. That's where all the bad mouthing of the South came from."

I looked over at Mason. He gave me a look of concern—wondering no doubt how I was handling this information. I did my best to keep from showing how shattered I felt.

"Was Frank Peterson part of your fiefdom? He was a year ahead of us. What could you offer him?" I asked.

"Frank and I were two of a kind. We both wanted power, money and prestige. It was a live and let live mutual respect."

"The cheating scandal?" I said.

"I'm not admitting any part in it, but you can imagine how intriguing it would be to figure out how it might be done. Sally was all in. If it meant she could stay in school and not have to work hard, she was for it. The others went along. They saw it as a prank and a way to boost their GPA's. It wasn't going to continue long term."

"Andy didn't go along with it," I said.

"No, he didn't know anything about it. Ryan didn't either."

"So, you're saying—you, Frank, Harper, and Sally cooked up this scheme." I couldn't believe I was saying this.

"All hypothetical, Ditie. It was amusing to realize how easily it might be accomplished. Theoretically."

"You expect me to believe that?" I asked.

"You and I both know I didn't need to cheat. Hypothetically, I may have told Sally who she could talk to, that kind of thing, but I kept my hands clean."

"Somehow Carl got wind of it and when he accused you he was only half wrong."

Phil paused. "I was furious of course. I didn't need that bulldog on me, and I was pretty sure Sally had confided in him. She never knew when to keep her mouth shut."

"So you threw her under the bus," I said.

"She was cheating, Ditie. I didn't make that up."

"How did it all end?" Mason asked.

Phil looked at Mason as if he'd forgotten he was there.

"Sally left school. A techie got fired. My father read me the riot act and said if I didn't get myself under control he'd disown me."

"That's when you started dating me seriously," I said.

"Yes. But I wasn't just using you, Ditie. You were good for me. You believed in me. The rest of them turned against me. Then, when they saw me with you, they thought I really had reformed."

I excused myself, went to the bathroom, and threw cold water on my face. Phil hadn't just used me at the end of our relationship. He'd used me all the way through. I didn't have doubts any longer about whether or not Phil was capable of murder. What I didn't know for sure was whether or not he'd actually committed the crimes.

I dried my face and walked back to the table. Mason and Phil were sitting in silence.

I couldn't bear to sit down again at the same table with Phil.

"One last question," I said. "If *you* didn't commit the murders, do you know who did?"

Phil's face went white. "You can't believe I would ever do something like that."

"Harper seems to think it's possible. She claims you wanted to marry her and Ryan would never give her a divorce."

"Harper is full of stories. You should know that."

"You didn't lead her on," I asked, "the way you did me?"

"I might have told her how much I enjoyed her company, nothing more than that."

"And you know nothing about an accounting book that Carl had?"

"What are you talking about?"

For once, Phil seemed genuinely surprised.

"Never mind. What's the end of the story?" I asked. "Why did you bother to tell us all this?"

"Because you have to see there are a lot of people who would want to frame me for these murders. I always knew I couldn't trust the bunch of them, but until now, I thought I was still in charge. Someone's out to destroy me. You have to realize that."

Mason stood up. "Let's go," he said. "It's clear this conversation's finished."

Phil nursed his drink as we walked away.

Chapter Thirty-Seven

I turned back when I remembered one last question. "You never told us what Frank was doing here," I said.

"He wasn't here to see *me*. I have no idea why he was in the building. You sure you saw him?"

"Yes. Is anyone else staying in the hotel?" I asked. "Anyone we know?"

"Sally Cutter," Phil said.

"How did we miss that?" I asked, looking at Mason.

"I'm sure the police didn't miss it," Mason said. "Makes it a cozy gathering, doesn't it?"

"I don't know what the hell you may be driving at," Phil said, "and I don't want to know."

Mason and I walked to the lobby.

"Shall we see if Sally is in?" I asked.

"Might as well. We're here."

I called up to Sally's room. She picked up.

"It's you, Ditie? Why are you calling me so late?"

"Mason and I happened to be at the Whitley, talking to Phil. He told us you were here. Do you have a few minutes? Can we come up?"

"Phil never knows when to keep his mouth shut," she said, "not that it's a secret I'm staying here. You can come up."

Sally and Phil were accusing each other of saying too much. Maybe they both had something to hide.

Sally greeted us in a pair of Escada hand-bleached jeans and a Dolci and Gabbana silk top. I only knew because Lurleen liked to keep me up on the latest fashion trends.

"Were you entertaining?" I asked.

"Why would you say that?" she asked.

"It's a gorgeous outfit, and we saw Frank Peterson leave."

"Leave my room?" Sally said. "You're spying on me?"

Funny that Phil had asked exactly the same question. I didn't correct her about where we'd seen Frank.

"All right, Frank was here. It's no big deal. We're all upset about what happened."

Mason and I sat down on the edge of the bed.

"Make yourself comfortable," Sally said sarcastically, "but if this is some kind of interrogation, I'm calling my lawyer."

"Everyone seems to have a lawyer," Mason said. "I wonder why?"

"I'm really trying to get some old history straight," I said. "You told me Harper was the woman involved with Phil and Carl. I've heard from more than one source, it was you, not Harper, who was the woman in question."

"Seriously, Ditie, the woman in question? You make it sound so sinister. Yes, I was involved with Phil and Carl. That's all ancient history."

She stood up, walked to the mini fridge and pulled out a beer.

"You like my clothes," she said with a smile. "I can afford these clothes because I had the good sense to leave school and go into finance. So, you see Phil did me a favor when he let the authorities know I was cheating. And Carl was trying to defend my honor when he worked so hard to get Phil kicked out as the ringleader."

"You stayed close to Carl?" I asked.

"Close enough," she said.

"You continued to sleep with him?" I asked.

"You have such an old-fashioned way of looking at things," Sally said. "Yes, we slept together occasionally. We were friends with benefits, but we both moved on. We looked out for each other."

"Did that mean helping him embezzle money from Frank and then Andy?" I asked.

"How dare you say that!"

"You worked in the financial department of both Frank's and Andy's businesses and knew nothing about Carl's scheme?" I asked.

"That was all Carl. He wanted to get ahead fast and didn't like to go through normal channels."

"It's hard to believe you weren't involved," I said.

"I don't care what you believe! You have no proof I did anything wrong."

"Why was Frank really here?" I asked. "Maybe with Carl's death, he thought you should pay him the rest of the money he was owed."

"It's none of your business."

"We suspect *you* were the one who attacked Phil when you found him in the room with Harper," Mason said.

Sally's demeanor changed. She shook her head in disgust.

"Attack Phil! You mean hit him with a book? If I'd meant to kill Phil, he'd be dead. I just wanted him to get the message that he couldn't get away with murder."

"Literally?" I asked.

"No! You keep putting words in my mouth." She stood up, finished her beer, and dropped it in the trash. "It's entirely possible Phil did murder Carl and then tried to make it look as if *he* was the actual target. I wouldn't put anything past him, but that isn't what I was talking about." She sat in the chair by the desk and leaned forward. "I was talking about his relationship with Harper. Phil still thinks he can have any woman he wants with no consequences, and I wanted him to know there were consequences even if it was just a headache."

"You chose a med school yearbook to throw at him," Mason said.

"Nice touch, don't you think? It was heavy and it was handy. I didn't mind making Phil worry that his past indiscretions were catching up with him."

"So you are still involved with Phil," I said. "When you asked if I was interested in Phil, it was to see if the coast was clear for you."

"I didn't reckon on Harper, but she hasn't changed since I first met her. She's all about the conquest and she doesn't care who she hurts in the process. I'm ready to settle down, and Phil will be available in a few months. Then Harper pops up causing havoc the way she always does."

"You sound so angry," I said.

"I'm tired of playing second fiddle," Sally said.

"Phil dumped you twice, first in med school and again now."

"Phil's like Harper. He thinks about only one person, himself. They deserve each other!" This she nearly screamed at us.

"I heard Carl was ready to ask Kathy for a divorce and then when she thought she was pregnant, he changed his mind."

Sally's face flushed. "I guess you heard that from Kathy. Yes, that's true—what of it?"

"I wondered if you hoped you and Carl might marry finally."

"I told you I never loved Carl in that way. This conversation is over! Get out."

Sally went to the door, but I stayed put.

"I don't think the conversation is quite over. Have the police contacted you about the accounting book with your handwriting in it?"

Sally froze. She turned slowly. "I only know about that book because Kathy told me she'd found it."

"I think you know all about it," I said. "I think it was your book, and you ripped out the pages you wanted no one to see."

"You're crazy!" she said.

Mason had remained silent through most of the interview. I took that as a sign I could keep talking.

"You've always had such nice clothes. I started to wonder how you afforded them. Maybe the book was about payments Frank was making to you and not money he was receiving from Carl. That's easy enough to check. In fact we already have. We talked to Frank on his way out. All he wants to do is get out of this mess."

"I don't believe you," she said, but it was clear she did. "What did Frank say?"

"That's confidential," Mason said. "The more you lie to us, the worse it is for you. This is about more than blackmail, it's about murder."

Sally crumbled at that point. "I never took more than I deserved or than people could afford to pay. It was always a business transaction, nothing more."

"What about Carl? You took money from him as well?"

"Only at the end. Carl said he was going to move on with his life and told me I'd have to find my own way. I said he'd have to make it worth my while."

"So you were the blackmailer. Were you the embezzler as well?"

"I'm not admitting to that, but it would have been child's play to skim off some of the profit, and make it look as if Carl was doing it. Carl knew nothing about finance. I'd had my own business transactions with folks in med school for years. I told Carl I'd talk to the senior Dr. Brockton if he didn't pay me, so, of course, he did."

"Or perhaps, he refused to pay you, and you killed him," Mason said.

"I'm not a murderer," Sally said. "I'm simply good with numbers and getting what I need to live."

"Who else were you blackmailing?" I asked.

"I wasn't blackmailing anyone. I was a secret keeper. I kept Harper's secret for a small monthly sum. And Phil's about the cheating scandal. And then, when it was clear Frank didn't want anyone to know he'd been duped, that was an easy sell."

She looked at both of us.

"I will deny all of this to the police. You have no proof. You never read me my rights, and nothing I've said can be used in court."

"I wouldn't be quite so confident," Mason said. "You were present for both murders and may have had reasons to wish to see both men dead. Perhaps Carl was going to turn you in, and you had only one way to stop him. "

"And Ryan? Why would I kill Ryan?"

"Perhaps that was a way to frame Phil," I said. "Phil seemed to get everything he wanted and he didn't want you—not in med school. Not now."

Sally looked at me. "How could Phil have chosen you over me in med school? And how could he choose Harper now? I should have killed *her.*"

Mason and I looked at each other. Had Sally just confessed to murder?

He took out his phone and called Inspector Barden. Sally sat on the bed staring straight ahead. We both stayed until Barden arrived twenty minutes later with two Atlanta policemen.

When Mason told him about our conversation after the police had taken Sally downtown, he just kept shaking his head. "You know how difficult you've made my job," he said. "What were you thinking, Mason? None of this is admissible as evidence. The book may belong to Sally, but the handwriting experts aren't certain of that. And she didn't actually confess to anything. We'll see if we can shake anything out of her, but her lawyer will be all over us."

Mason didn't say much. When Barden was done, Mason said simply, "I don't think Sally would have admitted to anything if she'd had time to think about it. At least now, we know she was blackmailing people and that the book belongs to her. That's a place to start. I'll bet Frank Peterson will talk to you if it means he can get out of Atlanta and back to his work. Or maybe you'll discover he's more involved than we know. We didn't find out why he was visiting Sally tonight."

Barden let us go.

"I'm sorry, Mason. I really botched this."

"I meant what I said. If Sally hadn't been caught off guard she never would have said anything. I don't know if she murdered two people or if the police will be able to prove she did, but all the secrets of Phil's little group are starting to unravel. Who knows where it will end?"

Mason left me to my thoughts as we rode down the elevator.

Sally loved reenactments, probably because she'd loved Phil and saw this as a way to win him back. She knew about cannons. Perhaps when it was clear Phil was more interested in Harper than in her, she decided to take revenge. She might have planned to murder Phil and then Carl stepped in the way. Her next best bet might have been to frame Phil.

When we got in the car, Mason turned to me.

"Okay, what have you figured out?" he asked.

I told him what I was thinking.

"You're saying she might have killed Ryan to frame Phil?" Mason said.

"A woman rejected—not once but twice."

"She's a hard read, I'll give you that."

"A chameleon. Isn't that what Phil said?"

"Hmm," was all Mason said.

"What are you thinking?" I asked.

"You want me to be frank?" he asked.

"Yes."

"Okay, when I found out about my wife's affair, she wasn't the one I wanted to kill. It was the boyfriend."

"Wow," I said. Imagining Mason angry enough to kill anyone took my breath away.

"Did I shock you?" Mason asked. "It took me all of five seconds to remember I had two young boys to worry about, but I *was* that angry."

"Got it," I said. "You mean why isn't Harper the one lying in a morgue if Sally is our killer. Just like she said—'I should have killed her.'"

"Exactly."

Mason dropped me at the house. He kissed me good night and promised to call the county sheriffs in the morning to see what progress was being made and what was happening with Sally.

I checked on the kids and fell into bed exhausted. Then I spent the night wrestling with imaginary murderers, all of them with familiar faces.

Chapter Thirty-Eight

My cell woke me up a little before seven.

"Hi, Mabel. It's Harper. I hope I didn't wake you. I assumed you were an early riser."

"I am. You beat my alarm by five minutes."

"I wanted to check on your schedule and see if I might come over to visit sometime soon. You remember, I wanted to talk to you about adoption."

Was Harper actually thinking of adopting or did she have some other motive for talking to me? Maybe I could find out about her relationship with Phil. She wouldn't be the only one gathering information.

"I'm available this afternoon," I said. "Where shall we meet?"

"I'd love to meet at your house. Get the feel for a home with children and see how you manage as a single parent," she said. "Do you think your darling friend, what's her name, Lillian, could take the little ones out of the house? That way we could talk more freely."

"It's Lurleen. We need to meet in a coffee house, so the kids can do whatever they want at home, and we'll need to keep it short."

I'd promised Mason I wouldn't meet with her alone, and I certainly didn't want her in my house with the kids.

"Whatever you say. It won't take long, I promise."

We settled on Java Monkey at three. I left a message for Mason about the time and place I'd be meeting with her. I knew he'd want to be there.

I spent the morning with the kids and tried to put the investigation out of my mind. We took a long walk with Hermione, who appeared to be as delighted as we were to wander through our Virginia Highland neighborhood. When we got home, Lurleen was there, and we had an hour before I needed to leave to meet Harper at the coffee house.

"Lillian? She called me Lillian?" Lurleen was in a state. "I've never liked that woman."

"I know. I don't either. She has some idea she wants to adopt children, and if she's for real, I need to talk her out of it."

I thought Lucie and Jason were in the backyard playing with Hermione when Lucie poked her head into the living room.

"I got too hot, so I came inside," she said.

"You heard what we were talking about?" I asked.

Lucie gave me a devastated look. "You…you don't want to adopt us?"

I knelt down beside her. "I want to adopt you and Jason more than anything in the world. What you heard was half a conversation, and sometimes that can lead to a lot of misunderstanding, Lucie. Harper thinks *she* might want to adopt, and I don't think she'll make a very good mother. She's the one I want to talk out of adoption."

"Oh," Lucie said, letting out the breath she'd been holding. "Aunt Di, do you think Harper might be the one—you know the one…

"The one who killed two people?"

"Yes. Does she have an alibi?"

"What do you know about alibis?"

"I know that's when a person says they were someplace else when a crime happens."

"That's exactly right, only Harper doesn't just say she was someplace else, she has witnesses to prove it."

"Maybe she's like a magician," Lucie said. "Like Uncle Tommy. He makes you look somewhere else so you don't see the trick he's playing."

I didn't say anything for a minute and let that sink in. Lurleen seemed to be doing the same thing.

Then the doorbell rang. It was Harper.

Hermione was still out back with Jason, so she didn't do her usual robust barking.

"What are you doing here?" I asked Harper. "We agreed on the coffee house at three."

"I know, but I was in your neighborhood and thought it would be so much more convenient to meet here." She looked around. "I'm relieved your dog isn't here," she said. "You said she's a sweetheart, but she wasn't a sweetheart with me at your party."

Then she saw Lucie and Lurleen.

"I thought the kids would be swimming, it's such a beautiful day, and I know that Lill—I mean Lurleen—takes them there all the time."

"How would you know that?" I asked.

"We talked about it at the party—about how lucky you are to have Lurleen available to entertain your kids."

"It's you, Hunter, oops I mean Harper," Lurleen said. She smiled sweetly. "I'm going to go check on Jason."

"We're not meeting here," I said. "If you still want to talk we'll do it at Java Monkey at three."

"Oh, dear," Harper said. "I've gotten off on the wrong foot with all of you. I only meant to be helpful. Java Monkey at three no longer works for me. I'll call to reschedule."

She left before I could say a word. Lucie just stared after her.

"Where'd she go?" Lurleen asked when she reappeared with Jason.

"She disappeared like magic," I said. "Why don't you three go on to the pool. I'll catch up on a few things here and join you later."

The kids grabbed their swimsuits and Lurleen gave me a peck on the cheek before she got the kids into my car. She looked at me. "You'll drive my Citroen?"

"I may walk, but don't worry about me if I don't make it."

They left and I sat for a moment with Hermione before she wandered upstairs to take a nap. Harper was a strange one, so eager to see me and then suddenly not. I thought about Lucie's comments. Now you see it, now you don't. How could she have managed to orchestrate two murders?

I gave Mason a call to say the meeting with Harper was cancelled and walked into the kitchen to look for a cornbread recipe to go with chili for dinner. I'd have time to think about how Harper might have pulled it all off without being close to either man when he died.

I'd just grabbed my cast-iron skillet when I heard the front door open and close.

"What did you forget?" I asked as I headed for the front door, skillet in hand.

There stood Harper.

"What do you think you're doing barging into my house?"

"I wasn't sure you'd hear the doorbell. I see you're cooking. That's fine. We can talk while you cook." She walked past me into the kitchen, and I caught a whiff of what smelled like alcohol on her breath.

"This won't take long, but it really can't wait," she said and settled herself onto a stool at my island. "The social worker wants to come to my house as soon as possible, so I really need your help now, Ditie."

Ditie? Since when did Harper call me Ditie?

"Now is not a good time," I said. "I'm asking you to leave."

"What's wrong with you, Ditie?" she asked. "You act as if you don't want me in your house. Are you expecting someone your detective friend doesn't know about? I promise I won't be long."

This she said with a smirk, and then she looked around.

"You are alone, aren't you?"

Harper was making my skin crawl. "Mason will be here any minute."

"Then we'd better hurry," Harper said. She stared at me for a moment. "You aren't a very good liar, Mabel. I don't believe anyone is coming. What I don't know is why you seem frightened of me? I just want help with this adoption business. Nothing more."

What could I do but play along. "You have the paperwork? You can ask me questions while I cook."

"Everything I need is in here." She showed me her large Hermes crocodile handbag. I recognized it as a bag similar to Lurleen's, only Harper's was undoubtedly the real deal.

She settled herself on a stool at the island, her bag beside her. "Do you have anything to drink?"

"Coffee," I said, "or lemonade."

She shook her head. "Any bourbon or scotch?"

I pulled a bottle of Chardonnay from the refrigerator and poured her a glass. "This is the best I can do."

Then I returned to the stove and began talking, the way I always did when I was nervous. "I'm working on a cornbread recipe for dinner. Mason enjoys it when I do real Southern cooking."

"That's quaint," Harper said. "I'm sorry to bother you, Mabel, on your time off. I'm just really worried about a few things."

"I'm listening," I said.

"I'm frightened of Phil!"

"Phil? So this conversation has nothing to do with adoption?"

"No, I was afraid if I told you the truth, you'd tell me to go to the police again."

"You're right about that. The last time you were here, you said everything was fine. What's different now?"

"Phil won't take no for an answer. He scares me. He took our relationship too seriously."

"So you *were* involved with him before Ryan died," I said.

She stared at me. "I never expected you to be so judgmental, Mabel. You've always been fair-minded. I like to feel men are attracted to me. There's no harm in that."

"No harm in that, Harper?" I said. "You kissed half the men at my party."

"I'll admit I had too much to drink, but it never went beyond kissing."
I shook my head.

"Mabel, you haven't lived the life I have. You always relied on your
brains, not your looks. Maybe you could have been a beautiful woman—
you do have a lovely face—but you never seemed to care about your body.
I've had to rely on my body. I'm smart enough. Plenty smart as a matter
of fact, but that isn't what men want. They want a beautiful woman and
beyond that a woman who will be a good mother to their children."

Here she stopped for a moment. I thought I saw a flicker of what might
be genuine emotion. She gulped down the glass of wine.

"Could I have another glass?" she asked.

I poured her more Chardonnay and left the bottle beside her.

"I was a person who was meant to have it all. I don't mean that in a
grandiose way. I was gifted with brains and beauty. My father always
made sure I knew that, and he was very clear about his expectations. He
wanted the finest line of offspring I could produce. He could never accept
less, even with the domestic animals we had."

She paused to finish off a second glass of wine.

What would my psychiatrist friend have advised me to do? Keep her
talking. And drinking, I suspected.

I topped off her glass.

"I had a favorite dog," she continued, "a walker coonhound. We were
inseparable. Daddy bred her and sold her pups, but somehow she got
pregnant with what my father called rotten mutts. When they were born
my father made me drown them one by one."

"That's horrible," I said and meant it.

"That wasn't the worst. He said if it ever happened again, he'd kill the
dog."

Harper stopped talking, drank wine, and poured herself more. She
drank as if I'd given her a pitcher of ice water on a hot day.

Her speech was slightly slurred when she continued. "It did happen
again, and my father said it was my fault. He made me shoot my own
dog—one bullet to the head."

Harper took a single breath and let it out in one anguished cry. "After
that, I swear that dog haunted me. Every dog seemed to know what I'd
done, and every dog was waiting to rip me apart." She caught herself. "So
when my father said he wanted pure offspring, I knew exactly what he
meant. And then my future got taken away from me."

She lost me there.

"Your future got taken away? How?"

"You know how! I was sterile. Sterile at twenty-five. Can you imagine that?"

"No," I said.

"No one can. Who wants a woman who can't get pregnant? I'll tell you who—no one. Not Phil that's for sure. Not even Carl. Men and their dynasties. Disgusting! They made me feel like half a woman. A good woman to screw. In fact, a perfect woman to screw, since I couldn't get pregnant. But not wife material. Never that."

"Ryan didn't feel that way," I said.

"No, he didn't. He loved me desperately, and when I couldn't get pregnant he said it didn't matter." She shook her head. "I couldn't settle for Ryan. I thought everything would be all right when Frank asked me to marry him. Daddy wasn't excited because Frank wasn't Southern. But he knew Frank was smart. He thought we'd produce good offspring."

"Your father didn't know you couldn't have children?"

"I couldn't tell him that. All he ever talked about was the good lineage that would carry on the ranch. When Frank broke off our engagement, Ryan was there. He was Southern, and he could keep a secret. We stalled Daddy for three years. I even thought we might adopt a baby that looked enough like me, so he'd never have to know. Then my father up and died. It was horrible. And it was a relief."

"I'm sorry for what you've been through, Harper, I really am."

"I didn't mean to tell you any of that," she said. "It just came out. I'm here to warn you about Phil. I'm scared of him, and you should be too."

"Why?"

"I think he planned the whole thing, the two murders. You know how meticulous he is about everything. He made it look as if he were being framed."

"But why would Phil kill Carl? To settle an old score? Because his father brought Carl into the practice?"

"Yes and yes. Phil could be very vindictive when he felt threatened. You know what he did to Sally. He sold her out and had no regret about doing it."

"Phil isn't the man I thought he was, but why would *I* be in danger?"

"Phil thinks you're too close to the truth."

"He told you that? He admitted to killing two people?"

"Not in so many words. He said, 'everyone should let this go.' He was sure the police bought his idea that someone was framing him."

"I see."

"I hope you do see, Mabel. I hope you'll back off the way Phil wants you to."

"I'll do that," I said. "I have my children to think about."

Perhaps I said it too quickly.

Harper gave me a hard look. "Don't ever think of acting as a second career," she said. "You're not good at it."

My heart began to pound. Was I sweating?

"You look so frightened. We won't be alone much longer," Harper said.

"What do you mean?"

"I mean that I spoke to Phil on the phone, and he's coming over."

She watched me like a hawk.

"And you think he means to harm me?" I asked.

"Yes, I do."

"Then we'd better leave."

I tried to usher her out of the kitchen, but she wouldn't move.

"You don't believe me," she said. "It's written all over your face."

My giveaway face! I tried hard to recompose it. "Harper, let's talk somewhere else. We need to get out of here before he comes!"

"You've already figured it out, haven't you?" Harper said. Her words were garbled, but she spoke with a deadly calm. "I'd hoped I might not have to kill you. Now, it can't be helped. You know I killed Carl and Ryan."

"I don't know any of that," I said.

"Come on, Mabel, don't play me for a fool. The great pleasure of the cannon exploding was that I didn't care who got killed. I would have been happy if the whole lot of them were dead. Every one of them betrayed me in some way, and I always get even. I did that with the men who gave me all their nasty diseases and left me infertile. Some are still alive, but every one of them will never be able to do anything sexual to a woman again. I saw to that."

"And Ryan?"

"Ryan was smothering me. It was easy enough to fill Phil's cartridge with a live bullet and urge him to fire at Ryan—just for fun. I told him Ryan would be aiming at him. I didn't know enough about ballistics to realize a smaller bullet couldn't be traced to the original gun. That was the only thing my father didn't teach me."

"Did you send the photo to Kathy?"

"Yes. Carl was ready to leave Kathy and marry me. He was going places unlike Ryan. And then Kathy got pregnant again, and all our plans fell through. Carl wanted to work out his relationship with her. Both of them deserved to suffer."

"*You* were the one who pushed me in the tunnel," I said.

"I hoped I could scare you off, but I didn't know if you'd recognize the hat I was wearing, so I gave it to Sally. I didn't want to kill you. I don't want to kill you now. You've never done anything to me, but now it's too late."

She reached into her giant handbag and pulled out an antique derringer. She pointed it at my head.

I backed away from her. "Phil's?"

"Of course."

"You can't possibly imagine the police will believe Phil came to my house to kill me with an antique gun."

"You overestimate the police." She looked at her watch. "Phil should be arriving in a few minutes. I told him that you had important information for him that you couldn't share over the phone. This is the pistol he brought for the reenactment. It's probably the only handgun he owns. The police will believe he killed you because he feared you knew too much."

I did what I could to keep her talking.

"How did you get the gun?" I asked.

"I have the key to his lockbox," she said. "I made a copy during one particularly passionate night, when Phil fell asleep after too much alcohol and carrying on. The sedative I put in his drink didn't hurt either."

My cell rang. I tried to pick it up, but Harper waved me away.

"No rescue for you, Mabel." She waved the gun erratically in my direction. "We have to get a move on, so Phil will find you dead, and I'll be gone."

I stood with my back to the stove and reached behind me for the skillet.

"What, Mabel, you're going to hit me over the head with a skillet?" Her speech was almost unintelligible. "Only you would think of such a lame defense. Put it down."

She waved the gun again in my direction and almost fell off the stool. She tried to steady herself with an elbow on the island.

Harper was drunk, and I had only one option.

I made a motion as if I were lowering the skillet to the ground.

I heard the click as Harper fully cocked her gun.

She aimed it unsteadily in my direction, and that was when I ducked and charged her with the skillet in front of my face.

The sharp crack of a gunshot stopped me.

Was I hit? My ears were ringing. I thought I'd heard the bullet ping off the skillet. Nothing hurt.

Thank God for cast-iron, and thank God Harper was drunk.

I stayed crouched and peered around the skillet. Harper looked as dazed as I felt. She struggled to reload, but she fumbled and dropped the bullet. Hermione roared into the kitchen barking ferociously, teeth bared.

I ran toward Harper, skillet in one hand, but Hermione reached her first and pounced on her. That seemed to completely unnerve Harper. The gun thudded to the wooden floor, as she fell to the ground and covered her face with her hands. Hermione was on her, yapping and jumping.

That's all the time I needed. Hermione stayed on top of her, front paws on her chest, growling, as I called 911 on my cell. I kept my iron skillet at my side to use as a weapon if I needed it.

"Get her off me!" Harper screamed. "She'll kill me!"

The police arrived in two minutes.

Mason was right behind them. "I tried to call you, and when you didn't answer I got worried."

Fortunately, Lurleen and the kids weren't due home for another hour.

Chapter Thirty-Nine

Everything seemed to unfold at once. Harper was led away in handcuffs. Mason took me to the living room to allow a forensics team to work in the kitchen. He made sure I was okay, and then we waited in silence for the investigator to do the actual interview.

Two officers took me into the family room, closed the door, and listened to my account of what had happened. There would be more questioning at headquarters later.

I called Lurleen and caught her just as they were headed home. I could imagine Lucie trying to listen in, so I made sure I started with the fact that everything was fine. When Lurleen and I had finished I asked to speak to Lucie.

"You were right about Harper," I said. "She was behind every bad thing that happened."

"Really, Aunt Di?"

"You gave me the clues, Lucie. When you talked about a magic trick, it made me start to think about Harper's alibis and that led to everything else."

"I helped solve the case?"

"You did, Lucie."

"Wow!."

I could hear Lurleen in the background asking Jason if he wanted ice cream with sprinkles.

She took the phone from Lucie. "Why don't you come to my house when things are…settled," she said.

"Great idea."

I hung up and went back to sit beside Mason. "Do we have all the answers now?"

I asked.

"I think we'll have them soon. The police had Brockton picked up for questioning. I suspect he'll confirm what you suggested—that it was Harper who encouraged him to let Carl participate in the way he did and that she suggested he fire at Ryan."

I shifted on the sofa. "What I don't understand is why Phil never said anything about that. He must have suspected Harper was the murderer."

"Maybe the interrogation will get that out of him," Mason said.

"And Sally? Did she admit to planting the accounting book in Kathy's apartment?"

"She did. Once she realized she was a murder suspect, she was desperate to get the focus onto someone else—like Frank Peterson. She ripped out the other pages because it would show payments from Harper, Phil, and Carl."

"There is another remaining mystery," I told Mason.

"And that is?"

"What was the secret meeting Kathy had with Andy? Andy says he can't tell me."

"I assume with your insatiable curiosity, you will call Kathy and find out."

"Brilliant, Mason. Of course I will. I need to tell her about what happened anyway."

Mason stood up and walked to the kitchen to see what was going on and to give me some privacy.

Kathy listened as I recounted what I'd just been through with Harper.

"Thank God you weren't hurt," she said. "I never would have forgiven myself for asking you to get involved if something had happened to you. If there is anything I can do to repay you, please tell me."

I smiled into the phone. "There is one thing, Kathy. About that secret meeting with Andy. Andy won't tell me one word about it. He said I'd have to get the information from you. I'd like to call in that favor you offered."

Kathy laughed, a full-throated chuckle. "I'm sorry I didn't come clean the first time you asked. Lucie doesn't miss a trick apparently, and she was right. It was meant to be a secret meeting."

She took a deep breath.

"I didn't want anyone to know for a while, but Andy and I are getting married at the end of the next school year. We've always cared about each other, but I swear we never did anything while Carl and I were married. After Carl died, Andy was so good to me. I think we both realized we could make a happy life together. I wanted to keep our relationship secret for a while because I knew people would think it was happening too fast. I was afraid they'd imagine all sorts of things."

"What about the money you gave him?"

"That money was to reserve the florist. I insisted on going in halfway with Andy on the wedding, so that was my part. The papers were about venues and caterers. I haven't felt this happy in years. I suppose that sounds terrible."

"Not to me," I said.

"Finally, I feel as if I'm living my own life, not the life Carl or my parents expected me to live."

"I couldn't be happier for you, and your secret is safe with me."

"Thanks. We'll announce our engagement in a few months, and then I hope you'll come to the wedding in June with the kids. Mason, Lurleen, and Danny are invited as well. You've been a godsend to me, not just by helping me find out what happened to Carl. It's good to know there are happy, healthy families out there."

I was about to hang up. "May I tell Mason about your news? He's the most discreet person I know."

"Of course. You can also tell Lurleen and the kids if you want. I'm tired of secrets, so if the word gets out I can live with that."

"Thanks. You'll move back to South Carolina?"

"Yes. Andy and I will buy a new house together and start fresh. He says you might bring the kids out for a visit soon. We'd love that."

"Good as done," I said.

I hung up and found Mason waiting for me in the breakfast room. The kitchen was cordoned off and we could see three members of the forensics team dusting surfaces and taking photographs.

"They found the bullet," Mason said. "Luckily for you it was a derringer that held only one bullet. It bounced off the inner surface of the cast-iron skillet and tore a giant hole in the side. You won't be using that skillet again."

"I may frame it," I said. "It saved my life."

Together we walked out to the porch and sat in the swing. I told Mason about Kathy's engagement.

"That's good," Mason said. "Really good. You need to be around people who get engaged and married. It'll get you used to the idea."

Mason put his arm around me, and I rested my head on his shoulder. "I'm already getting used to the idea," I said. "Just a few hundred more questions for you to answer and I'll be there."

Mason chuckled and kissed my unruly curls. "Promise you won't change one thing about you," he said.

"That's a promise I can't keep, but if you mean will I ever stop loving you, I can't imagine that."

We sat outside as it started to rain. It was a hard rain that felt cleansing, washing away the unbelievable history of classmates I thought I knew. We didn't speak. Mason let me be and when I sighed, he simply squeezed the arm he held around me, as if to say everything would be all right.

When the rain let up, we made plans to go to Lurleen's and pick up the kids. I was finally settled enough to do that, but before we could leave, Mason got a phone call. He checked the number.

"It's Officer Barden. You want me to take it or call him back later?"

"Take it now, please. Can you put him on speaker phone?"

"I'll check."

Barden agreed to let me listen in.

"I just finished a preliminary interview with Philip Brockton and Harper Hudson. He acknowledged it was Harper who told him to let Carl do whatever he wanted on the day of the reenactment—she convinced Phil it would sit well with his father."

"Did she confess to both murders?" I asked.

"She did. She admitted to filing down the barrel of the cannon once we agreed to take the death penalty off the table. She couldn't manage the placement of people around the cannon, but she didn't care who got killed."

"Why not?"

"It seems most of the men around that cannon had rejected her," Barden said. "You may understand this better than I do, Dr. Brown. She kept referring to the fact she couldn't have children, and how that meant she wasn't marriage material."

"I think I do."

"How did she manage to get Phil to fire at Ryan?" Mason asked.

"Not that hard," Barden said. "She told Phil Ryan would be aiming at him and that he should do the same. She admitted she led Ryan to believe Phil was after her. She suggested Phil needed to be out of the picture in order to leave them in peace and encouraged Ryan to consider using live ammunition. Harper didn't care who was killed and who was brought up on charges. She'd get rid of both of them one way or another. Ryan apparently couldn't do it in the end."

"Did she show any remorse?" I asked.

"None. She seemed proud of the fact she pulled it all off like a magic act."

"Why did the DA take the death penalty off the table?" Mason asked.

"I guess he thought a prominent female physician in Atlanta, well connected, wasn't going to be executed regardless of what she'd done. I had to agree, and it let us get the facts straight. She's likely to get life without parole, but on the other hand she's an attractive woman with a good team of lawyers. We'll have to see how this plays out."

"I have another question, Inspector Barden," I said.

"Go ahead."

"Phil must have realized Harper was framing him."

"Dr. Brockton is an odd fellow, if you don't mind my saying so. He went away with Dr. Hudson at her insistence—wasn't supposed to tell a soul, which is why Danny didn't know where he was. He said Harper convinced him she wasn't the murderer."

"How did she do that?"

"Harper went into a long story about how Sally made her living—by blackmailing people to keep their secrets. Phil knew some of that was true from personal experience."

"But why would Sally kill Carl?" I asked.

"According to Harper, Carl wasn't willing to protect Sally any more from the charge of embezzlement. Sally had been the mastermind of the operation with Frank and Andy, and Carl supposedly had proof. Sally had no choice but to kill him."

"Phil bought all that?" I asked.

"He said Harper was very persuasive. Maybe it was safer to go along with Harper than to challenge her," Barden said.

"He now knows what really happened?" I asked.

"Yes. But I have to tell you he didn't show much emotion. He did say he was glad you weren't harmed."

"That would be Phil."

Barden hung up.

Mason turned to me. "That finishes it, doesn't it?"

"I wonder if Phil will work for his father now. Will it bother you if he does?"

Mason shook his head. "No. I think I'm beginning to work through some of my own issues—with your help, and we've both seen the kind of man Phil is. I'm not jealous of him anymore."

"How could I have been so blind?"

"You were young, Ditie. You knew the man your father was and you expected other men to be like that."

"I did. I always thought Phil chose oncology to help people, but I know now he did it so he could make a good salary through grants and drug studies. It also gave him a chunk of time free for his reenactments. There aren't many emergencies in research."

Mason took my hand and pulled me up from the swing. "Let's go see your kids. I bet I can talk Danny into grilling some of his famous barbecued chicken. The forensics team will be done in an hour or so, and then we can get your house and our lives back in order."

"It's starting to feel like *our* house and *our* kids," I said, squeezing his hand.

"I like the sound of that."

He looked at me with those soft gray eyes and that generous smile, and I knew I was finally old enough to recognize a good man when I saw one.

Old Recipes

from the

North and South

Deep South Old Fashioned Tea Cakes

This recipe came from the internet and Divas Can Cook (which is a fantastic website and worth a long visit). The desire to include such a recipe came from the number of friends in the South who talked about their grandmother's tea cakes. They are not quite a cookie, not quite a biscuit, but always delicious.

Servings: 24 or so. Depends on how hungry people are.

Difficulty: This one takes a little skill, time, and practice. The less flour you use, the lighter the tea cakes will be but the more difficult the dough will be to work with. It gets and stays quite sticky.

Ingredients:

1/4 cup unsalted butter, room temperature
1/4 cup butter-flavored shortening (or use lard)
1 cup granulated sugar
1 egg, room temperature
lemon zest from 1 small lemon
1/2 vanilla bean, scraped, or 1 1/2 teaspoons vanilla extract.
(It's fun to scrape a vanilla bean and see all those little dark flecks in your creation, but you can get by with vanilla extract and save yourself a little wear and tear. Also a considerable amount of money—vanilla beans are pricey. Conversion seems to be 1 teaspoon extract for 2 inches of vanilla bean or 3 teaspoons for a typical vanilla bean.)
2 cups flour
2 teaspoons baking powder
1/2 teaspoon salt
1/4 teaspoon nutmeg
1/4 cup buttermilk

Instructions:

In a large bowl, cream together butter and shortening until creamy.

Mix in sugar until well combined.

Mix in egg.

Mix in lemon zest and vanilla bean or extract. Set aside.

In a medium bowl, sift together baking powder, salt and nutmeg.

Mix the dry ingredients into the wet ingredients, alternating with the buttermilk.

Turn dough onto a smooth surface and knead until dough is soft. (Dough will be sticky and hard to work with, but try to do this without adding too much flour. The less flour you use, the lighter your tea cake—even if you don't get to knead as much as you might like)

Shape into a disk and cover with plastic wrap.

Refrigerate for 1 hour or freeze for 30 minutes.

Preheat oven to 350 degrees F.

Line a large baking sheet with parchment paper. Set aside.

Remove dough from fridge and plastic wrap.

Knead dough to soften it.

Roll dough to 1/4 inch thick. (I roll the dough between parchment paper to prevent sticking.

Use a round cookie cutter and cut out circle shapes

Place cookies on ungreased pan about 2 inches apart. (The dough should be cold when going in the oven, so if need be pop the cut cookies into the fridge to chill again before baking)

Bake for 8-10 minutes but don't overbake! They will not get golden on the tops and will continue to cook as they cool.

Remove from pan and place on cooling rack to finish cooking.

Once cooled store in an airtight container—if they are not all immediately consumed.

If you want to know the way to the heart of a Southerner—this recipe may be it. Not easy but worth the effort.

Captain Sanderson's Boiled Pork and Bean Soup

Any time you look for old recipes (Civil War Vintage) this recipe will pop up.

I've started with the original recipe below. It provides a pleasant tasting, authentic soup.

If you want a little more flavor, as I did, try adding the ingredients below the original list. These were provided by two chefs (Mandy and Paula Haddon) who make the best soup in Falmouth, Massachusetts and own Molly's Tea Room on Main Street.

Servings: 8-10
Difficulty: Moderate (more time-consuming than difficult)

Ingredients:

1 pound dried navy beans
1 pound pork shoulder or butt
1 onion (diced)
1 leek (diced)
1 garlic clove (diced)
1 sprig thyme
1 tablespoon apple cider vinegar
2 tablespoons bacon fat.

Additional ingredients to make the soup more flavorful:

1 teaspoon dry mustard
1 tablespoon salt
1/2 cup molasses added the last 15-20 minutes of cooking (can be added when the pork goes back in)

Instructions:

Soak beans overnight in cold water.
Dice pork into 1-inch pieces (I had the butcher do this for me) and boil in water about 1 hour until tender.

Save the stock.

In a soup pot, add bacon fat, onions, garlic and leek. When the onions become translucent (a few minutes) add thyme and vinegar.

Add soaked navy beans and the pork stock.

Simmer for 30 minutes, and then add pork back to the pot.

It was at this point that I added the additional ingredients listed above.

Cook for 15-20 minutes, until the beans are tender. (My beans needed more cooking time.)

Season with more salt and pepper as needed and slightly mash the beans

Serve with cornbread or confederate biscuits.

Confederate Biscuits

You will find any number of variations on this simple recipe.

Servings: 6-12
Difficulty: Easy

Ingredients:

2 cups flour
2 teaspoons baking powder
1/4 teaspoon baking soda
1 teaspoon salt
6 tablespoons shortening
2/3 cup buttermilk

Instructions:

Preheat oven to 450 degrees.
Sift together flour, baking powder, baking soda, and salt.
Cut in shortening until mixture is the consistency of meal.
Stir in buttermilk.
Form mixture into a ball.
Place on a floured surface and knead a few times.
Pat out to about 1/4 inch thick.
Cut with a small biscuit cutter. (The rim of a small glass works fine.)
Place on an ungreased baking sheet and bake for 8-10 minutes. (You can do this in a cast-iron skillet as well and be even more authentic)
Cut open and spread with a little butter. (I'd say a lot of butter!)

Filled Cookies

This recipe came from a very old recipe card. It turns up everywhere—North and South.

Servings: 12-20
Difficulty: Moderate

Ingredients:

1 cup sugar
1 egg
3 1/2 cups flour
2 teaspoons cream of tartar
1 teaspoon baking soda
1/2 cup shortening
1/2 cup milk
1 teaspoon vanilla

Filling:
1 cup chopped raisins (chopped dates or figs work as well)
1/2 cup water
1/2 cup sugar
1 teaspoon flour

Instructions:

Filling

In a saucepan combine flour and sugar.
Stir in water until smooth.
Add raisins.
Bring to a boil over medium heat; cook and stir and cook for 3 minutes or until thickened.
Cool.

Cookie Dough:

In a large bowl cream sugar and shortening.

Add egg and beat well.

Beat in vanilla.

Combine the flour, cream of tartar, and baking soda.

Add to creamed mixture alternately with milk.

Cover and refrigerate until easy to handle.

On a floured surface, roll out dough into 1/8" thickness.

Cut with floured 3" round cookie cutters. You can make these cookies smaller if you like.

Spoon 2 teaspoons filling on top of half the circles and top each with another circle.

Pinch edges together and cut slit in top.

Place 2" apart on ungreased baking sheets.

Bake at 350 degrees for 10 13 minutes or until lightly browned.

Remove to wire racks to cool.

Ozark Pudding and Old Fashioned Vanilla Ice Cream

These two desserts are best served together. Both of these recipes are old and easy.

Servings: 6-8
Difficulty: Simple and foolproof

Ozark Pudding

Ingredients:

> 1 egg
> 2/3 cup sugar
> 1/3 cup flour
> 1 1/2 teaspoon baking powder
> 1 cup raw, peeled, chopped apple
> 1/2 cup walnuts, chopped
> Pinch of salt
> 1 teaspoon vanilla.

Instructions:

> Preheat oven to 350 degrees.
> Beat egg until thick and lemon colored.
> Beat in sugar.
> Mix together flour, baking powder, pinch of salt and add to sugar and egg mixture.
> Add apples, walnuts, salt and vanilla.
> Bake in buttered pie pan at 350 degrees F. for 30 minutes.
> (This will not look like a pudding but more like a dry crumble or a golden topped pie)

Old Fashioned Vanilla Ice Cream

Ingredients:

4 cups heavy cream
3 egg yolks
3/4 cup granulated sugar
1 vanilla bean, scraped, or 3 teaspoons vanilla extract.

Instructions:

In a medium sauce pan bring the cream, half the sugar to a simmer.

Remove from heat and add vanilla.

In a medium bowl, whisk together egg yolks and remaining sugar until light.

Slowly add hot cream to egg mixture, 1/4 cup at a time, whisking all the while.

Return mixture to the sauce pan and cook over low heat, stirring constantly with a rubber spatula, until it is thick enough to coat the back of a spoon.

Refrigerate mixture until cold. Place mixture in an ice cream maker for twenty to twenty-five minutes.

Classic Skillet Cornbread

You can find dozens of variations on this recipe. The Southern variety, below, is more crumbly and savory. Northern cornbread is sweeter, more dense, and cakelike. Make your cornbread in a skillet, and people will think you really are a Southern cook.

Servings: 8
Difficulty: Easy

Ingredients:

> 1 1/2 cups fine stone-ground yellow cornmeal
> 1/4 cup all-purpose flour
> 2 teaspoons granulated sugar
> 1 teaspoon baking powder
> 1 teaspoon baking soda
> 1 teaspoon kosher salt
> 1 3/4 cups buttermilk
> 2 large eggs
> 3 tablespoons salted butter

Instructions:

Place a 10-inch cast-iron skillet in the oven and preheat oven to 450 degrees F.

Leave skillet in oven for seven minutes as oven heats.

Meanwhile, stir together the cornmeal, flour, sugar, baking powder, baking soda, and salt in a large bowl.

Stir together the buttermilk and eggs in a medium bowl.

Add butter to the hot skillet and return to oven until butter is melted, about 1 minute.

Stir buttermilk mixture into cornmeal mixture until just combined.

Pour melted butter from skillet into cornmeal mixture, and quickly stir to incorporate.

Pour mixture into hot skillet and immediately place in oven.

Bake in preheated oven until golden brown and cornbread pulls away from sides of skillet 18-20 minutes.

Remove from skillet and cool slightly before serving.

About the Author

Photo by VagabondView Photography

Sarah Osborne is the pen name of a native Californian who lived in Atlanta for many years and now practices psychiatry on Cape Cod. She writes cozy mysteries for the same reason she reads them—to find comfort in a sometimes difficult world.

Into the Frying Pan is the second novel in her Ditie Brown Mystery series.

She loves to hear from readers and can be reached at doctorosborne. com or visit her Facebook Fan Page at Sarah Osborne, Mystery Author. You may email her at Sarah@doctorosborne.com.

Printed in the United States
by Baker & Taylor Publisher Services